THE STORY OF OUR SECRETS

SHARI LOW

Boldwood

First published in Great Britain in 2021 by Boldwood Books Ltd.

Copyright © Shari Low, 2021

Cover Design by Alice Moore Design

Cover Photography: Shutterstock

A CIP catalogue record for this book is available from the British Library.

Paperback ISBN 978-1-80048-726-0

Large Print ISBN 978-1-80048-725-3

Hardback ISBN 978-1-80280-976-3

Ebook ISBN 978-1-80048-727-7

Kindle ISBN 978-1-80048-728-4

Audio CD ISBN 978-1-80048-720-8

MP3 CD ISBN 978-1-80048-721-5

Digital audio download ISBN 978-1-80048-723-9

Boldwood Books Ltd
23 Bowerdean Street
London SW6 3TN
www.boldwoodbooks.com

To Myla Ina Taggart.
Welcome to the world, little one.
We love you beyond words and can't wait to watch you grow.

PROLOGUE

COLM O'FLYNN – AUGUST 2016

This isn't going to work. My hands are shaking so much I can't hold the phone still. Change of plan. I rest the phone against the pile of books on my bedside table. The thrillers and crime novels belong to my wife, Shauna, but she brought them in here for me because she hasn't had time to read for months. My fault. My bloody incredible wife of fifteen years has been working so hard to make up for the income I've lost that she crashes into a deep sleep within seconds of crawling under the duvet. Another UCoADH. Unintentional Consequence of A Dying Husband. Especially one who's self-employed in a fairly new company.

My business partner and best mate, Dan, is paying me as much as possible every month, but there's no way one guy can bring in as much as both of us together, no matter how hard he tries. Reduced earnings. An UCoADBP. See what I did there? The last couple of letters are interchangeable, depending on whether the effect is on my role as a husband, a business partner, a dad to our six-year-old girl, Beth...

Sorry. Had to stop there. Bloody big lump in my throat. An Unintentional Consequence of A Dying Me. Forty years old and

I've barely shed a tear in my gifted life, and now one wayward thought can have me choking back a tsunami of liquid pain.

Not that I'll tell you that, my darling Shauna.

We did the whole 'falling apart' thing a while after we got the prognosis that the end was inevitable. I'm not saying imminent. Hopefully, it'll be a while yet. We allowed ourselves a weekend of grief, while Beth was having a sleepover with Dan and Lulu, then we dried our eyes on the Sunday night, five minutes before Beth arrived back home, and there's been nothing but relentless cheeriness ever since.

Our immediate friends, Dan and Lulu, and Rosie know, but we've both agreed not to tell Beth. She's too young and I don't want her to worry a day in her life. Besides, I don't do bad news. I much prefer denial and avoidance. Two of my very favourite things. Shauna is usually more one for straight talking and realism, but she's come over to my side lately. That's what a chat with a doctor delivering a death sentence can do for you. Twelve to eighteen months. That's the average survival rate for this particular bastard of a brain tumour. Not that I'm accepting that. Nope. That's not happening to me.

Although, I guess I'm dropping the denial on a temporary basis, just long enough to make this video for Shauna to watch after I'm... well, you know.

I could save myself trying to balance this bollocksing phone if I just told it all to her face, now, while I'm still here, but I know she won't listen. She'll brush it off, say she doesn't want to talk about it. I know ma darling wife. I knew her inside and out the minute I set eyes on her beautiful face, fifteen years ago in a bar on the riverbank in Richmond upon Thames.

And that's why I'm lying here, in a hospital a few miles from our home in Richmond, trying to get my head straight enough to tell her everything I need her to hear, while she's out putting in another fourteen-hour day at work. I'm being unusually, yet impressively, practical, if I do say so myself.

Brainwave. I lift a Michael Connelly novel the size of a Hovis loaf from the top of the pile and put it in front of the phone to stop it sliding down. Bingo. The brain might be under siege from this bastard tumour, but it still conjures up the occasional moment of inspiration. That's how the idea to do this thing with the phone came about.

Years ago, long before the first headache led to so much more, Shauna persuaded me (I think there was emotional blackmail or bribery involved) to watch one of those romcom movies she likes. I'm not a fan. They always end up marrying the bloke who was their best friend and secretly in love with them all along. Anyway, despite the fact that there was football on the other channel, I gave in. We ended up watching that movie... agh, what's it called? The one where Gerard Butler has an Irish accent and a brain tumour and he sends letters to his missus, Hilary Swank. *PS I Love You.* That's it. Really bad choice, in hindsight. There's a dose of sick irony, if I ever saw one. Life imitating art here. Anyway, when the movie finished, she binned the half a box of tissues she'd gone through in the sad bits, then we went to bed, made love, and afterwards... please don't judge me, I swear I was joking... I looked into her gorgeous green eyes, brushed back a lock of her blonde hair and whispered, 'If that was me in that movie, I'd have finished those letters differently.'

She grinned that gorgeous, sexy, irresistible smile. 'Oh yeah? And what would you say, Colm O'Flynn?'

I put on my best serious face. 'Something more profound. More spiritual. Something that only you and I would know.'

She waited as I paused, then went on...

'I was thinking, *PS I love that you're a smashing shag.*'

She skelped me with a pillow, but she laughed until I hushed her with a kiss that lasted until we were ready to love each other again.

God, I adore her. I haven't always shown it. I've been a pretty shit husband at times, I admit, but I've always loved her. I still find it fucking miraculous that she loves me too.

And that's why I owe her this.

I plump up the pillow and wedge it under my head, feeling that familiar tug as the scar across the back of my scalp stretches. I stare at the ceiling for a few minutes, looking for inspiration. None there. Surgery, followed by months of chemo and radiation therapy, has officially wiped out any imagination I ever had, but it hasn't wiped out my burning need to get this done.

Okay. Let's do it. I still haven't worked out what to say – I've just got a list of headlines and I was planning to make the rest of it up as I go along. Not exactly a shocker. That's pretty much how I've lived my life. Dan and I own a management consultancy and when you think about it, I've got a cheek advising people on how to organise and manage their business, considering I haven't organised or managed anything in my own life for... let's go for honesty and say forever.

I roll on my side, reach over and press 'record' on the iPhone.

'Hey, ma darlin',' I say, as always. It's how I start every day, every call, every conversation. I feel a catch in my throat, and I swallow it back. Not doing the sad thing. No way. There will be enough of that later. This needs to be happy, to be positive, to make her smile.

I force a grin and some levity into my voice and go on...

'So, I was thinking that we should probably have a chat about some stuff. I know what yer thinking... *Wow, my husband is sexy and look at him lying there in bed like some kind of drop-dead gorgeous hunk in an aftershave advert...* but try to focus on what I'm saying.'

When she watches that bit, she'll shake her head, she'll roll her eyes and whisper that I'm a fool, but we both know she'll laugh too. What's the chances that someone as beautiful and funny and fecking brilliant as Shauna would find my lame line in chat amusing too? It's up there with all that loaves, fishes and walking on water stuff.

'The thing is, ma darlin', we both know what's coming. You've been refusing to discuss it and, well, we both know that denial is one of my superpowers. No one wins a coconut for guessing that I don't want to give a single day of what's left to talking about what will happen down the road. But we have to, love. I'm planning to tell you what's on here at the last possible minute, so I know I won't be around when you watch it. You might wanna go get a coffee and get comfortable because this will take a while and I can't promise I won't ramble on or insert inappropriate jokes to break the tension. I can't have you keeling over with dehydration when I finally find the courage to get to bits that matter.

'Just in case, let me start with the good stuff. Shauna O'Flynn, I've adored you every day of my life. Even when I've been a daft prick or an insensitive arse. You're everything. You always were. And if I had the choice of living these fifteen years with you, or fifty years with someone else, I'd choose you in every lifetime. But this isn't forever, Shauna. We both know that, so I've got some stuff to tell you. About the past. About now. But mostly, about after I'm gone. You know I don't believe in all that "watching over you" stuff – and yep, I'll feel like a complete eejit if it turns out I get a ringside seat to the future – that's why I need you to know my hopes for the lives you and Beth will have without me. I need to know that you'll take care of the people I love. And I need to ask your forgiveness for...'

The words get stuck somewhere between my heart and my mouth. I can't open with that. If I do, she might never watch another minute, and this will all be wasted. I swerve and change tack.

'Actually, I'll come to that one later, m'darlin'. I've got a whole load of other stuff to get through first. Let me start with a few messages that I need you to pass on for me. Okay, here goes...'

1

Friday night. Nine o'clock. I was pretty sure that I was setting a giddy new level on the saddo scale. I'd been sitting on the floor of the utility room watching my washing go round since the ten-minute pre-wash, through the soapy stuff and at least two rinses. The glass of Prosecco that was on the tile floor beside me began to vibrate and I knew from experience that we were about to switch it up to the heady excitement of the spin cycle. Yes, I'd been here before. More times than I could count or wanted to admit. Tonight didn't feel any better, or any worse, than the others. Okay, maybe slightly worse.

I'd been feeding organic chicken goujons and mini-hamburgers (one hundred per cent beef, gluten-free buns) to forty kids at a six-year-old's birthday party in Chiswick this after-noon, when – some time in between little Araminta smacking little Camilla in the face with a dairy-and-gluten-free cupcake from the dessert tray, and little Theobald throwing an almighty hissy fit because he didn't get an iPhone 12 in his gargantuan mountain of gifts – I realised today's date. It's 25 May 2021. Which makes today exactly twenty years since I was in a bar on the riverbank in Richmond upon Thames, and Colm O'Flynn walked in. Five minutes later and I'd have missed him, and my whole life would have been oh so different.

I could see still see that night so vividly. I was there with my closest friends back then, Lulu, Rosie and Vincent, celebrating the launch of Vincent's new catering company. Rosie. Wow. I hadn't thought about her for ages. She lives in New Zealand now, after going over there a couple of years ago, to meet a farmer she'd hooked up with online. Her occasional emails told me she was loving life and I was happy for her. Our friendship had fractured long before that, when I discovered that despite a twenty-four year age difference, she was in a relationship with my dad in the years before his death in 2016. That would never stop being a shocker. Afterwards though, we'd stuck a patch on the wound and found a way to live with it, but now it was a closed chapter that I chose not to re-open.

Back in 2001, though, we were oblivious to what else life had in store for us. As we knocked back a few cocktails, we had no idea that one day Vincent and I would merge our companies and become partners, and that we'd have a spectacular fallout that would end with him leaving the country. I could never have predicted what the future held for Lulu. And I had no clue that just as I was about to leave and head home, Lulu's boyfriend, Dan, would arrive, and his best mate, Colm, the love of my life, would walk in behind him.

Actually, it was more of a swagger. Colm had this walk that made you smile, a kind of casual, easy-going physicality that was matched by the twinkle in his eye and his easy grin. He was the kind of guy that wore his goodness on the outside and that, combined with a couple of deadly one-liners, a self-deprecating humour and the sexiest Irish burr I'd ever heard, caused something in my head – and my heart – to explode.

When the bar closed, he walked me across Richmond bridge to my flat on the Twickenham side of the river, and I heard myself asking him in for coffee. This stranger that I felt I'd known forever. We sat on my tired old balcony until the sun came up, watching the flickering lights in the sky of the planes stacking in the airspace above Heathrow. Sometime in those hours, I fell in love. I also sustained a large bruise on my left buttock, thanks to the combination of an enthusiastic smooch and a collapsing balcony chair, but his laughter made the pain – and the chiropractor's bill – easier to bear.

My eyes closed as I rested my head on the wall behind me, the throb of the spin cycle blocked out by my focus on bringing the memory of his face to the front of my mind. For a while after he died, there would be days that I'd fall apart because I couldn't seem to remember what he looked like. How ridiculous was that? The man I was with for fifteen years, the father of my child, the love of my life, and I was devastatingly sure that I couldn't pick him out in a line-up.

It's hard to say when that passed. Now, five years after he left us, I can see him clearly, I can even hear his voice and sometimes, I'm sure I can feel him around me. At least, that's what I choose to believe. I'm not sure if that makes me miss him more or less. It helps that even though she's only eleven, Beth already looks so like him. The same green eyes and hair the shade of walnuts. The same smile – wide and quick – and a laugh that is so contagious it makes you forget that you're knackered, stressed or ready to hunt down the driver who dented your car door in the Tesco's car park. Although, if you're the driver of the blue Volvo who left a ruddy great big dent on a van with my company logo, Constant Cravings, on the side, be afraid because I will find you.

The sudden realisation that the door beside me was opening startled me. Beth was at a sleepover at my mother's house this weekend, so, as far as I knew, I was alone. This was it. I was about to be murdered in my own home by an intruder and my soapy knickers would languish in the washing machine until someone found my body.

'You know there's a box on the wall in the living room that shows far more interesting stuff than your clothes going round? It's called a TV. There's also a thing called a sofa, which is far more comfortable for a woman of your advancing years. Every minute on that floor is a minute closer to a hip replacement.'

Not a burglar, but close: a home invader with a pretty decent line in sarcasm.

Jess O'Flynn, my late husband's first wife, reached the wall I was leaning against and slid down it, joining me on charcoal tiles.

Jess held out a bottle of Budweiser, but I shook my head and gestured to the Prosecco on the other side of me. As I did, I realised it was empty and revised my answer, taking the beer. It saved my allegedly crumbling hips from getting up and taking me through to the kitchen for a refill.

She nudged my shoulder with hers. 'So... want to tell me why you're sitting here drinking plonk while staring at your washing machine, or is this some kind of weird fetish thing? "My name is Shauna and I get off on soapy bubbles,"' she teased, doing a breathy, sexy thing when she was mimicking me. 'Is your safe word Ariel or Daz?'

That would usually make me laugh, but not tonight. 'I really need to take your key off you. I only gave it to you because I was hoping you'd come in and fill my fridge while I was at work.'

Her auburn, chin-length bob quivered as she shrugged her shoulders. 'You can tell yourself that, but we both know it's because I'm a free babysitting service.'

'That's also true,' I agreed, deadpan.

'All part of the shared husband's ex-wife service,' she quipped, before taking a slug of her beer and nudging me again. 'Go on, admit I'm the best ex-wife in a co-dependent blended family that you've ever had.'

It took a bit of effort to shrug off my sadness, but I'd had plenty of practice at masking the hollowed-out canyon in the pit of my stomach. And, let's face it, she was right. Twenty years ago today, I met Colm, which was approximately one month after his divorce from Jess was finalised. During the next decade and a half, Jess and I rubbed along in polite civility, mostly, if I'm honest, for the sake of their twins, Davie and Joe, who were four when we met. Later, after Beth was born, we did a few blended-family Christmases and birthdays, but it was only after Colm got sick that we became friends (despite a couple of revelations about their relationship that I've compartmentalised into a big box with a 'Do Not Open' sticker on the top). Since we lost him, I think we've surprised ourselves by becoming close and now she's like the sister I never had, the older, cooler one who frequently turns up uninvited, regularly acts like the boss of me but who I can always count on in times of crisis and childminding.

I gave up trying to resist her attempts to distract me from my rare but heartfelt moment of self-pity. 'Okay, you're the best ex-wife in a co-dependent blended family that I've ever had.'

She made a 'touchdown' gesture. 'Yaaaasssss!' A pause. 'But you still haven't told me why you're sitting here.'

'I realised this is the twentieth anniversary of the night I met Colm.'

That gave her a moment of pause. 'I should have known it was around now.'

'Because it was twenty years last month since you got divorced?' I filled in the blanks.

Her sad smile as she nodded told me I was right.

Both of us sat there with that for a minute.

I cracked first. 'What are we like?' I sighed, putting my head on her shoulder.

'Pathetic, sad, but aging well and gorgeous on the inside?' Jess offered, her wit restored, but her words lacking her usual enthusiasm.

I couldn't remember the last time I cried over losing Colm, and the tears didn't come now either. It was more of a numbness, an emptiness where a whole stack of emotions – joy, attraction, passion, excitement, and yup, even lust – used to be. 'I just... miss him.'

I felt her rest her chin on the top of my head. 'I know, hon, I do too. Not that I'm trying to steal your thunder or make this all about me. I'm his ex-wife, I'm not Lulu,' she said, getting a playful dig in about my lifelong best friend. Even Lulu wouldn't have argued with her. Being completely self-absorbed was one of the qualities Lulu put on those surveys that asked for your biggest strengths. 'I invented self-love before it was a thing,' she'd say proudly, before going off to do as she damn well pleased.

Jess's barb made the corners of my lips turn up. Down deep, waaaay deep in their hearts, Jess and Lulu loved each other, but they clashed and both seemed to absolutely relish opportunities to wind the other one up. Most of the time, I wasn't sure if I was a friend or a referee.

'I just got a flashback to Colm, standing in my kitchen, telling me that he'd met you. Can't believe that was twenty years ago. You'd only been going out together for a few weeks and I couldn't comprehend what I was hearing. I still had some slices of my divorce cake in the freezer and he'd already met someone new and had decided to marry her. I'd already met Steve, so it wasn't that I was jealous of the relationship, but I was definitely pissed off that he was getting married so quickly. I'd been hoping that he'd find it impossible to do the till death do us part stuff for years after our divorce. Or at least until I married Ben Affleck.'

This wasn't news. Years ago, not long after Colm passed away, she'd confessed that she'd felt that way at the start of our relationship.

'You're a really terrible person, you know,' I told her.

'But a great babysitter,' she pointed out hopefully.

'True. I forgive you.'

'Anyway, karma bit me on the arse. A few weeks later you were married. I mean, who does that? Who gets married that quickly?'

'We did.' It was a totally unnecessary answer, but sometimes I just liked to say it out loud, to remind myself of the thunderbolt that was my husband. Six weeks after we met, Colm asked me to marry him and we tied the knot a few weeks later. Not once did I have a second of hesitation or doubt. I knew. He knew. At least, at the start. It wouldn't always be that way. It wasn't always the fairy tale I thought it was going to be. I squashed that thought and stuck with the happy memories. 'Three months. That was how long it took to completely change my life, my future, everything. And now...' I struggled to finish the thought. 'He's been gone for five years and I still think he's going to walk back in the door, Jess. When is this going to get better?'

My head was still on Jess's shoulder, but I could tell she was thinking about what I said because I could hear her heart thudding. Or that might have been my pipes. This building was gorgeous but ancient.

Jess's dramatic sigh made her hair flutter. 'Okay, Shauna, do you want me to tell you what I really think, or just stick with clichés and platitudes?'

I didn't hesitate. 'Clichés and platitudes.'

That made her laugh. 'Well, tough, because I've been thinking about this for a while and waiting for the right moment to talk to you. I've just done a whole module on grief and it's made me realise a few things...'

Jess was almost done with her master's in psychology. Since she left university with a social science degree, Jess had worked in both teaching and recruitment, but now she'd decided to retrain and become a life coach. I had a feeling I was about to become her guinea pig and I stifled a groan. This didn't sound like it was going to be a light, breezy conversation. She wasn't going to tell me some piece of witty gossip or about a 20 per cent off sale on ASOS. Jess and I hadn't had a deep and meaningful conversation for years, and to be honest, that kept me sane. Superficiality and forced cheer had been my two best friends since I buried my husband. For the first time, I really did wish that I hadn't given her a key.

'Jess, don't...'

'Sorry, Shauna, but this comes from a place of love. You need to move on. You need to start living again. It's been five years. You can't spend the next five years shut down like this, just surviving, getting through the days.'

There was no point arguing with what she'd just said because she was accurately describing my life.

'Do you want to know what I think will help?' she murmured.

'Could I stop you telling me?'

'Only if you magically pull some gaffer tape out of that ironing basket and apply it to my gob,' she retorted.

I knew when I was beat. 'Go on then.'

I closed my eyes and waited for Jess to dole out her words of wisdom. Whatever she had to say would no doubt be honest and heartfelt, but that didn't mean I wanted to hear it.

Jess took a breath. 'Okay, you're not going to like this, but I think that...'

That was as far as she got before the phone lying on the floor next to me began to ring. I felt her head lifting off mine as we both checked the screen. Lulu.

Jess rolled her eyes 'Bloody hell, she's thousands of miles away and she's still managing to make this moment all about her.'

Grateful for the reprieve, I answered the call and put it on speaker. 'Hey, shouldn't you be lying on a beach in the Maldives, drinking a pina colada while your shiny new husband rubs sun cream on your buttocks?'

'I'm doing that too. I can multitask,' Lulu fired back.

'Shall we chat about your history of doing two things at once?' Jess interjected cheekily. The statement was loaded and I could envisage Lulu's eyes narrowing as she tossed back her wild mane of red corkscrew curls, preparing for battle.

Lulu's current and very new marriage to property mogul, Bobby Jones, was the result of a relationship she'd started while still married to Dan.

My teeth clenched as I prepared for Lulu to go full Predator and annihilate Jess, but, to my surprise, she giggled. And Lulu didn't do giggling. Either she was a few cocktails in or Bobby had a superpower that allowed him to defrost the icy edge on my best friend's personality.

'Ah, is that Jess? The one who hasn't had a life since about 2012? Must be great up there on your moral high ground, but I much prefer the view down here in a cabana on the edge of the Indian Ocean.' And there she was. My shameless, smart-mouthed pal.

This time it was Jess who hooted with laughter.

I just shook my head. Ribbing each other was like a blood sport for these two and they both seemed to derive such twisted amusement from it. I really needed to find a softer pal. Someone who was sweetness and light and had a circle of butterflies above her head when she woke up in the morning. Or Dolly Parton. She would definitely lighten my day.

Lulu cut back to the point. 'Anyway, what are you two doing right now?'

'Sitting on the floor of the utility room feeling sorry for myself. Jess brought beer and I've dragged her down to my level,' I admitted, knowing that Lulu could picture the scene perfectly, because she'd been in here countless times. Dan owned the building I lived in, and Lulu had lived here with him until their marriage crumbled. He still occupied the bottom two floors, while Beth and I lived on the level above him.

Jess spoke up. 'Yeah, come home. It's going to take two of us to get her off the floor.'

'Oh honey...' Lulu said softly, and I knew that was directed at me. 'Your heart hurts because today is twenty years since you met Colm?'

That shocked me silent for a few seconds. Lulu was rarely aware of much that was going on in anyone else's life. Except Beth. When it came to my daughter, she was all over it, making sure that she felt loved and secure and seen. It was like she'd taken all the angst and disfunction of our teenage years growing up together, flipped them upside down and channelled the result into a blueprint for raising a happy, grounded, secure, loved child. Say whatever you wanted about Lulu Jones – and many did – but she was an incredible godmother to my child.

And she never failed to surprise.

'How did you know that?' I asked, so touched she'd remembered something so important to my life.

'Because that was the first night I hooked up with Jake, the Australian bloke who worked the bar and it was his birthday. I ended up seeing him on and off for years. For some reason, the date always stuck in my mind.'

Ah, right then. What she failed to mention was that her boyfriend at the time, the lovely Dan, arrived while she was outside hooking up with the Australian bloke and I had to keep him talking for an excruciating twenty minutes, while making excuses for her. I think I said she was taking ages in the loo because she had cystitis. I know it would be easy to hate Lulu. Her principles are dodgy and she's unapologetically wild, but I understand her. I know where all that comes from.

I sighed. 'Good to know. So now that you've crushed Jess's ego and crapped all over my sacred memories, was there a reason for this call?'

'I need the two of you to get off the floor and go downstairs and check on Dan. I'm worried about him.'

Like I said, she never failed to surprise.

Jess pointed out the obvious. 'Dan, your ex-husband. The one you left and divorced so you could marry a bloke with a Lamborghini and blonde highlights.'

'Yes. And they're not highlights, that's his natural hair.'

'Yeah, well, Rod Stewart wants it back,' Jess drawled.

I stuck to the important stuff. 'Why are you worried about him?'

Dan had been Colm's best mate for most of their adult lives. They worked together, played together and shared almost every important moment. He was like the brother I never had and without him I'd never have met Colm. I didn't get in the middle of his relationship with Lulu, but I'd been gutted when they split. Now, I walked a tightrope between them, caught in the middle of two of my favourite people in the world.

'Because he's not answering his phone...'

'Probably because you're his ex-wife and on your honeymoon with your new husband?' Jess suggested unhelpfully.

Lulu ignored her and carried on explaining her concerns.

'... And that's not like him. You know we've managed to keep things amicable, and we speak most days, but yesterday and today there's been no answer. I've got visions of him lying in a pool of alcohol, having choked on the last remnants of edible food in the cupboard. If he dies thanks to a jar of olives that's been there since 2018, I'll never forgive myself.'

'I'm sure he's fine,' I assured her, racking my brain to pinpoint the last time I'd spoken to Dan. Was it yesterday? I ran through the day in my head. No, it was the day before, because we were still hung-over from Lulu's wedding. He'd called to cancel lunch, citing an aching head due to overindulgence of fine wines and champagne at the nuptials. It had been a spectacular affair at Clivedon House, the stately home that had once been the residence of generations of the Astor family. It was an apt choice, given that it was originally built by a duke to house his mistress, and then was a pivotal location in the Profumo affair, the scandal that rocked the British government in the sixties. Just Lulu's kind of place.

Some people might find it odd that Dan was invited, but, as Lulu said, they'd kept things amicable and up until last week Lulu still worked for COMP Consultants, the company Dan and Colm founded and that Dan had continued to run after he lost his best mate and partner.

I knew it would take more than words to reassure Lulu, so I added, 'But I'll pop down now and check on him.'

'I'll come too, in case the olives got him. I'm fully trained in the Heimlich manoeuvre,' Jess said.

I flicked her arm. She wasn't taking this seriously at all.

'Thanks, Shauna. Will you drop me a text and let me know he's okay? Bobby and I are just about to go out to a club, so I might not hear my phone if you ring.'

I calculated the time difference and realised it was now close to midnight over there. Lulu had always been the queen of stamina.

I pushed myself up off the floor. 'Sure will. But I'm sure he's fine. You know, Lu...' I paused. Sentimentality wasn't Lulu's thing, but I decided to forge on with my thought anyway. 'I miss you.'

'Yeah, I miss you too.' I was feeling warm and bubbly until she added, 'Christ, would you listen to me. I think I must have sunstroke. Bye, Shauna. Bye, Satan.'

'It's Miss Satan to you,' Jess quipped back, earning another giggle before the click of the call ending.

I reached down, took Jess's hand and pulled her up. It wasn't difficult. Since the day I met her, almost twenty years ago, she'd never varied from a size ten. That's what daily yoga and a 5K run every morning did for you. I was a size fourteen. That's what twenty years of talking about taking up yoga and running but not actually doing it did for you.

'Right, come on then. Let's go downstairs and pay a visit to the lonely hearts club and check Dan's okay. And then, when we come back up here, I'll wallow in sadness and loss for a while longer, then we can finish the conversation where you were about to tell me how to fix my life. Or we could just watch senseless reality TV until we're numb. I think I prefer option two.'

Jess flashed her perfect white teeth. 'I'll give you one more night of moping. Let's eat popcorn, drink beer and watch a chick flick – a high-grade snot one, that will make us cry our eyes out and get all the sadness out of our system. How about that one with Gerry Butler? The one where he pops his clogs?' She wouldn't be winning any prizes for sentimentality.

'*PS I Love You*?'

'That's it!' Jess exclaimed. 'I love that film. It's a three box of tissues and swollen eyes for two days kinda movie. If we're going to be sad, let's do it with a bit of Gerry Butler.'

Hadn't I just been thinking about that movie? Sometimes it felt like the universe was telling me exactly what I needed.

'Sounds like a plan,' I agreed, smiling at the memory of my darling husband's horrified reaction when I coaxed him into watching it a million years ago.

If he was looking down on us now – his wife and his ex-wife planning a night in with a sob-a-thon, featuring a heartthrob with an Irish accent – he'd be shaking his head as he grabbed his jacket and sought refuge in the Pearly Gates pub.

As we headed for the door, I wondered if the noise I could hear was the washing machine, or Colm spinning in his grave.

It took seconds to descend the stone stairs and reach the dark carved mahogany and stained glass of Dan's door on the ground floor. Dan had inherited the gorgeous three-storey Georgian townhouse on Richmond Green from his uncle when he was in his early twenties. Over time, he and Lulu had converted the two lower floors into a stunning duplex apartment. After Colm died, I'd sold our home and rented the third floor, which Dan had refurbished and turned into a three-bedroom flat for Beth and me. I'd never regretted the move. Our old house had a big mortgage, an unruly garden and way too many memories, both good and bad. Living here gave me the security of my closest friends downstairs (until Lulu upped and left Dan for Bobby), handy childcare and a family atmosphere for Beth to grow up in.

I knocked on the door and waited. And waited.

Jess was leaning against the wall of the hallway, eyebrows raised expectantly. 'Don't you have a key?' she asked.

'I do, but I don't like using it unless I know for sure that it's a good time. For all we know, Dan could be in there on day two of a sex marathon with a new girlfriend. How would it look if two women burst in, demanding to know why he wasn't answering his phone? That's a passion killer right there.'

'Even if we bring beer?' Jess asked, holding up the four-pack of Budweiser she'd grabbed on the way down.

'Fair point, that could swing it,' I shrugged, as I knocked again. Nothing.

Jess filled the gap. 'If this was a cop show, one of us would kick the door down and we'd run in and find him passed out on the floor, and I'd throw myself on him and give him CPR and save his life.'

'Why do you get to save his life?' I asked. 'Why can't I save his life? Today is the anniversary of meeting my dead husband, surely I should get the glory moment?'

I know. Completely inappropriate. But Jess and I had used gallows humour to get us through pretty much every day of the last five years and it was a force of habit now.

She sighed. 'S'pose so. But if there is a burglar or violent criminal in there, I get to tackle them to the ground and knock them out with a handily placed heavy object.'

'Deal,' I agreed reluctantly, as if I was making some major concession on a global arms negotiation.

I banged on the door again, louder this time, then waited a few more seconds.

Nothing.

'Maybe you should forget the whole privacy thing and go get the key,' Jess suggested. 'If he's in the middle of orgasmic sex, we'll avert our eyes. Actually, it's been so long, I'm not sure I'd recognise it.'

I ran back upstairs, grabbed the key and was back down, a little breathless, in seconds, trying to push down the triffids of anxiety that were beginning to creep around my gut. Everything was fine. Dan was great. Hadn't he told me that a hundred times?

Hadn't he sworn he was over Lulu and wished her well? Hadn't he vowed to move on and build a new life on his own terms? He was probably out right now, shooting tequila with a date. Or at the gym. Or hiding behind the sofa because he knew two women who were sitting on the floor of a utility room ten minutes ago were about to descend on him.

After glancing at Jess and getting a nod of encouragement, I put the key in the door and pushed it open. Silence.

'Can't hear an orgy,' Jess observed, unhelpfully.

'He must be out. Or away.' Yep, that's what it was. He'd gone off somewhere for the weekend.

Jess wasn't convinced. 'Wouldn't he have told you?'

Good point. Of course he would have.

Out on a date then. Maybe he wouldn't have shared that info with me. We were as close as siblings, but that didn't mean he had to give me a heads-up about every romantic encounter and to be honest, I wasn't sure I wanted to know.

As I pondered this, Jess gave me a not-so-subtle shove, propelling me forward, to the end of the short hallway. Ignoring my hiss of objection, she nodded more encouragement as I tentatively opened the door to the open-plan living, dining, kitchen area, a gorgeous white-walled space with herringbone oak floors and glass doors spanning the full length of the wall out to the garden. Lulu had updated the kitchen the year before, swapping out the gleaming white gloss units for matt black cabinets with bronze handles and white quartz worktops. The oversized copper drop pendants above the massive island and the wood and metal bar stools gave the place an industrial edge that was softened by the welcoming vibe of the live-edged oak dining table that separated the kitchen from the huge white leather sofa in the lounge area. The times we'd had at that table. For almost twenty years, every decision, every event, every drama had been discussed around that huge slab of well-worn but utterly beautiful wood.

That's not where my eyes were now though. They were transfixed on the top of the kitchen island, on the countless empty beer bottles and used plates that were piled there. This wasn't normal. Dan was usually fastidiously tidy and the place was always pristine.

'Bloody hell, it looks like there's been a rave in here,' Jess whistled. 'I'm just gutted we weren't invited.'

I was already over at the bottom of the stairs. 'Dan! Are you up there?' I didn't expect an answer. Surely, if he was in, he'd have answered the door? 'Dan?' I tried again.

At first I didn't recognise the noise as human. It was a low hum. That then morphed into a groan. Then a mumble. Then a raspy cough.

My gaze shot round to the other side of the room and fell on the back of the U-shaped sofa, which faced the TV on the furthest wall. There, inch by inch, a head was emerging from the seating area of the couch.

'Shauna?' The voice was that of an eighty-year-old man who'd been on forty cigarettes a day since he was a lad. The hair looked like a straw bale that had been through a wind turbine. And the face? That was Dan's. Or at least, what I reckoned Dan would look like twenty years from now, after being stuck in a desert storm that sucked every drop of hydration out of his pores.

'Dear God, tell me you're Dan's grandad,' Jess blurted, as more of Dishevelled Dan appeared over the top of the sofa.

'Nope. Dan's grandad ran a marathon last weekend and he's dating someone half his age. He's in much better nick than this one,' I countered, gesturing to the creature from the white sofa.

I went straight into *Grey's Anatomy* mode, heading into the kitchen area to prepare urgent medicinal supplies: aspirin, water, strong coffee and a bargepole to keep Dan at least five metres away until he'd had a shower and burned his clothes.

Why was there never a Hazmat suit around when I needed one?

This was the question I was pondering on the inside. On the outside, my focus was elsewhere, as I took in the full vision of the man who was now standing in front of the couch. The tuxedo trousers. The white, wing-collar shirt. The cufflinks at his wrists.

'Is that the outfit you wore to Lulu's wedding? Oh, Dan...' A wave of sadness and guilt killed my words and I paused for a moment, trying to cover up my reaction by fighting with the buttons on the coffee machine.

No one else spoke – even Jess was uncharacteristically quiet – so I knew I had to finish my thought. The coffee machine burst into life, wiping out my delay tactic.

'That was three days ago. Why didn't you give me a call? Or a text? Or knock on the ceiling? I had no idea you were down here drowning your sorrows.'

He began unbuttoning his shirt, then slipped it off and ran his fingers through his hair, calming it down from The Clash circa 1982, to Duran Duran in the Rio years.

That was all it took. After a three-day bender, I'd have needed a week at a spa and a professional makeover to bring myself back to something recognisably human. Dan made a couple of minor adjustments and went straight from Swampman to the month of June in a Hot Builders calendar.

Jess noticed, and continued being the unhelpful gift that kept on giving. 'Did you spray-paint those abs on?' she asked, taking in his naked torso a tad too intensely. 'Surely they should have been enough to stop Lulu leaving you for Rod Stewart?'

Sometimes I forgot that she'd known Dan for much longer than I had. He'd been Colm's best mate since the early days of their marriage, and even after Colm remarried, Jess and Dan had managed to maintain a friendship that was more distant, but just as deep.

That made Dan attempt a laugh, which I suspect was the point. 'I know. I must have a really shit personality to cancel out these bad boys,' he said, with a rueful smile, his voice still raspy.

A piece of my heart chipped off. He was one of the best people on this earth. Bloody Lulu and her fickle bloody ways. Dan didn't deserve to be tossed aside by his partner of over two decades, But he did deserve friends who could keep him company in his swamp.

I switched into boss mode. 'Right. You go and get a shower and don't come back until you're peachy fresh, and Jess and I will sort this lot out.'

'We will?' She didn't look thrilled, but then she caught my expression and changed her tune. 'We will,' she repeated more forcefully, pushing her sleeves up and joining me in the kitchen.

Dishevelled Dan managed a sad smile. 'How did I manage to get rid of one bossy woman and gain two new ones?'

'That isn't the level of gratitude we expect, Dan Channing,' I chided playfully, desperate to lighten the mood. 'Now go.'

'And bring those abs back when they're clean and shiny,' Jess joked. At least, I think she was joking.

We waited until he'd headed upstairs to the shower before I met Jess's doleful gaze with one of my own. 'We're rubbish pals,' I began. 'I had no idea. I was so wrapped up in my own stuff...'

Jess swatted the air. 'Look, it's not your fault. Or mine. This is how Dan has chosen to react and that's his right. The important thing is that we're here now. And we've got rubber gloves and disinfectant,' she added, pulling a pair of Marigolds from under the sink.

We worked in silence and small talk for the next half-hour,

cleaning counters, loading the dishwasher, filling a black bin bag with the rubbish and loading bottles into the glass recycling tub outside. The whole time, my shoulders were slumped with sadness. A year ago, I wouldn't have predicted this. Even then, despite many splits and reunions, wandering eyes (mostly Lulu's and on several occasions), I'd really thought Dan and Lulu were just one of those couples that thrived on drama and discord, but would last forever. Wishful thinking. Lulu had met Bobby Jones when she went along to a networking event for highflyers in the property sector, hoping to pitch COMP Consultants to some of the larger enterprises. Instead, over a lunch of salmon and truffle linguine, she'd pitched herself to the multi-millionaire sitting next to her. Bobby Jones, the famously private, fabulously wealthy East End boy made good. This time, she didn't just have a harmless flirtation, or even the kind of brief, meaningless fling that she'd succumbed to a few times in the past. Oh no. This time, she bloody well fell in love and left the bloke who was now upstairs trying to wash off three days of grime and a thick layer of devastation. Within a month of meeting Bobby, she'd left Dan, within six months, she'd divorced him, and within ten months she'd marched up the aisle and said another round of the 'I do's.' A whirlwind romance that was more of a tornado, leaving a path of destruction in its wake. And as usual, both emotionally and physically, I was on clear up.

We'd just given the floor a mop when Dan reappeared, bearing no resemblance whatsoever to the man who'd emerged from the depths of the couch. He'd shaved, so the angles of his jaw were back on full view. His hair had been grey now for a couple of years (it had always been a standing joke that Lulu was the cause of that), but he rocked it in a younger George Clooney way. The bags under his eyes were still there, but they'd subsided enough to get a peek of the bloodshot blue peepers above them.

And somehow, the shower seemed to have washed some of the weight off his shoulders, because he looked like he towered above us again, well over six feet tall when his head wasn't down.

I handed him a mug of fresh coffee, poured another two, then let muscle memory automatically draw us all to the dining table.

Dan opened the conversation with an embarrassed shrug. 'Sorry about that. I guess I wasn't as okay with Lu remarrying as I made out to be. It's just... strange, you know? We've been together for pretty much half my life. I figured I deserved to give her a bit of a leaving party.'

I knew what he was trying to say and I understood. 'You could have invited us, though,' I chided softly. 'It's not like I've got far to travel.'

Dan took a sip of his Colombian roast. 'I know. But I guess... I wanted to wallow. Is that pathetic?'

'No,' I said, at exactly the same time as Jess blurted, 'Yes.' At least that made him laugh.

I threw in my own personal low point of the week. 'You're talking to the woman who was sitting on her utility room floor watching her knickers on a spin cycle an hour ago.'

His brow knitted with a question. 'Hang on, where's Beth?'

'At my mum's,' I explained. 'So I was wallowing too.'

He was still confused. 'Because of Lu?'

'Nope, because today is twenty years since the night I met Colm.'

His whole body sagged again. 'Shit, Shauna, I'm sorry. I should have known that.'

'Why should you?' I countered. 'Colm couldn't have told you the date we met if his life depended on it.' It was true. Colm just about managed my birthday, Beth's date of birth, and the year we met, but all other significant dates went right over his gorgeous head.

'Jesus, would you look at the state of us,' Jess said, shaking her head. 'We are three relatively attractive, relatively successful, relatively balanced people in the prime of our lives and we've had the joy sucked right out of us.'

Fair assertion. Dan and I didn't argue.

'I'm supposed to be a life coach and yet the three of us are sad specimens of humanity. If we were clients of mine, I'd have a few blunt truths for us.'

'Go on then,' Dan prompted, probably realising that it was coming anyway.

I scanned the room for the exits. I knew my problems. I didn't need them to be pointed out.

Jess didn't get that memo. As she took a deep breath, and then began to speak, I was one hundred per cent sure I wasn't going to like anything she had to say.

3

Jess didn't hold back.

'Shauna, since the day Colm died, you've spent your whole life putting on this happy, positive exterior for Beth's sake. And when you're not doing that, you're working your arse off. Meanwhile, on the inside, you're sad, and lonely, and you've never given yourself permission to grieve or allowed your heart or your head to move on.'

Again, no point in arguing with the obvious, but I gave it a shot. 'So what would you have had me do? Fall apart?'

'I'd have had you take care of yourself a bit more.'

'Yeah, well, if we're talking about wishes, I'd have had my husband here a bit more.' My voice was calm. Pragmatic. One of the side effects of losing Colm was that I rarely lost my cool now. All of these minor issues meant nothing when the worst thing had already happened. 'Sometimes you just have to deal with things the best you can,' I added, not that I needed to justify myself. I was proud of how I'd kept going, maintained my business and watched Beth grow into a happy, balanced almost-teenager. Colm died when she was so young that her memory of him had faded, so she'd escaped the worst of the pain. In a way, much as part of me wanted her to have vivid memories of him, I was grateful that she didn't, and that she wasn't carrying the scar of losing a parent. I put that down to her having Colm's easy-going genes, my determination to keep it together, and the fact that Lulu, Dan, Jess and Beth's brothers, Joe and Davie (technically half-brothers, but we rounded up) had wrapped her in love and laughs.

'I know that,' Jess replied, 'but you also have to get to a point where your happiness is real and not an act that you put on for everyone else.'

'Okay, fair point. Can you move on to Mr Peachy Fresh over there because there's only so much of your loving commentary and life-coaching theories I can take. I can't believe people will actually pay you to do this to them.'

'My last lecturer says I have a gift for insight and resolution,' she said, grinning.

'Yeah, well remind me about that when I block your calls and take away your keys to this building,' I said, thinking I might ditch the coffee and raid Dan's fridge in the hope there was some form of alcohol he hadn't yet consumed. 'Right, Dan, your turn. Brace yourself,' I warned him. 'Tune her out and think happy thoughts until her mouth stops moving.'

Jess kicked me under the table, then took another deep breath and focused her attention on the guy with the mighty hangover.

'Okay, Dan, here's the headline: Lulu didn't deserve you. I love her, but she's a fricking nightmare, and you spent twenty years trying to change her, when everyone else could sew their eyes shut and still see that would never happen. It's over. You deserve better. But you need to let go of your marriage and start living for yourself, instead of existing in some kind of twisted co-dependent mess of a relationship.'

Dan visibly bristled and I didn't blame him. 'You make me sound like a total doormat who let someone walk all over them for two decades. Look, I know she had her flaws...'

I choked on my coffee. I adore my darling Lulu, but that was the understatement of the decade.

'... But Lulu and I had some great times. For the most part, we were happy. And I wasn't perfect either, so she doesn't get all the blame.'

'Okay, I'll give you that,' Jess conceded, 'but ending the marriage wasn't your choice. You'd have stayed married to Lulu for ever, despite the fact that you had the peaceful contentment and stability of a war zone.'

'But...' Dan started to argue and she put her hand up.

My toes were curling – I hated emotional confrontations – so I got up to refill the coffee cups.

Jess was unstoppable. 'Dan, there's no arguing with that. And the fact that you're still challenging the truth shows that you haven't accepted it yet.'

'When did you get this bossy and harsh?' he asked, and thankfully I could hear a glimmer of amusement in his voice. 'This has turned into one of those SAS programmes where unsuspecting contestants allow some bloke to bollock them for a week.'

'Sorry. But not really. You need to hear it and just remember it comes from a place of love.'

'That doesn't make it any better at all,' Dan retorted, laughing for the first time since we'd got there.

I jumped in. 'I get it, Dan, I do. And you have to know that Lulu still loves you in some way too.' As I said it, I realised that he didn't know what had prompted us to bang on his door. I wasn't sure if it would make it better or worse, but I went with full disclosure. 'It was Lulu who called and asked us to check on you. She's been trying to call you and was worried because she couldn't get hold of you.'

I could see by the way he flinched that this was a surprise to him. 'My mobile ran out of charge on the way back from the wedding. And then when I got in, I had a beer, and then... Well, you saw the results of what happened next. Why was she trying to reach me?'

'Just to check you were okay,' I said.

He rolled his eyes. 'Great. So now I'm a pity case that the ex feels the need to check on. How pathetic is that?'

Neither of us pointed out the obvious, but it soon dawned on him anyway.

'Yep, she had a point. Right, I need you two to make me a solemn promise that you will never tell her the truth about today. I want you to say I was out cruising in a new Ferrari, with... with...' he seemed to be consulting a database in his mind... 'Stephanie from Bracal Tech. She's the Sales Director and Lulu was always convinced I had a thing for her.'

My curiosity kicked in. 'Did you?' Dan had been trying to land the training contract for Bracal Tech for years and he'd finally succeeded a while ago when the HR department was taken over by the delectable Stephanie – a fact that Lulu didn't let him forget.

'No. Maybe. I'm not sure. I'm so out of practice, and right up until the last minute, I didn't think Lu would marry Bobby, so I'm not sure.'

'This is why you and Colm were best mates,' I interjected. 'Denial and optimism. Those were his default settings.'

'You honestly didn't think she would go through with it? What part of the affair and her moving in with Bobby did you not think gave a heads-up as to her intentions?' Jess questioned him, unable to hide her astonishment.

Dan grimaced. 'Yeah, okay, so in hindsight there were clues. Look, nobody likes a smart-arse.' His sense of humour was definitely emerging, slowly but steadily, from his hangover.

Jess gave a rueful laugh too. 'Okay, well, if it's any consolation, I'm not letting myself off here either.'

My coffee paused in mid-air. 'Oh, I can't wait for this. On you go, oh wise one.'

She paused for a second and I saw a couple of drops of water pool in her bottom eyelids. That was the thing with Jess. She had always appreciated the therapeutic value of a good cry, whereas I'd rather stick forks through my knuckles than sob my heart out in normal life. I saved my tears for things that didn't directly affect me. Sentimental adverts on telly. Programmes about rescue dogs. Danielle Steel books. Sad movies.

After blinking back the tears and clearing her throat, Jess began, 'Since my, erm, *second* divorce, I've completely shut down the prospect of finding love again. Not interested. Absolutely, definitely not. I decided I'd rather stay single forever than go through that again.'

Colm had been waiting for Jess the first time she walked up the aisle. They'd been nineteen when they'd met at uni, and were in their final year there when they discovered Jess was pregnant with the twins. They were happy for a while, but just too young to stick together when they suffered the heartbreak of losing another baby a few years later. After they divorced, Jess met Steve and tried again, but it didn't work. Several years and a whole load of tears later, they split. It was around the same time that Colm was dealing with his illness, and trying to navigate their boys through the imminent loss brought them closer than they'd been for years.

Too close. Way too close.

A memory tried desperately to pop to the surface, but I squashed it back down. I wasn't going there. Not now. Not today. Maybe not ever.

Jess started speaking again.

'I think it was one of the reasons I decided to become a life coach – I knew that if I was going to help other people forge happy, balanced lives, then I was going to have to confront the problems in my own.'

Jess's ability to understand and articulate her own feelings always astounded me. I come from a long line of women who had mastered the art of swallowing their pain and getting on with it – which is probably why I was still spending my private moments sitting on the floor five years later.

'So that's what I'm going to do,' she declared, before turning the heat on me alone. 'And earlier, when we were upstairs, I was about to tell you that I've decided to make you my first client. How can I turn a paying client's life around if I can't sort mine or yours? Plus, I've got to find two willing suspects for case studies for my dissertation, so I'm making you my first victim...'

'Do I have a choice in this?' I asked, stomach knotting in dread. I am, if nothing else, a control freak. I don't do surrender. I keep myself on a tight leash. Since I was a child, I've had to look after myself, with only Lulu, my late gran, Annie, and Colm being allowed into my sphere of influence. Now Jess wanted to take over my life? I felt myself starting to twitch.

'It's amazing, I can almost see your inner core freaking right out,' Jess teased me. 'Take a deep breath. You can do this. I'm not going to wreck your life, I promise. I might even make it better.'

'Get me out of this, Dan,' I begged him, only half kidding. 'I'll give you anything. I'll leave here right now and go slash the tyres on Bobby Jones's Lambo.'

Jess leaned forwards and put her elbows on the table. 'Eh, no. Dan's going to be too busy to bail you out because – thanks to tonight's little debacle – he's my other new client. You two are the case studies, but I'm including myself in the experiment too. We three sad pathetic souls are going to be transformed back into the positive, emotionally balanced, fully functioning human beings that we once were, before life came along and crapped all over us.' She finished on a note of positivity. It was like a politician's campaign speech when they promised to deliver the impossible. Which was probably about six months before they'd forgotten everything they'd vowed to deliver, and instead were plastered across the papers for shagging an aide on the desk of their Parliamentary office.

However, that wasn't what I was thinking at that moment. Another wave of fear consumed me, as I thought about the reality of what she was saying, of what she wanted me to do.

Showing vulnerability was up there with hostage situations in my list of my least favourite things to do in a day, so it took me a minute to find my voice and even then, I had to force the words out. 'What if I don't want to move on? What if hanging on to the memory of the man I loved is all that gets me out of bed every morning, and all that keeps me going until I go back to sleep?'

Dan reached over and took my hand. 'He wouldn't want that, Shauna. You know that.'

'I don't,' I replied honestly. Colm loved me and he'd have wanted me to be happy but... 'You know, we never, ever talked about what would happen after he was gone. Never. He was denial and optimism, with a whole lot of inappropriate laughter, right up until the day he died.'

The two of them stared at me, open-mouthed. Dan found his voice first. 'What, he said nothing?'

I shook my head. 'No. And despite my rampant need to plan

and prepare everything down to the last detail, I said and did nothing either. I felt if I did, then he would think I was giving up on him. So I went along with it. Stayed positive. Didn't bring us down with talk of a future without him. But now I wish we'd had those conversations. I wish we'd talked it all through. I wish we'd made plans for Beth and discussed how I'd handle all the important milestones in her life. I just wish...' I swallowed what felt like a gobstopper at the back of my throat. 'I just wish that I knew I was doing everything the way he would want it to be.'

'Shauna, you are,' Jess assured me, based on absolutely no knowledge or factual evidence whatsoever, just a desire to reassure me and make me feel better. Then she hesitated for a moment. 'But wow, he didn't even leave you a note? A letter?'

I shook my head. After he'd died, I'd gone through his things, expecting to find something. I don't know why. Colm had never been one for thinking things through and planning for the future. Or planning for no future. Still, I was sure I'd find something, but I never did. Since then, I'd been winging it, filled with regret that neither of us had the courage to face the pain of sharing our wishes.

'Sometimes I wonder if that's why I'm stuck. Why I can't make changes or take risks. I can't stand the thought of him looking down on me and being disappointed or hurt.'

'You know he never believed in all that afterlife stuff,' Dan tried to console me, but it didn't work.

'I know that, but what if he was wrong? You know I've always believed that Annie is up there, watching over me and Beth, even though she died before her granddaughter was born. I need to think that. Makes me feel like part of her is still here.' My gran had been a force of nature and I'd always been convinced that if there really was a heaven, the first thing she'd have done up there was knock someone out of an observation post, set up her telescope and do daily checks on our well-being, sending down subliminal wisdom in tough times and the same waves of love she'd shown me when she was alive. Now, I hoped she'd set up a chair right next to her for Colm and the two of them were there, playing cards, drinking bourbon and singing long into the night, stopping only to have a peek down the telescope and keep Beth safe.

It was Jess who finally broke the silence and the sombre moment. 'Okay, I'm pulling rank.'

Both Dan and I looked at her questioningly, which seemed to give her the impetus to carry on.

'I knew Colm longer than both of you, so I'm taking charge. Honestly, if you meet him in the afterlife and he's pissed off with anything that happens from here forward, just blame me. I'm happy to take the rap. He's already divorced me once, so his options for retribution are limited.'

It was such an absurd statement, said with such sincerity, that it made me laugh. Chuckling at inappropriate moments had always been one of my defence mechanisms. I'm mortifying at a funeral. Except Colm's. And my gran's. When my gran passed, every bit of me was broken and I didn't have Beth to keep me strong. And when we said goodbye to Colm, I detached from what was going on so that I could focus on taking care of Beth.

My eyes met Dan's and I saw surrender there. That was all it took for the last shreds of my strength to resist Jess's plan to crumble. Fine. What did I have to lose?

Jess spotted our shrugs of defeat and put both her palms on the table. 'Right then. Let's do this.'

'Do you have an actual plan or just a rough notion?' Dan asked her.

She squirmed slightly. 'To be honest, I didn't think for a second that Shauna would agree, so my plan to turn your lives around is yet to be fully formulated,' she admitted sheepishly. 'But I know where we're going to start.'

'Where's that?' I asked, all resistance gone.

'Dan, pass the remote control and a box of tissues. Let's see if I can pick up any tips from Gerard Butler.'

4

COLM – 2016

I check the notes on my phone for the list that I'd prepared in the two hours I'd been waiting on my latest MRI scan last week. There was a backlog and I was stuck in the waiting room. It was a patients-only area so Shauna went for a cup of tea in the hospital cafeteria while I sat there in one of those blue gowns that tied at the back and flashed your arse when you walked. Who invented those? Surely there had to be a more innovative design than one that could have you up on charges of accidental exposure. It could cause a major incident if anyone put it on the wrong way round.

Anyway, I passed the time thinking through all the things I wanted to say in these videos, all the people I wanted to talk about, all the messages I wanted to pass on, and yes, I hated every second of it. Shauna has always said that I'm emotionally stunted and, like I said earlier, she's right. I'll choose denial and optimism every time. It cost me my first marriage and since I met Shauna I've let her down on so many occasions when I should have been there for her but I just didn't know how. Anyway, I'll get to that stuff later. I'm going to start with the things that are easier for me to talk about.

I check the list again. Yep, I know where to kick this off.

I reach over and place my phone back on the makeshift stand I set up earlier, then I shake out my shoulders. Okay, I've got this. Come on Colm, ya useless fecker, let's get this done.

I make sure I'm already smiling when I press 'record'.

'Right, m'darlin', let's get this started. By the way, I miss you. I miss you now when you're not with me, and I'm pretty sure that when you finally see these videos, well, I'll be missing you then too, because you're the other half of my soul.'

I feel myself choking back up, so I clear my throat and try to shake it off with flippancy. 'Och, listen to me getting all senti-mental again. Honest to God, I'm sure it's the drugs. Anyway, here's the first thing that's on my mind. Babe, after I'm gone, I need you to keep an eye on Dan for me, because much as I pray I'm wrong, we both know that Lu will break his heart again.'

I lean back on the pillow, making sure I'm still in view of the camera.

'Sometimes I wonder if I should have stopped him getting married that morning in Spain. He asked me outright if he should go ahead with it and I said it was up to him. I bottled out. You know what they were like back then – on again, off again, but God, they loved each other. They probably always will, but we both know sometimes that isn't enough. And you know I'm not saying this because I don't love Lu, because I do, but she's...'

I struggle to find the words. In fact, I struggle to find a lot of words when it comes to Shauna and Lulu. Or rather, the life they grew up in. First day I met Shauna's parents, Debbie and Jeff, was at their twenty-fifth wedding anniversary party in their stock-broker belt garden with all their stuck-up golfing chums. They made a big speech thanking their friends, Charlie and Gwen, Lulu's mum and dad. The two couples, posh as can be, have always been inseparable. Quite literally. When we were leaving, we went to say goodbye and Shauna's dad was in a bedroom with Lulu's mother. I know. It's a total mind warp. Shauna and Lulu grew up with parents who pretty much ignored them, while the adults were inter-shagging their way through the years. Seriously messed up.

I realise I've drifted off topic again, and flick my gaze back to the camera and try to finish the point I was attempting to make. 'Lulu is… a free spirit. You know that next month, next year, maybe five years from now, she'll wander again. It's who she is and our mate, Dan, well, he knows it. He'll stick in there though, because even though deep down he knows she's going to do it, he tells himself that she won't. Just keep an eye on him, will you, love? And I'm not asking you to betray Lu's trust, but if you can see a disaster on the horizon, could you give him a heads-up and try to prepare him for it? And then help him through whatever happens? If I'm not around, then you're the only one who can be there for him.'

I smile. 'I know what you're thinking, m'darlin'. Dan and I have had about three serious conversations in our life and the rest stuck to footie and beer, but there's something in that. If Lu breaks his heart again, he'll just need someone to be there. Although, if you do fancy taking his mind off whatever is going on, cracking open a few beers and taking him to a Chelsea game is the equivalent of a month in therapy for blokes like us.'

It is pretty shallow, but it is also true.

'Anyway, that's me going to cross Dan off my list, because I know you've got his back. I love you, Shauna. Always will.'

As soon as I press the red button to stop the recording, my fake smile fades and I sag with relief. One down. Just need to get through a few more before I say goodbye.

5

'I would just like to state here and now that I agreed to all this when I was in a compromised state and my bloodstream was pretty much one hundred per cent alcohol,' Dan announced, as he pulled out a bar stool at the breakfast bar in my kitchen.

Just over a week after the whole three-day bender incident, Dan was restored to his usual handsome, together self. He'd come straight from the office, so he was still in his suit, and as always, the minute he walked in I felt a twinge of loss in my gut. Colm O'Flynn, in a suit, when he came home from the office, used to be one of my favourite sights. He and Dan trained in the gym together five times a week, so they both had similar body shapes – the broad, muscular shoulders, the slender hips, but Colm... well, he had a way of way of working smart clothes that made me melt. The tie was always loose, or sometimes discarded altogether, the sleeves would be rolled up, the dark waves of his hair would be haphazardly pushed back from his face, with one lock always determined to fall on his forehead, and almost always, unless he'd had a really bad day, there would be the glint in his eye and his ever-present grin as he walked in the door.

I took a moment to let that image go, then slid a coffee in front of Dan. 'I hear you. I keep hoping Jess will get a real job and let us continue to wallow. I can do wallowing. I'm great at it.' I was joking, of course, but there was a grain of truth there – the same one that got us into this in the first place.

'Anyway, how are you doing? Things any better?' In the last week, I'd texted him every day and popped in to see him a couple of times and he'd insisted he was fine but I could sense he wasn't back to his usual laid back, chipper self.

He shrugged. 'Yeah, I think so. It's probably just a bit weird because Lulu's still on honeymoon, although she's stopped calling me now since you told her I was out with Stephanie from Bracal Tech. I owe you one for that.'

That made me smile. Not, of course, that I enjoyed telling lies to my lifelong friend, but the stakes were higher for Dan on this occasion, so I had his back. Lulu had gone suspiciously silent when I told her that, which, to be honest, just irritated me. She'd moved on, so what if Dan had too? I found it strange that she still seemed to feel a need to speak to him every day, although, they'd been joined at the hip for twenty years, so maybe it just took time to adjust. I was pretty sure the guilt of leaving him contributed to that too. 'All part of the upstairs neighbour service. Thai food okay?'

He raised his eyebrows. 'Is that anywhere near the Maldives?'

'Definitely not.'

'Then it's perfect.'

I'd just fetched the takeaway menu from the kitchen drawer, when there was a loud knock at the door, then Jess came in. Her cute, cropped jeans and white Bardot top, her make-up-free face and ponytail, made her look at least ten years younger than her forty-five years. I really needed to change the lock.

'You showed up!' she exclaimed, her gaze going from Dan to

me and back again. 'I was sure the two of you would suddenly remember an urgent engagement or a long-lost auntie who needed to be visited.'

I pulled another cup out of the cupboard. 'I was going to try that, but I've only got one aunt and she's in Scotland. It's a long way to travel to get away from you.'

'And I knew you'd hunt me down, so I figured it was easier to come quietly,' Dan told her. 'Plus, Shauna promised to feed me if I came here so that swung the deal.'

Jess plonked her bag down on the worktop. 'What you really mean is that you've thought everything through and realised that you could really benefit from my expertise and insight, and that you're thrilled I'm your new life coach, so you couldn't wait to get here to begin the process of working with me to transform your lives.'

Dan's eyes widened, then he nodded slowly. 'Sure.'

Before Jess could answer, Beth wandered in, backpack slung over one shoulder. 'Aunt Jess! I thought I heard you,' she exclaimed, opening her arms and giving Jess a hug. That, right there, was the biggest gift that came from being close to my husband's ex-wife. I'd been Joe and Davie's stepmother since they were four, and even now that they were grown, twenty-five-year-old men and living their own lives they still texted me most days and came for Sunday lunch when they could. And on the flip side, Beth had a second mum who treated her like her own, loved her to bits and who was part of her everyday life.

'Mum says you've got a mad plan to change her life,' Beth said, her easy smile exactly the same as her dad's.

Jess threw me a pointed glare. 'Mad plan?'

I shrugged, laughing. My daughter had yet to fully under-stand tact and subtlety. Then again, her father had never managed either one of them, so I wasn't sure that would change.

'Am I allowed to make requests?' Beth asked, flicking back her dark curls. At eleven, she was already the same height as Jess, and only a couple of inches shorter than my five foot eight. It made her both self-conscious because she stood several inches above her friends, but also the star of the school netball team, so she was getting an early lesson in pros and cons. 'Could you make her change my lights-out time to 11 p.m. and tell her it's a great idea to go to Ibiza this summer? Marcy goes every year and she says it's brilliant. She met Calvin Harris once and he signed her hand. She didn't wash it for weeks.'

Another of her dad's qualities: her enthusiasm for life oozed out of every pore.

Jess nodded. 'Only if I can come too,' she said. 'And if Calvin Harris signs my hand, I won't wash either.'

'Deal! Can we, Mum? Can we go?'

'Maybe. But we're taking soap and you two are getting lessons in hand hygiene. Right, are you ready? Marcy's mum will be here any minute.' I wrapped my arms around her and squeezed. Thankfully she hadn't quite reached that phase where she rejected her mother's affections and pretended she didn't know me if she met me in the street. Although, I'm forty-five and still have the urge to hide when my mother is around. But then, my mother, Saint Debbie of the Eternal Disapproval, has that effect on most people.

Beth returned the hug, kissed Jess on the cheek, then did the same to her beloved Uncle Dan.

'Have a great time, kiddo,' he replied. 'If you get arrested, phone me instead of your mother,' he added, as he always did, and every time it made Beth chuckle. Our self-made family. I would always be grateful for the people in Beth's life.

A ping on my phone told me that Linda, Marcy's mum, was outside. I had a quick glance out of the window and waved, getting a thumbs up in response. Linda was a single mum too, and for years we'd traded childcare. She took the girls to netball on a Thursday night, then they stayed over at her house, and I did the same on Monday nights.

I gave Beth another quick hug as she dived out the door, then watched at the window until she'd climbed into Linda's car and waved.

'Prawn curry and noodles,' Dan was saying as I got back to the breakfast bar in the kitchen.

Jess took my order too, and fired it all into an app on her phone, then lifted her coffee mug.

'Okay, people, I hereby announce that the first session of the Thursday Life Coaching Club is now in session.'

Dan groaned. 'I prefer the Thursday Sad Git's Recovery Club. I'm a sucker for accuracy.'

'I feel like we should have a brass band or a ribbon that we can cut,' I said, ignoring him, too busy seesawing between being amused and dreading this with every iota of my being.

'I'll bring those next week,' Jess quipped, pulling a folder out of her bag and opening it on the table. 'I've given this lots of thought, and I've come up with a programme for us. It's like AA, only without the strangers and with a few steps less. The important thing, the crux of this whole project, is that we understand that in order to move forward, we have to let go of the past.'

I suddenly had no appetite for my curry. This was fine when it was a vague notion, one of Jess's mad ideas, but now it was actually happening, I could feel my anxiety rising.

I returned to my previous objection. What if I didn't want to let go of the past? For the last five years I'd been hanging on to it until my knuckles went white.

'And to do that, we have to talk about it, revisit it, make peace and lay it to rest.'

Dan was looking decidedly uneasy too. 'I preferred you when you only talked about superficial stuff, like celebrity gossip and what the boys were up to,' he murmured.

Jess gave him her very best death stare. 'And I preferred you when you weren't moping around wondering where it all went wrong.'

Ouch. Jess The Friend was loving and warm and an unlimited source of care and compassion. Jess The Life Coach was a whole other bitchy ball game.

'Okay,' she moved on, consulting her notes again. 'Every week, we will have a new task or conversation topic, all of them designed to make us confront what's happened in our lives and find some kind of resolution.'

Was it too late to cancel? Could we just break out the popcorn and watch a Chris Hemsworth movie instead?

I was thinking these things, but nothing was coming out of my mouth, which was just as well because Jess was in full flow now.

'So tonight, we're going to start with the easy stuff, the positive things that made us give our heart to that person in the first place. We're all going to share one memory, something that sums up why we loved that person.'

Nope, didn't want to do this. No way. Not ever. I couldn't. Wouldn't.

But Jess wasn't getting the message.

'Shauna, why don't you go first?'

6

'You know, I think this might be my favourite place on earth,' I said, with a contented sigh. It was one of those rare days when neither of us were working and we were sitting in a lush park on the bank of the Thames. We were just a mile or so from where we'd first met, yet it felt like a different world. Marble Hill Park was only a few streets away from our home on the Twickenham side of the river, and it was the first place we headed for when the sun was shining. Today it was high in the sky, so we'd put up a little pop-up sun tent on our blanket to protect Beth from the rays.

Other groups were dotted on blankets around the grass, gatherings of mums with toddlers, couples with their arms entwined, families with squads of children and then there was us: Colm, me, Beth, our own little world.

'Lean over so I can put more suncream on you,' I said, my gaze on the faint redness that was starting to creep over the back of his shoulders. It was a standing joke that the only thing that would sufficiently protect his fair Irish skin from the sun's rays was a duffle coat.

'Tell the truth – you just want an excuse to touch the ravishing gorgeousness of this body,' he teased, sucking in his almost-a-six-pack, before adding in a high, breathy voice. 'But can you do it quick because I can't hold my breath for much longer.' My laughter floated over the heads of the sun seekers nearby and a few turned to smile.

Colm O'Flynn made me laugh almost every day in life. Even the bad ones, when I was furious with him for some triviality, or irritated by his refusal to take anything seriously, or narky because he'd left his pants on the floor again, or stressed because our bills were higher than our bank balance. On those days, he'd get that glint in his eye, and he'd pull me close, and say something like, 'Hey, m'darlin', don't worry. This is just today. Me and you are always.' And then he'd usually finish off the moment of sweet romance with something along the lines of, 'Now come to bed and I'll let you take your frustrations out on my body. Just to take your mind off your woes, you understand.'

The only times in my life that his charm hadn't been enough to sooth my soul was when we were trying and failing to conceive and when Annie died. Those were rough patches and there were many days when it looked like we might not make it through them in one piece, but somehow we did. Now, apart from a crippling work schedule and tight finances – I was working insane hours to support us while Colm and Dan got their management consultancy up and running – life was bliss. And we had Beth. Our gorgeous Beth.

I noticed Colm's gaze drift a few metres, to where a dad was playing football with his son. I could tell what he was thinking before he said it out loud. He rolled towards our five-year-old daughter, who was happily colouring in a unicorn with purple crayons, while singing quietly. We were still in her *Frozen*, 'Let It Go' phase and she sang it all day long, until I was having malicious thoughts about what I'd do to a Disney princess should she find herself in my kitchen.

'Bethy,' he whispered. 'Can you see that kid over there?' he pointed at the mini footie player, probably around eight or nine, who was running back and forward with his very chiselled dad, kicking a ball in between two trees.

Beth glanced up. 'Yep.'

'I reckon we could take them. Whad'ya think?'

Beth's eyes narrowed. 'Deffo, Dad.' I wasn't sure what was melting my heart more – her confidence or the shorthand she shared with her father.

'Hey, mate,' Colm shouted over to the other dad. 'D'ya mind if me and my girl have a kick around with you?'

I watched as the little boy's brow lowered in horror at the sight of a curly-haired girl in an Elsa costume staring at him expectantly.

The adult was a tad more diplomatic. 'Sure, no problem.'

As he scrambled to his feet, Colm leaned towards Beth and spoke in hushed tones. 'Okay, when I give you the nod, I want you to take the ball, I'll go left, you go right, you know what to do...'

I watched Beth unconsciously move her hands, as if confirming her right and left in her head. That done, she nodded with a surety that I don't think I've ever possessed. My heart exploded as this man and his daughter straightened up and headed into battle.

The other kid had the ball and clearly wanted to show off his skills. Colm allowed him to kick the ball straight through his legs, then little Beckham ran around him, got the ball again, shot for the space in between the trees and... missed.

Beth took a few steps towards where the ball came to a stop, but the boy cut her off with a sharp nudge of his shoulder.

'Still my turn,' he insisted.

'Isn't,' Beth countered. 'It's our turn now.'

'It's my game, so it's my rules,' little Beckham snapped. 'I keep the ball until I score.'

To her credit, Beth didn't bite back, but I saw the teeth clench and her eyes narrow with laser focus. She despised unfairness. Hated being told she was wrong, when she was right. And wasn't too fond of obnoxious little kids either. Tiny Beckham had no idea what he'd just done.

His father didn't chide him, just shrugged with a half-hearted apology. His kid clearly had free rein to do as he pleased.

The boy dribbled his way back to his father, turned round and headed for the makeshift goal again. His head was down, focusing on the ball, so I'm pretty sure he didn't even notice the nod that Colm gave our daughter. It was all she needed. Wee Princess Elsa morphed into Dash from *The Incredibles*, sprinted forward and deftly swiped the ball. She then passed it to her father, who took a couple of steps then swerved it back to her, at which point she blasted it with a left kick that sent it soaring through the space in the trees.

'One nil to us. I'll show you how to do that if you want,' she told miffed Beckham, with genuine kindness, but he was already storming off, shouting something about wanting an ice cream. Beth just shrugged and came back to her little shaded area and resumed colouring. 'Let It Go...'

I gave Colm an admonishing glance as he slumped back down beside me. 'And what did that teach our daughter?' I asked, with mock chastisement.

He grinned. 'That there's nothing she can't do better than a little emperor with a big ego?'

I flicked his arm. 'Has anyone ever told you you're incredibly immature?'

He wore that like a badge of honour. 'Absolutely,' he said,

leaning over and kissing me. 'But I reckon that must not be a bad thing because I still managed to get a pretty cool chick to marry me.'

'Oh yeah? She must have the patience of a saint,' I teased.

Chuckling, he kissed me again, then reached over for the picnic bag and broke out the sandwiches, the fruit, and the chocolate chip cookies that Beth and I had made that morning.

We spent the rest of the afternoon lying on the blanket, with his head on my stomach, just chatting about something and nothing. He didn't even complain when Beth pulled a purple nail varnish out of her little backpack and asked to paint his toenails – or when she applied it so haphazardly, it ended up looking less like a pedicure and more like some kind of tropical infection.

I loved that Colm was up for any game or activity when it came to Beth.

For the next few hours, we gabbed, we sang songs. We broke out a swingball set and had a ferocious competition that ended with Beth adding another win to her athletic achievements for the day. We chilled with our daughter, colouring, playing cards, reading from the book that she'd stashed next to the nail varnish in her backpack. And when she dozed off for her afternoon nap, I kissed my husband like I used to do when we first met, milking the moment for every ounce of pleasure, because my weekends were fully booked with work for the next few months, and I had no idea when we'd get to do this again.

By late afternoon, the sun was beginning to fall. Some of the families had packed up and left, but a second shift had arrived, a scattering of solos, couples and families, perhaps parents who'd been working during the day and were now snatching a couple of hours of fresh air.

'Snap!' Beth exclaimed, as her hand flew in to cover the king of hearts that Colm had just put down on a king of spades.

The three of us were sitting cross-legged on the blanket now, a pile of cards and a bag of popcorn in the centre of our triangle.

Colm threw his cards up in the air with a dramatic flourish. 'That's it. I'm not playing with you any more,' he told Beth. 'Are you sure you're five, because I think we've got that wrong. At least Davie and Joe waited until they were ten before they beat me.'

Beth giggled. 'I'm five and three quarters. And it's not the winning, it's the taking part that matters, Dad. My teacher always tells us that.'

'How did you get to be so grounded and mature?' Colm groaned. 'You're supposed to be a kid. You shouldn't be that sensible until you're....' he turned to me. 'What age am I, Shauna?'

'Forty,' I told him. He didn't miss a beat, turning straight back to Beth. 'Until you're forty-one. Maybe forty-two.'

I shook my head, amused as ever by his ability to see the fun in everything.

It was probably time we headed home and got Beth into a bath and then bed, but I was in no rush to burst this little bubble of happiness. Family days like this were so rare and so precious, I didn't want to cut it short by a single minute.

We grazed on the rest of the fruit and bread in the picnic basket that I'd overpacked, then Beth struck up a conversation with a boy roughly the same age who was eating ice cream with his grandparents nearby. As the two kids played a few feet away, Colm wrapped his arms around me and pulled me to him, so that my back was against his chest, his arm across my collarbone, his cheek at my ear.

'Let's have another one,' he murmured in my ear.

'They're done. I think there are only a couple of bananas left.'

That made him howl and it took me a moment to get the joke.

I thought he was talking about bread rolls. He was talking about something far more important.

His shoulders were still shaking when he explained, 'I meant another kid.'

'Oh.' My cheeks flushed as red as his shoulders. It had taken years for us to conceive Beth, and it only happened after I'd convinced an incredibly resistant Colm that having another child would be a good idea. Arduous rounds of fertility treatment had failed, but suddenly, by some miracle, I'd fallen pregnant naturally. We'd taken no precautions after Beth, but there had been no blue line on a test kit. 'Babe, I don't think it's going to happen.' I didn't tell him that every month I still felt a desperate hope, followed by a twinge of disappointment. We had Beth. We were luckier than some families who never managed to conceive. I should take the win and stop dreaming of more.

'Let's try. Really try. Talk to the doc about more fertility treatment...' That astonished me – Colm had absolutely hated every minute of the process the first time round. His pathological avoidance of tough situations and the monthly blow to his relentless optimism, combined with the fear of history repeating itself, of losing another child before it had even had a chance of life, was too much for him.

The fact that he loved me enough to even suggest this, made my heart melt.

'And just so you know, I definitely think we should start putting extra practice in. I'm thinking tonight...'

He was nuzzling my ear now and I swear my ovaries were conducting the 'Hallelujah Chorus'.

Later, we strolled back to our house, the two of us holding Beth's hands and swinging her between us. At home, I gave her a bath, while Colm cleared out the picnic bag and poured a couple of glasses of wine.

'Can you both read me a story tonight?' Beth asked, as she pulled on her Batman pyjamas. Disney princess by day, super-hero by night.

I hugged her tightly, inhaling the intoxicating smell of her freshly washed hair.

'Of course we can, my darling,' I told her, relishing the prospect just as much as she did. Having us both together was a rare treat. Colm and I were usually a tag team in the evenings. If I was catering an event, he made sure he was home to put Beth to bed. If I was home, he put in the extra hours that were needed at the office while he and Dan grew their fledgling company. Colm and I knew why we were doing it – it was a short-term sacrifice for the long life we were going to have together. It was all part of our grand plan. We were going to carry on working our hearts out for the next five years or so, establish our compa-nies, then we'd be able to recalibrate our work/life balance and focus on quality of life, on enjoying the moment, on travelling and having fantastic experiences, on each other. And on the family that my gorgeous husband had just committed to expanding.

As I dried off Beth's hair, we sang 'Let It Go' at the tops of our voices, Beth chuckling as I adopted a ridiculously operatic, out-of-tune soprano voice. I'd just switched off the hairdryer when a noise at the bedroom door made me look over. Colm was standing there, his grin wide, eyes twinkling. He scooped Beth up and tossed her over his shoulder, making her squeal with laughter until he deposited her under her Scooby Doo duvet. Our girl had every genre of children's entertainment covered.

Her ten-minute story turned into twenty, then thirty, and only ended when she could no longer fight the urge to close her eyes.

I tucked her duvet around her, kissed her forehead, then took Colm's hand and led him to our bedroom. For once, I wasn't too tired. He wasn't too distracted by work projects or preparation for his next meeting.

'C'mere, m'darlin',' he whispered, pulling me close, his hands on my face, his thumbs grazing over my cheeks. 'God, I love you, Shauna O'Flynn.'

'Mmmmm,' I murmured, as I moved closer, until my lips were almost touching his. 'I think you're just saying that because I'm about to be naked.'

His chuckle was low and sexy. 'You could be right. Let's test that theory out.'

And we did. For the first time in a long time, we made the kind of long, slow love that had been one of our very favourite pastimes in the early days of our relationship, before the ups, downs and stresses of life got in the way. I'd almost forgotten how incredible it could feel when it wasn't rushed or grudged or make-up sex after a stupid row because we were so tired that we'd snap at the least little thing.

Afterwards, my head was on his chest as he idly played with my hair. 'Yep, definitely love you more when yer naked,' he mused, making me laugh again.

'And I love you more when you're not making really bad jokes,' I retorted archly.

He responded by rolling over, so that he was above me, our noses almost touching.

'I'm going to make you so happy, you know that?' he said. 'Forever. Me and you.'

'Colm O'Flynn, are you getting all mushy and romantic in your old age?'

He blushed a little. 'I am. I'll be reciting poetry next. There once was a woman from Nantucket...'

I clamped my hand over his mouth. 'I love you back, you gorgeous man. And I like the sound of forever.'

He kissed me again, then we snuggled in tight and were asleep in minutes. We didn't realise it then, but that was the perfect end to our last day of carefree happiness.

The next day Colm had the first headache.

And our family was never the same again.

7

The weight on my chest felt like it could crush me, squash my lungs, squeeze every breath from my body. I'd never told anyone about that day before. The memory had been locked in my mind somewhere, yet another file in the 'Do Not Open' box, the one that I avoided at all costs, the one that I never reopened because I was way too scared of the pain.

'I thought this was supposed to make me feel better,' I blurted in Jess's direction. Not even her expression of pure compassion was enough to ease the turmoil inside me.

Dan, meanwhile, was fetching my bottle of Prosecco from the fridge and filling my glass back up to the brim. He was just like Colm in so many ways – hopeless with emotional stuff, but great with the essential practicalities.

'I'm so sorry, Shauna,' Jess said sheepishly. 'I really am. But it's going to be a process and it's going to hurt sometimes. We have to acknowledge what we had, in order to face our feelings and deal with them.'

My gaze went to Dan. 'Make her stop. Can we not have a Thursday night book club instead of this?'

Dan was on my side. 'I reckon a bit of crime fiction with serial killers and the odd bite of cannibalism would be preferable to this.'

Jess gave us a glare of disgust. 'My skills are wasted on you two, they really are. Would you rather I just let you stay stuck in this barren no man's land between the life you used to have and your future?'

'Definitely,' Dan retorted, just as I said, 'Absolutely.' I appreciated her efforts, but we were only on week one and already I felt like my soul had been sucked out by a Dyson.

She shook her head, determination all over her face. 'Nope, not happening. I'm going to get us all out of these slumps we've descended in to and one day you'll thank me.'

I nudged Dan, who was climbing back onto the stool next to me at the breakfast bar. 'Do you think anyone's ever written a crime novel about a widow who knocks off her dead husband's ex-wife because she's become a power-crazy life coach?'

'I think if we stick around long enough it'll be a true-life story,' he said, jumping right onto the same wavelength.

Jess ignored us and just carried on as if we hadn't spoken.

'Okay, I'll go next,' she said. 'My favourite memory of being with Steve was the day he asked me to marry him. It was a Saturday morning, the rain was pouring down and we were watching Joe and Davie play in a football match. They were maybe five or six years old. Actually, you and Colm were there too, standing over by the goal, huddled together and you were wearing a bright red bobble hat. For some reason that always stuck in my mind.'

As Jess carried on talking, her memory became mine too. I remembered that morning. It was early December, a few months after we married. Davie and Joe were the cutest little guys, but I was feeling a little self-conscious, gate-crashing the event with

Colm, walking into an environment where everyone knew each other, and I was the new wife. Even more so because Jess was there. I'd met Colm's first wife a couple of times and she'd been perfectly pleasant. Why shouldn't she? She'd moved on – she'd met someone else before Colm and I got together – and in fact she was here with him now. I was curious. Did she have a type? Was he anything like Colm?

A quick glance. Nope, nothing like Colm. This guy was slicker, with his sharp haircut and his Barbour jacket. Years later, every time I watched *Suits*, the main character, Harvey, would remind me of Steve, but back then I just thought he was a good-looking man, who seemed perfectly pleasant and treated the boys well. That was good enough for me.

That morning, out of the corner of my eye, I'd watched them interact. They were tactile, but not too over the top with cringy displays of affection. What struck me most was that both of them seemed to be happy, despite the fact that we were in danger of getting some kind of horrendous foot infection from standing on sodden grass for two hours.

Yeah, they were good together, I decided. At ease. Natural. Meant to be.

That's why I wasn't surprised when, just after the full-time whistle went, Joe and Davie ran over to them, and stood on either side of Steve, their little faces pictures of concentration. Jess was clearly puzzled though, until Steve fell to one knee and pulled a tiny box out of his pocket. Jess's hand flew to her mouth in shock, but her delight was obvious, especially when Joe and Davie kneeled too, and all three of the men in her life held up boxes. I found out later that it was all pre-planned: that Steve's box had an engagement ring in it, and Davie and Joe's both had Haribo gummy rings.

Jess burst into tears, accepted the rings, hugged them all and then took a bow as the rest of us cheered. Colm was genuinely happy for them and that made me love him a little bit more. There was no jealousy, no resentment that another man was going to be such a strong influence in his sons' lives, just genuine delight that Jess and the kids were happy.

Jess's voice was wistful now. 'I was so touched that he'd included the boys and couldn't believe he wanted to take us all on. To be honest – sorry Shauna – he was the type of guy I'd always wanted Colm to be: someone who would step up and care and provide for our family, someone who could handle life's curveballs and stand strong and steady. A grown-up.'

She threw me an apologetic glance, but it wasn't necessary. I completely understood what she was saying. I'd loved my husband beyond words, but there had been many times when I'd wished that he would sort out a problem, instead of ignoring it. That he would take care of fixing issues instead of leaving everything to me. That his talent for denial and oblivion would take a back seat to grown-up planning and organisation. Jess had felt the same when they were married and his inability to support her when they lost a baby had ended their marriage after only four years.

I could see why Jess would look for a guy she could count on after Colm, someone who would take equal responsibility for their lives.

'At that time, in that moment, I honestly thought we would last forever,' Jess admitted, tears streaming down her face. 'God, how wrong was I?'

I climbed off my stool and went round to her side of the table so that I could hug her tightly.

'Maybe…' she sniffed, '… this is a shit idea after all. Maybe I'm a crap life coach.'

'You're not crap at this,' I murmured into her hair, as she sniffed again on my shoulder.

Over the top of her head, my eyes met Dan's cynical gaze, as he mouthed, 'She is!'

I retorted with a silent, 'I know!'

In what world could this help us? All we were doing here was contributing to a mass pity party. It was a truly terrible idea, but I wasn't going to tell my sobbing friend that, because I couldn't kick her while she was down.

Still holding her close with one arm, I reached over for a roll of kitchen towel and pulled a sheet off.

Jess blew her nose with a volume that was up there with a fighter jet doing a fly-by outside my window.

'Okay,' she spluttered, getting herself together.

I let her go and she inhaled deeply, then shook out her shoulders, as if shrugging off her sorrow.

'I need to revel in someone else's misery. Dan, you're up. Let's go. Tell us about your best day with Lulu.'

Dan's very handsome face twisted into something resembling horror. 'Why would I do that? Shauna is traumatised and you're on the edge of hysteria. I'm thinking we swerve this whole thing, grab some beers and see if there's a good movie on TV. I'll even watch a romcom, as long as Reese Witherspoon is in it and I can have inappropriate thoughts about how we'd pass the time if I was stuck in a broken-down lift with her.'

Jess responded with the kind of glare usually reserved for Davie and Joe, back when they were teenagers and made the occasional mistake of challenging her when she'd asked them to do something. And, of course, it was accompanied by high-grade sarcasm. 'Yeah, because you'd definitely stand a chance there, Romeo. I hear Reese Witherspoon has a thing for emotionally stunted blokes who only get truly passionate when they're watching twenty-two men chasing a rubber ball on a big bit of lawn.'

Dan didn't argue, but neither did he seem particularly perturbed about this accusation, mainly because there was a grain of truth in it. Colm and Dan spent hours together every week, yet they rarely discussed anything deeper than Chelsea's chances of winning the league or something called the transfer window. I was never exactly sure what that was because every time they started talking about it, I slipped into a coma.

Dan held his hands up. 'Okay, okay. But you're getting the pamphlet edition, because I totally don't see the point in this.'

Jess opened her mouth to bite back, but I got there first with a more conciliatory approach. 'That's okay. You do this whatever way you want.' I shot a loaded glare to Jess and she got the message, clamping her mouth shut before she pushed him to the point where he would dig his heels in and refuse to participate.

Instead, she got him another beer from the fridge, then slid it along the breakfast bar like we were in an old Western saloon. 'There you go, buttercup. Some liquid courage in case your inner macho explodes when you're trying to access authentic emotions.'

That made Dan laugh, and thawed out the atmosphere as he summoned up his favourite memory. I wondered if it would be his wedding day, a gloriously beautiful ceremony on a picture-perfect beach in Spain. Or perhaps the night he and Lulu got engaged as we ate and drank under a Balinese moon.

But no. He surprised me by going back even further, to the earlier years of their relationship.

'It must have been about a year after we started seeing each other. I'd already introduced you to Colm and five minutes later you guys were married.'

I gave a 'what can you do' shrug that made him laugh, before he went on.

'You two were so happy, but over in our house, we were struggling. Actually, that's not completely accurate – I was struggling, and Lu was being Lu. She was just storming her way through life, taking no prisoners and living like there was no tomorrow. It's strange, because that was what excited me and terrified me in equal measure.'

I knew exactly what he meant. Lulu and I had been like sisters our whole life, and she'd had exactly the same effect on me for as long as I could remember. There was something intoxicating about being in the presence of someone who grabbed every opportunity for enjoyment and pleasure, who had a tireless thirst for joy. It's what made it possible to live with the challenges that also came with the package.

'Anyway, it was her twenty-fifth birthday and we'd been living together for a few months, so we threw a party downstairs. Even though it should have been a fantastic time for us, she was restless. I could sense it, but I thought I was imagining it. I mean, why wouldn't she be happy? As far as I was concerned, everything was cool. We had a smart home, good jobs, great friends...'

I wasn't sure exactly what was coming – there had been so many dramas over the years that I couldn't pinpoint which one this was – but I suddenly had that feeling that came at the start of a roller coaster, when you knew you were about to climb to a spectacular point at the top, but you were fairly sure that you'd plummet to earth pretty soon afterwards.

'You and Colm had helped us set everything up for the party...'

Jess cleared her throat. 'For the purposes of this process, I'm not going to mention the fact that I wasn't invited to this little soirée.'

Dan winced. 'Sorry. You know that Lulu wasn't your greatest fan at the start.'

'Sometimes I'm not sure that's changed,' Jess retorted.

I knew she wasn't being serious. In the beginning, Lu was being protective of me by keeping Colm's ex-wife at a distance. It took her a moment to thaw out and accept Jess as a true friend. And by 'moment', I mean about fifteen years.

'So, as I was saying...' he moved swiftly on. 'Big party, I'm happy, Lulu is happy, all is good, although there's definitely an undertone that I can't put my finger on. I'm ignoring that, though. Turns out I'm pretty good at ignoring shit I don't want to see. Everyone arrives and it's going great and I feel like the luckiest guy in the world. Someone hooks up a karaoke machine and...'

'Lulu and Colm did the whole Sonny and Cher act!' I blurted, pinpointing the memory in my mind. That had been a fantastic day, until...

Dan headed off my thought with, 'Yep! They rocked that, but they couldn't get enough of it. They did about four duets in a row, and after they were George Michael and Elton John, we prised the microphones from their hands and told them to give someone else a turn.'

Yes, we did. Colm was crushed that his moment in the limelight had ended, and Lulu threatened a full-scale diva strop, but we calmed them down with praise and alcohol.

'Sometime after that, I noticed Lulu outside talking to some bloke. Didn't give it much thought because I recognised his face – it was that Australian bloke that used to work at the bar. She looked like she was flirting, but then, Lulu flirted with everyone she ever met. It was like breathing to her. That's when I realised that the uneasy feeling I'd had in my gut was fear and for a split second, I acknowledged it, then I blew it off, but I couldn't help keep an eye on her. That's when the parents arrived. All of them. Your mum and dad, and Lulu's mum and dad. They came in, all fecking winter suntans and respectability, and I saw Lulu spot them and she had the same reaction she always had. Her shoulders slumped and she looked pissed off that they were even there.'

That was a pretty accurate assessment. As kids, Lulu had always desperately wanted their approval and love, but there came a point when we were teenagers that she realised it would never happen and that's when she'd flipped to scorn and general disdain. I remember her summing the situation up one afternoon when she told Colm that her and I were 'the less than perfect daughters of the two most self-centred couples in the free world'. She wasn't wrong.

Jess chipped in with a quick question to me. 'Can I ask, did your parents always have an open marriage? Every time I met them, I thought they were so proper and terrifyingly strait-laced – I couldn't believe it when I found out they had a whole interchangeable thing going on. And your dad's thing with Rosie was an even bigger shock.'

I thought about it for a moment. Articulating the two couples' intertwined existence had never come naturally to me but I gave it my best shot. 'Pretty much. My dad and Lulu's mum had a sexual relationship for most of their respective marriages, and Lulu's dad and my mum just ignored it and had occasional dalliances of their own to balance things out. The bizarre thing was that my mum and dad really did love each other and never even contemplated splitting up. They just believed that they should live their lives the way they wanted, and for them, that meant having more than one sexual partner. They all just maintained this façade of upper-middle-class respectability and acted as if absolutely nothing was amiss. I've seen my mother more upset about her highlights coming out the wrong shade than about the fact that my dad was shagging her best friend, Gwen. She genuinely didn't mind. And that's how Lulu and I grew up, with four parents who were best friends, and lived in a twisted dynamic of casual infidelity, while pretty much ignoring the kids that they had absolutely no time for.'

'Did you ever wonder if you and Lulu were... were...' Jess trailed off.

'Related?' I asked, spotting the obvious question. It was one we'd thought about many times. 'Sure. When we were teenagers, we used to fantasise that we were actually sisters, but no, our parents didn't start their affairs until a couple of years after we were born, so there was no chance of that. And as for Rosie... well, that one shocked us all. Basically, my dad had a fling with Lulu's mum for more than two decades, and when that was done and we were all well into adulthood, he took up with Rosie. I'll never understand why we didn't spot the second affair but... I shrugged. 'It's done. Over. I can honestly say I never give it any thought. There's no point.' I left it there. I understood the curiosity of such a bizarre set up, but to me it was old news. My dad was dead, my mum had moved on, I rarely saw Lulu's parents and Rosie now lived on the other side of the world. Besides, now that Dan was opening up and on a bit of a roll, I didn't want to sidetrack the conversation any further.

Dan put his beer bottle down after a taking a swig. 'Anyway, they joined the party, and for a couple of hours everything was great. At one point though, I realised Lulu was missing, and I don't know why, but I had a really bad feeling. The Australian bloke wasn't around either and I remembering thinking, is this it? Is this the minute that I find out that my girlfriend is cheating with some guy who looks like that bloke from INXS? And do you know what's weird? For a split second, I thought about letting it go, about ignoring my missing girlfriend and pretending that nothing was going on. That's how much I loved her. How pathetic was that?'

'You do know that this is supposed to be the memory of a favourite day in your relationship,' Jess asked doubtfully. 'Because this doesn't sound like it's heading anywhere good.'

Dan gave a rueful grin. 'Don't worry, I got the memo. I'll get to that bit. Anyway, I thought "fuck it", and went to look for them. I took the stairs two at a time, and got to our bedroom just as Lu was getting into full flow, but she wasn't with the bloke. She was standing in our bedroom, and the only other people there were your dad and her mum. She'd caught the two of them feeling each other up in our bedroom and lost it. Said it was one thing being cheating arses, but it wasn't happening under our roof, at her party. And she...'

'Tossed them out.' I didn't even realise I'd said that out loud, but now that I'd joined the dots, I knew exactly what Dan was talking about.

I'd been in the kitchen, trying to ignore the fact that my mother was flirting mercilessly with Dan and Lu's next-door neighbour. She knew how to work a room, my mother. She was twenty-five years older than me, so she'd have been around fifty, but she looked thirty-five. Her baby blonde hair was cut into a shiny shoulder-length bob, her skin flawless, her tan maintained to a shade of creamy caramel. Now, I couldn't picture exactly what she was wearing that day, but no doubt it was some variation of her standard uniform of very smart jeans, killer heels, a slinky little vest top and a Chanel jacket. Whatever it was, Rafe, the wealthy nightclub owner from next door, seemed extremely interested in it.

I'd put an extra few shots of tequila into the mojitos I was making in the hope they'd numb my mortification. As it turned out, no amount of tequila could head off what was about to come, when Lulu marched her mum and my dad down the stairs and told them to get the hell out of her house and suggested that my dad take 'his wandering dick' with him.

Even now, my face flushed at the memory. My parents, folks.

Dan took up the thread again. 'Yeah, she booted them all out and then she stormed into the garden on her own. I went after her and saw that she was crying. It was the first time I'd even seen her break down – it might have been the last too – and all I could do was just put my arms around her and hold her until she stopped. It took a few minutes, but finally she looked up at me, all streaky mascara and snot, and I melted, especially when she managed to speak. "I don't ever want to be like them," she said. "Promise me that won't happen to us. Promise me that we'll find a way to be faithful and we'll never be as screwed up as they are." "I promise," I told her, and I meant it more than I'd ever meant anything in my life.'

That hung in the air for a moment, Dan back in that moment, feeling every emotion all over again.

'I still don't understand...' Jess said softly, sympathy oozing as she reached over and took his hand. 'Why was that your favourite day? It sounds like carnage to me.'

Dan snapped back to the present. 'Because looking back now, I can see that those few hours after that were the only time that I didn't have a tiny grip of fear in the bottom of my stomach. Right then, just in that moment, I trusted her one hundred per cent. Every day before then, and every day after, although I couldn't see it at the time, a part of me knew that she wasn't completely mine, that she could throw it all away in a heartbeat. The irony was that she was exactly like them. Fidelity didn't come naturally to her and she showed it more times than I should have tolerated.'

Jess was still holding on to his hand. 'I'm sorry.'

Dan immediately flipped back to his laid-back, happy-go-lucky demeanour, the one that – like Colm – he used to brush off every negative feeling he ever had.

'Sorry that happened, or sorry that you're making us talk about all this stuff when we could be down the pub or doing something that wasn't going to give us PTSD?'

'The first one,' Jess said, wrinkling her nose in a half-hearted apology.

There was a pause, as we waited to see if Dan had anything else to add.

After a few seconds of staring at the table, he spoke again, this time peppering his words with his usual rueful humour.

'I still don't get why I chose someone who could never be faithful. I knew who Lu was, and yet I stuck with it, because I always thought she would reach a stage when she felt loved and secure enough to stop the constant search for excitement and for the affirmation she got from men desiring her. I mean, what's wrong with me that I picked a woman like that?' He gave a half-hearted laugh. 'Why couldn't I have ended up with someone as loyal and faithful as you two were to your husbands?'

The question was so sincere, so heartfelt, that it made my face flush with shame.

Without conscious thought, my gaze went to Jess, only to see that she was waiting for me with an expression that sat somewhere between embarrassment and guilt.

We both knew that Dan's characterisation of us was way off. Because Jess and I knew that we weren't the kind of perfect, faithful wives that Dan was looking for.

Jess and I were two ex-wives of the same man, a relationship that was commonly distant or fractious. There were many reasons that we'd managed to overcome that stereotype and build a real and deep bond. And, amongst the many ties that bound us, were a couple of duplicitous events in our past that we'd sworn to keep between us.

And I wasn't sure that we were ready to let anyone else in on the secrets.

8

'Honey, I'm home!' I heard Lulu's voice before I saw her, and my smile was automatic. For all her flaws, she was still the person I loved most in the world, after Beth of course. And Matthew McConaughey.

And besides, I was in no position to judge Lulu. It wasn't as if I'd lived a life without mistakes or transgressions either. It was almost a week after our session with Jess and I was still rattled by the turn the conversation had taken. There were some moments in my history, mistakes I made in the past, that I still wasn't ready to face, and most of them came with a thick coat of guilt.

Lulu burst through the kitchen door in a cloud of her favourite Jo Malone lime, basil and mandarin perfume, her mane of red corkscrew curls wild, shiny and falling way past her elbows. Never one to under-dress, she was wearing a stunning white trouser suit, that was miraculously uncreased and unstained by her travels. I know it's a cliché, but she was glowing. She threw her arms around me and hugged me as if it were a lot longer than two weeks ago that I waved her off on her honeymoon.

'Babe! I missed you. Don't ever leave me again!' she blurted, making me chuckle.

'I think you'll find it was you who left me,' I pointed out, my voice muffled by the shoulder pad of her jacket.

'Don't bother me with technicalities,' she joked, squeezing me even tighter, before finally releasing me and plopping her Gucci tote on the table as if it were a cheap knock-off instead of the birthday present Bobby bought her in Selfridges a few months ago. Speaking of which...

'Where's Bobby?' I asked, glancing behind her to see if her new, tanned, probably exhausted husband was on the way in too.

'Oh, he went straight to the office. His driver picked us up at the airport, so I got him to drop me here on the way to the city.'

I could see something about that sentence was pissing her off, but I wasn't sure what it was. No doubt it would come out soon enough. Lulu could never keep things to herself.

'Urgh, you've just stepped off a fifteen-hour flight from the Maldives and you look like that?' I groaned, taking in her flawless skin, bright eyes and immaculate outfit. 'God, I hate you. Anyway, how was the honeymoon? I want details. I want to hear everything, except the bits where there was nudity,' I demanded, pulling out two coffee mugs and filling them to the brim from the pot of strong black roast that was already made and waiting.

Lulu spotted what I was doing. 'Eh, can I have something stronger?' she asked, surprising me. It was barely 11 o'clock on a Tuesday morning. Day drinking usually only happened when we were on holiday or facing a crisis. As far as I was aware, neither applied.

I didn't comment. If something was wrong, she'd tell me in her own time, and putting her on the spot would only make her defensive. Lulu always needed to process things in her own way. I'd learned that when we were six and she punched Joey Simpson in the face at school. Turns out he'd been forcing her to give him her lunch money for a week and she'd decided to sort it out for herself. He never bothered her again and it set a precedent for life. Even now, she refused to be vulnerable, and she always handled her problems by herself, although thankfully, she'd stopped smacking people in the face.

'I'm still on holiday mode,' she added hastily, making me wonder if I was reading the situation completely wrong. Perhaps she was just blissfully happy and milking that feeling for as long as possible. Yeah, that must be it.

She slid onto a stool at the breakfast bar. 'Tell me first, how's my favourite girl?'

'I'm fine,' I responded, casually, making her laugh. I wasn't her favourite. Not even close. That spot was firmly reserved for Beth and I wouldn't want it any other way.

'Och, okay, Beth is fine too,' I added, uncorking a bottle of white wine from the fridge. I had a corporate buffet for twenty at a music company in Chiswick later, so I was sticking to the coffee. 'She asked for a pair of cowboy boots and a guitar at the weekend. She's decided she wants to be Taylor Swift.'

'Excellent,' Lulu said, as if this was an entirely feasible plan. 'Does this career direction involve trips to Nashville for her mum and her Aunt Lulu?'

I pulled out the bar chair across from her and climbed aboard, then sat forward with my elbows on the white quartz slab, cradling my mug with two hands. 'Undoubtedly.'

'Then I think it's a great idea. I definitely prefer it to her astronaut phase. What's the point of flying if you don't have duty-free shopping and a few champagnes mid-air?'

'No point at all,' I agreed, chuckling. 'Okay, so tell me how wonderful your honeymoon was then.'

'It was fantastic. We were in those wooden bungalows, the

ones that are on stilts and stretch right into the ocean. As soon as we arrived, our personal butler...'

On she went for about twenty minutes. The hotel. The restaurants. The bars. The people she met. The first-class flights. The sheer luxury and decadence of it all. Everything except...

'And did Bobby enjoy it too? You've barely mentioned him.'

'Oh. Yep, he loved it all. You know, it's so amazing having someone who just takes charge of everything. He knows exactly what he wants and I barely have to lift a finger.'

I saw right through her. 'You were bored, weren't you?'

A long pause, then her head flopped down on the table, and I heard a prolonged, 'Soooooooo bored,' from underneath the pile of red curls. When she finally lifted it back up, I saw that the glow was gone, and in its place was sheer despair.

'Shauna, I think I might have fucked up. I mean, seriously fucked up. What have I done? And more to the point, why did you let me do it?'

There were so many parts of that sentence that warranted discussion. I started with, 'Lulu! I don't know how to break it to you, but listening to advice, guidance or other people's opinions isn't your strong point.'

I was pointing out the obvious, so she brushed right over it with an ironic, 'I've no idea what you're talking about.'

Maybe I should have gone with the wine after all because this sounded like it was going to need more sustenance than a strong Americano. 'Okay, use your words. Tell me why you think you've made a mistake.'

She kicked off with a deep sigh. 'It started on day four or five. I was lying in a cabana, looking out over the Indian Ocean in the most perfect place on earth and where was my husband? Walking up and down on the terrace of our bungalow, barking into his mobile phone. Every day he buggered off for hours to do work stuff. At night, we'd have dinner and I'd get his attention for a couple of hours and what would he do? Talk about work. If I hear one more word about the revolutionary sewage system for a new block of flats in Hackney, I'll scream.'

'Why didn't you change the subject?' I asked, puzzled. Lulu was no wallflower, and she never shied away from a difficult conversation. It was so unlike her to put up with something she wasn't happy about.

'Because we seemed incapable of maintaining a conversation about anything. I know it's a total cliché – oh the mortification – but I think that before the wedding we spent our time together planning the ceremony, and the honeymoon and the changes I was making to his home.' Bobby lived in a fabulous penthouse in a gorgeous development in Kew. He actually owned the whole building, so every single aspect of it had been designed to his and Lulu's specifications. 'I was completely wrapped up in all of that, so by the time we actually got to the other side of it – the house was finished, the wedding was over, we were on the bloody honeymoon – I had nothing to occupy my mind.'

'Isn't that what your new husband is supposed to do?'

'Yes! But he's just so work-obsessed that he barely had any time for me. I used to think that it was great that he left me to plan and design everything exactly the way I want it, but now I realise it's because he couldn't give a toss if we had a big wedding, a small wedding or a honeymoon in flipping Seychelles or Skegness, just as long as he had a mobile phone signal and access to broadband.'

Another little nugget of realisation dropped into my mind. 'That's really why you called so often? Because you were bored and in need of a chat?'

She didn't even blush. 'Yes! Gave me something to pass the time. I even called Jess halfway through the second week. I must have been desperate.'

'I thought it was just to show off your fabulous life,' I teased her, trying to de-escalate her rant with some gentle teasing.

'Well, it was that too,' she admitted, flicking her hair off her shoulder. 'But it was mostly for a chat. You know, all I could think about was that I never had a problem finding conversations with Dan. We knew each other so well that we always had stuff to talk about, always found things to do together. Our honeymoon was a total giggle...'

Which, I couldn't help thinking, was the opposite of this conversation. I had a creeping sense of unease. Lulu was the queen of unpredictability when it came to relationships, and if she was now getting wistfully nostalgic about her time with Dan, anything could happen. The only way forward was to try to reason with her and hope that something landed.

'But maybe that's because we were all there with you too. That's what happens with destination weddings – all your guests come and stay for two weeks, milking every bit of sun and sangria we can get. You were sick of the lot of us by the time we left Marbella.'

'I wasn't,' she retorted. 'Well, maybe a little bit.'

'Exactly! The thing is though, Lu, we were one big group and nothing was ever boring because we all had each other. Things are different now...'

Leaning over, she squeezed my hand and I knew it was because we both thought of Colm at the same time. It was a conversation we'd had many times before. Lulu and Dan. Me and Colm. We were an interchangeable gang and we were together for decades of our lives, a dysfunctional family, that loved hard, partied hard, fought occasionally, laughed a lot and made sure there was never a dull moment. It was only natural that Lulu was struggling with all the changes. Colm was gone. And Lulu had given up her work, her home, and the man she'd spent most of her adult life with. That was a whole lot of adjustment for anyone. I just hoped it didn't come with a side order of regret.

'Wait a minute – so is that why you were calling Dan all the time too? I thought it was just to check on him because you were worried about him, but it was because you were wishing he was there?'

'No! Well. Kind of. Yes.'

'Oh, dear God, no...' I groaned, trying to throw up roadblocks to where I was suddenly sure she was going with this.

Again, she just kept on going. 'I mean, I know Dan and I weren't perfect, but we were never dull either.'

'Nope, you were never dull,' I conceded. 'But, Lu, you left him. You absolutely broke his heart, dumped him for a shinier, flashier model. Albeit a vintage one.'

She didn't even argue. Must be the jet lag.

'And you said Bobby was the best thing that ever happened to you. That you finally knew how it felt to be loved. That...'

She put her hand up. 'Stop! Your ability to remember every detail of every conversation you've ever had can be really irritating sometimes.'

As I said before, she could get mighty defensive when she was put on the spot. I didn't take offence. 'It can also be a good way of reminding you of how you were feeling,' I said, staying calm. Lulu did dramatics and volatility, I did calm, measured reasoning – that had always been the balance on the seesaw of our friendship.

'Yeah, well, maybe I don't feel that way now,' she shot back, with a weak shrug, before she knocked back a good two fingers of her vino. 'The thing with Dan was that we knew each other inside out and liked the same things, especially on holiday. If he'd been with me, we'd have been paddleboarding, or surfing, or scuba diving out on a reef. Instead, I was lying on a sunlounger listening to Celine fricking Dion's greatest hits wafting over from the next bungalow. I swear Elton John and David Furnish were staying in that one. Day three of listening to "My Heart Will Go On" and I was starting to have fantasies about going down with the bloody Titanic.'

Trying not to laugh, I nudged her back on point. 'And if Dan had been with you, you'd have had a fantastic few days, followed by an explosive argument and an occasional episode of drama.'

'I know! I missed that,' she said, again not quite getting the message I was trying to give her. 'I'd much rather have been bickering with Dan than listening to Bobby moaning about the price of imported steel.'

I could feel my body begin to slump. This wouldn't, just couldn't, go anywhere good.

'So what are you saying? That you want to leave Bobby and go back to Dan? I really hope not, Lu,' I said, irritation clipping my words, 'because you've put him through enough. Let's get real here – you and Dan were great together, but only about eighty per cent of the time. He was never enough for you...'

'But maybe he was and I just didn't realise it,' she argued.

Both my hands were gripping the edge of the breakfast bar now, as I fought to stay calm. I didn't often lose my temper and I rarely got heated with Lu, but she was pushing my buttons here. Dan was my family too and I couldn't bear the thought of him being dragged back into Lu's Hadron Collider of a life. This would have pissed Colm off too. I could almost hear his voice in my head and I knew what it would be saying, the same thing he'd said on many occasions while he was alive. It went along the lines of, 'I love Lu, but, Jesus, she's a fecking nightmare. We need to look out for him, Shauna. Don't let her wreck him.'

Somehow, knowing that if he was here, he would have my back, made it easier to have the conversation that my friend needed to hear. I leaned forward, voice calm again, but low and forceful. 'Listen to me, Lu, don't do it. Don't even think about getting back into Dan's life in that way. You know where we found him last week when you called and asked us to check on him? On the floor. On. The. Fecking. Floor.'

'I thought he was out with Stephanie from Bracal Tech?' she shot back.

Shit. I forgot about that small white lie. 'Yeah, well, he got off the floor and then went out with her,' I blustered, trying to dial that one back. 'The point is, your break-up devastated him, but now he's finally started to pick himself up and he's trying to move on. Let him have a chance to find someone who makes him happy, someone new who will treat him the way that he should be treated. Don't go near him, Lu. I swear I'll never forgive you.'

'Bloody hell, it sounds like you want him for yourself.' The petulance and downright bitchiness in her voice pressed yet another button.

'Seriously, Lu? That's where you're going to take this? Christ, you're an insensitive cow sometimes. I don't want Dan, and you know that.'

At least she had the decency to look like she regretted her words. 'I know. Sorry. I'm just a mess and saying crazy stuff.'

'Well, keep your crazy away from Dan. He can't take any more grief, Lu. Go home, make your marriage work, be happy. You're allowed that, Lu.'

I was beginning to soften. She was a grown woman, but to me, both of us would always be the little girls raised by parents who regularly reminded us that we were nothing more than an incon-venience to them. Perhaps that was why I cut her endless slack.

'I know. I'm just... I'm not sure what happy looks like any more. How can I keep messing up like this? I thought I'd found everything I wanted in Bobby, but now...'

'Give it a chance. You can't just walk away at the first blip.'

She thought about that for a moment and then I saw a slight nod, and she seemed to force her spirits up. 'You're right. I know you are.'

'What did you say?'

'I said, you're right.'

'Pardon?'

'Is there something wrong with your hearing...' She spotted my grin, and flicked some of her wine at me.

I squealed. 'Sorry, couldn't resist. Don't think I've ever heard you saying I was right, so I had to milk it for a minute.'

'No wonder I'm a mess. I've got terrible friends,' she said, but she was smiling for the first time since she arrived, so I took that as a positive.

'Eh, I think you'll find your friends are spectacular,' I joked.

She drained the rest of her glass. 'Well, how about I cook dinner on Thursday night for my spectacular friend, to make up for stressing her out today.'

This was classic Lu. She wouldn't apologise, wouldn't admit to being wrong, but she would just do lovely things in the hope that they'd balance out the strife she brought to the table. It usually worked.

'Can't make Thursday, we've got...' The words froze in my mouth. Damnit. I hadn't thought this through, but in the light of what she'd just said, I wasn't sure that telling her we had a 'moving on' club was a great idea.

'You've got what?' her eyes narrowed and my neck started to

itch under the scrutiny. I knew she wouldn't be impressed with the truth because first, she wasn't involved and second, despite the clear double standards, given her earlier confessions about mixed feelings, she wouldn't be happy that her two closest friends were helping Dan move on to new horizons.

'Well, Dan and Jess and I have been getting together on a Thursday night.'

'Cool. Where are you going and I'll join you?'

Did I already say dammit? Fricking dammit again.

'Well. Thing is, Jess is practising her life-coaching skills and she's got us working on her programme for people who are... erm... moving on after a relationship has ended.'

Silence. For a moment I thought it was going to be okay. After all, she was an adult. Of course, she should understand. Accept this with grace. Be magnanimous in victory.

Eh, no. The delay in her reaction was caused by the naked flame going along the wire, before it reached the dynamite.

'What? Oh, for fuck's sake. Is that one of those things where you all sit around encouraging each other to get on Tinder?'

'No, it's more about, well... Jess has a theory that you have to revisit the good and bad times in your past so that you can make peace with letting it go.'

'When you say "revisit", you mean what?'

'Well, we talk about it.'

'Woah! You're saying that Dan talks about the crap times in our relationship with Jess? What the hell has it got to do with her?' I was beginning to worry that her voice had reached a pitch that could crack her Prosecco glass. 'The traitorous git!'

I thought about de-escalating her fury again, but something in me snapped. 'Okay, first of all, you're the one who had an affair, so I wouldn't throw the word "traitorous" in Dan's direction. Second, he has every right to do whatever he damn well pleases when it comes to putting his life back together. You trashed it, so you don't get to have an opinion, Lu. It's none of your business. I'm telling you again, go home and make your marriage work, and don't you worry about what Dan is doing. He's been to hell and back. Give him a break.'

Oh, that did it. Bugger. An hour ago, my best friend rushed in and hugged me like she'd never let me go. Now I was pretty sure that she'd be happy if she never set eyes on me again.

'You know what, Shauna, you're right. I'll go home and you three can go sit on your yoga mats and chant and talk shit about me and whatever else you do in your snarky little group. I really couldn't care less.'

She was halfway to the door when my landline began to ring. Over on the worktop next to the fridge, the base immediately clicked on to answer machine. I kept it that way so that I never actually had to speak to those scamsters who called claiming I'd had an accident or I'd just won a two-week beach holiday in Magaluf.

'Hey Shauna, it's me. Vincent. Long time, no speak.'

Lulu froze, her jaw dropped, while every nerve ending in my body began to tremble. Vincent. My former friend. My ex-business partner. Now residing somewhere in the USA. I hadn't spoken to him for years, so this was a bolt from the blue.

'Look, I know this might not be cool, but I'm back in the UK and I just wondered if you fancied meeting up? I've still got the same mobile number, so drop me a text and let me know. Would be great to see you.' He sounded nervous. Unsure. 'But if it doesn't work, it's no worries. Hope you're… hope you're good.'

Click.

'Holy shit,' Lulu drawled, her stroppy exit abandoned. 'Now there's a blast from the past. You should invite Vincent to join your Thursday night gang too. He was never much good at moving on either.'

With that, she stormed out. If she'd glanced back, she'd have seen my jaw on the floor. She'd have heard my heart thudding. And if she could read my mind, she would know that I was thinking that she wasn't the only traitor in the room today.

The front door slammed shut just as I pressed the delete button. If only I could erase the past the same way.

9

COLM – 2016

I check my list again, searching for inspiration on what to talk about in the next clip. Beth, Davie and Joe are at the top of the page, but I can't. Not yet. If I talk about the kids and my hopes for them after I've gone, I'll crumble and then Shauna will have to remember me as a bloke with a red patchy face and swollen eyelids. They say that the living glamorise the dead, so I'd far rather she conjured up some super chiselled version of me, than a bloke with a face like a slapped arse. I'm going to start dropping hints that people think I look like Matt Damon. By the time I pop my clogs, I'll have her so convinced it's true, she'll think of me every time she sees a rerun of one of those Bourne movies. And they are never off one channel or another.

Christ, I'm talking shite again. My favourite avoidance mechanism when I'm putting off doing something that I really don't want to do.

Okay. Come on. You've got this.

Shite, I'm talking to myself as well. I need to get these tapes made pronto because there's every chance I'm losing it.

Back to my list. Jess is on there, and there's another couple of names too, but I'm not ready for those either.

Stick to the easy stuff, mate. You've got this. Come on. If that bloke in the *Bourne Identity* can take down international spy rings, you can do this.

I run my fingers through my hair, blow out my cheeks, and slap a smile on my face.

I absolutely refuse to think about the next few days, weeks, months. No headspace whatsoever is given to bloody meds, and treatments or this bastard tumour. And if one more person mentions a bucket list, I'll lose my shit. I don't need one. If, despite all evidence to the contrary, I make it through this, the only things on my bucket list will be going home with my wife and daughter. I need to keep believing that could happen. And even if I don't, no matter how I'm feeling, I need Happy Colm to be the guy she sees on the camera.

When I think I can pull that off, I reach over and press the 'record' button on my phone again.

'Hey, m'darlin', me again. In case yer wondering, I'm still missing you. Wherever I am, if I'm not with you, then I miss you. I always will. You know that, don't you?'

Shit, that bit caught me right in the chest and for a second I feel winded. I clear my throat, take a deep breath, keep the smile going and continue.

'You know, I've been thinking about how things will be when I'm gone...'

I don't know if I can hold this together. I really don't. If there's an Oscar category for Best Performance by a Dying Husband, I'm definitely taking home the statue.

Only the thought that I don't want to have to delete this and do it all over again makes me push through. I clear my throat again. Still smiling.

'... And I don't want me dying to take away all the things we've always done together. Please take Beth down to the coast for the summer and I know the boys are grown men now, but try to persuade them to come too. We always made great memories there and I want Beth to have more of them. Swimming, playing football, cycling... I know you always complain that the bike seat makes your arse sore...' For a moment my smile is genuine. '... By the way, that arse of yours is spectacular. Anyway, Beth loves the fresh air, so strap a cushion to the seat and you'll be fine. Take her to the cinema for every Marvel movie and don't ever let her tell you that any of them could beat Iron Man in a fair fight. Go out for Chinese food to our usual place every week and invite everyone we love – we've had some of the best times of our lives there. But don't touch the king prawn curry because I'm still pretty sure that's what caused the epic food poisoning bout of 2012.'

I'm on a roll now.

'Davie and Joe will be living their own lives soon, so they're going to be harder to pin down, but encourage them to still come see you guys as much as possible. I know Jess will do the same. I see how close you two have been over the last few months since the bastard cancer got me in a chokehold. I used to think that I was in the middle, keeping both families together, but I was kidding myself. It's you two who do that. You're both incredible mothers and I can see now that you made it all work so that the kids have a strong family unit. I owe you, babe. If I can arrange the occasional miracle when I get up there, I promise I'll send them your way. I'll try for a lottery win and two-week cruise round the Bahamas with that Matthew bloke you have the hots for...'

Feck, I can't get the guy's name. My mind has gone blank. That happens a lot now. The docs say it's a combination of the tumour, the damage done by the radiation therapy and the tiredness caused by the chemo. A triple whammy and it feels like it.

Focus. Come on.

Matthew... The actor. The one that was in *How To Lose A Guy In 10 Days*. She makes me watch that movie at least once a year and I pretend to object, but actually it's not bad. It's not *Fast and Furious* good, but it's watchable. Matthew...

'McConaughey! Mathew McConaughey. That's him. Anyway, if there's a miracle going, I'll make sure he's involved, even though you're way too good for any bloke.'

Shit, we're straying on to dangerous territory here. The bloke conversation. I know we need to have it, but it's on the sideline for now, sitting next to the Jess conversation.

I have a lot more to say about Jess, and it might blow any chance of a happy extended family out of the water, but now isn't the time. I'm not ready. I'm not sure I ever will be. That one might require a couple of beers beforehand, and a lie-down in a dark room afterwards. My only hope is that if, or when, I tell Shauna what happened between me and Jess, they can work it out and find a way to get past the roaring bollocks I've made of everything.

Jesus, I'm not even going to think about that one right now. Denial and avoidance. Stick to the happy stuff. I still don't know how I got two fecking magnificent women to marry me. There must have been a full moon. I just hope that if I get the balls to confess what I did, both of them don't think I was the biggest mistake they ever made.

10

SHAUNA – JULY 2021

'Okay, so this week's session of the Thursday Life Coaching Club – otherwise known as the Sad Git's Recovery Club – is now in session,' Jess announced with much grandeur, while snapping a prawn cracker and dipping it in her curry sauce. This was our group's equivalent of a field trip. For many years, we'd come to this Chinese restaurant in Chiswick at least one night a week: Lulu and Dan, Colm and me, Rosie in the old days, Vincent back then too, sometimes Beth, occasionally Davie and Joe if they were staying with us that week. In the last months of Colm's life, after Jess split with Steve, she would bring the boys over on her weeks too, and she'd stay and eat with us. I used to wonder if the other diners thought we were the fun table, because the laughter never seemed to stop. They would have been right. But we were also the table that was trying to savour every last minute of joy while all of us could still be there.

I hadn't been back since Colm died. For five years I'd even avoided coming down this street because the memories stung too much. When Jess had texted yesterday to say we were meeting here tonight, I'd broken off from loading 100 pale blue French fancies for a gender-reveal party in Barnes and hit the call back button straight away.

'Jess, I can't go there,' I blurted before she'd even managed to get out a 'hello'.

'Not bad,' she'd said, confusing me.

'What isn't bad?'

'I thought I would manage to count to ten before you called. I only got to five. The good news is that your reflexes are in spectacular working order.'

Now wasn't the time.

'Jess, I'm serious. It would kill me.'

'It wouldn't,' she'd countered calmly. 'It might inflict a couple of punctures to the heart, but it's all part—'

'If you tell me it's all "part of the process" one more time, I'm hanging up.'

'Okay, I won't say it, but that's exactly what it is. A part of reclaiming your life and your happiness is doing all the things that you enjoyed, all the things that meant something to you. And to Colm.'

'But how can it be the same?' I'd argued. 'Colm isn't there. Lulu won't be there either.'

This whole project was beginning to wear thin. In the beginning, I'd gone along with it for peace and because a tiny part of me thought it might make things better. So far it was having the opposite effect. I wanted to disown Jess and it was clearly making things worse.

All day I'd been contemplating asking Beth to stay home and miss her weekly sleepover with Marcy tonight, but I didn't have the heart. Okay, that's not strictly true. After school, I took her temperature twice in the hope that it was high, and then quizzed her for every ailment I could think of. Sore head? No. Sore tummy? Nope. How are your ears, Beth? 'Pierced,' she'd replied, with raised eyebrows of scepticism. I'd only pulled myself together when she began to look alarmed and said, 'Mum, is everything okay? You're freaking me out.'

Shame had made my cheeks flush. Dear God, this poor child already lost her father and now she had a mother who was acting like an A&E doctor in *Holby City*.

I was always telling her to be brave, so how could I admit that I was riddled with anxiety and dreading going back to our old haunt tonight?

'Sorry, love,' I'd said, giving her a hug. 'Everything is good. I just heard there's a few bugs going around school and wanted to check.' Oh, the shame. I'd moved away from the window in case a bolt of lightning struck me down. Although, on the plus side, at least that would have got me out of tonight.

My stomach had been in knots when Dan texted me to say he was waiting down at the entrance to our building. He'd already booked an Uber and it came just as I got there. I only had time to notice that he was as smart as ever – dark grey tailored trousers, a slim-fit white shirt that showed off his broad shoulders and narrow waist. Other than that weekend he'd spent lying on his floor with a bloodstream that was mostly alcohol, Dan had maintained the gym schedule he'd shared with Colm and it showed. I sometimes wondered if that's what kept Lulu with him for so long. It had always been a standing joke that no matter how pissed off she was with him, he would walk into a room and her sexual attraction to him would completely overrule all irritations.

He'd given me a hug and I appreciated the body heat in the unseasonably chilly July evening. 'Are you okay with this?' he'd asked. 'You know, we don't have to do it. We can say no.'

I shook my head. 'I tried that. Didn't work.'

'Yeah, me too,' he'd admitted, laughing. 'I'm sure I used to have balls before I met Lulu – if I find them again, maybe I'll become all self-assured and regain my power to resist being bossed around by Jess the Life Coach. I'm scared of no one, yet those two women slightly terrify me. Why is that?'

I'd plonked down onto the seat of the cab. 'No idea, but will you save me too? Protect me from the Jess's and Lulus of the world?'

'Sure will.' He'd given the taxi driver the address of the restaurant, then sat back in the seat.

Curiosity and apprehension had got the better of me. 'You know Lulu's back? Have you seen her?'

His weary expression had answered the question. 'Yeah, I know she's back. She's called a few times, but I only spoke to her once. She wants to come over, but I'm putting it off. Just not ready to see how happy she is.'

I'd thought about telling him otherwise, but I didn't. Interfering was never a good idea with those two. He'd turned the spotlight on me. 'What about you? You doing okay? Embracing this?'

'I think "embracing" might be a stretch, but I figure I've got nothing to lose and there's a slim possibility that it might help. Besides, and don't tell Jess this, but even hating this is a welcome distraction to the nothingness that was there before. I just miss him, Dan. So much. And all that bollocks about things getting easier with time is something that people say to give you false hope. I really wish someone had just said, look, love, this will suck for ever. There's no escaping it. At least then I wouldn't feel so pathetic for still feeling this way.'

Dan had taken my hand in his. There was more I'd wanted to say, but I knew I couldn't. Dan missed Colm as much as I did. They were inseparable and he left a hole that Dan knew he would never fill. 'I miss him too, Shauna. Every day,' he'd said, vocalising what I was thinking. 'Even at work, my heart isn't in it any more. We set that company up with huge plans to build something special, but without Colm, the joy has gone out of it. I want him here to share every success, and when it all goes tits up, I want him here to crack open a beer and talk entertaining nonsense to take the edge off. Without him, it's like the highs and lows just merge into one straight flatline of mediocrity.'

The restaurant had come into view a hundred metres or so down the street. 'At least we've got each other. The power of communal moping can't be overstated.' I'd squeezed his hand. 'I need to tell you something,' I began, biting my bottom lip.

'Oh God, what now?' he'd groaned, only half kidding.

'I love you,' I said. 'And I appreciate that you and I share something special.'

He'd nodded, acknowledging the truth in that.

'But if Jess asks, I'll deny this conversation and tell her we only spoke about positivity and new beginnings. Just until you find your balls of steel.'

He was still laughing when the car pulled to a stop.

Jess was already at the table, prawn crackers in a bowl in front of her. I'd glanced around the room, and saw that everything was exactly the same as when we used to come here. The same wall-paper, flocked with lotus flowers. The same tiled floor. The pagoda-shaped lanterns that dropped from the ceiling. Even the menus, wedged between bottles of soy sauce and a pot of paper-wrapped chopsticks looked like they hadn't changed. The only thing that was different was us. I'd been a wife. Now I was a widow. And there were empty chairs where Colm, Lulu and Rosie would sit.

I'd wondered why Jess hadn't chosen a smaller table, but she'd got right on with declaring our Sad Gits Club in session, and then it went right out of my mind. Nostalgia, I'd figured. More facing the past and confronting our feelings. At least here, that came with great food. As long as no one ordered the prawn curry.

'What are you smiling at?' Jess asked, amused, snapping me out of my reflection.

'I'm remembering the time Colm got food poisoning...'

'... From the dodgy burger he bought from a van on the way here,' Dan finished my sentence, puzzling me.

'No, it was from the prawn curry.'

Dan was laughing now, shaking his head. 'It wasn't. He just told you that because you had him on the "no fast-food" diet and he'd scoffed a quarter-pounder from El Salmonella, the grub cart near the station.'

'Oh my god, all these years I've been defaming this place while avoiding the seafood!' I blurted, just as the waiter came to take our order.

I didn't have the slightest hesitation.

'King prawn curry, please.'

If Colm was watching us right now, and I really hoped he was, I knew his raucous laugh would be making anyone who could hear it smile.

When our meals were ordered and our drinks were poured, I got the awkward subject out of the way first. 'Listen, we need to talk about Lulu...'

Dan was immediately alert. 'What's happened? Is she okay?'

After a generous sip of gin and tonic, I filled them in on her visit, omitting the part where she confessed that she'd made a mistake marrying Bobby and seemed to be second-guessing her decision to divorce Dan. It wasn't my place to share those details. And anyway, given that it was Lu, she may well have changed her mind before she reached the end of our street and I hadn't heard from her since, so I had no way of knowing. For the sake of diplomacy and crisis aversion, I stuck to relaying her outrage that we'd formed this group and her extreme case of FOMO. My gaze connected with Jess. 'She thinks Dan will be discussing her behind her back and she can't stand it.'

'To be fair, that's a pretty accurate assumption,' Jess conceded. 'Look, Dan, this is completely up to you. If you think it'll cause issues between you and Lu, then I'll understand if you bail out on this. Shauna and I have more than enough issues to keep us going for weeks.'

'True dat,' I drawled. One gin and tonic and I thought I was down with the kids' lingo. Beth was mortified every time I opened my mouth. She'd almost left home in a fit of embarrassment the time I called something 'cray cray' in front of her friends. I had to bribe her with a McFlurry to get her to stay. Somehow I didn't think that would work with Dan, though, and I really, really didn't want him to quit. For my sake, as much as his. I felt so much more solid and stable when he was around.

Dan shook his head. 'I think my time for appeasing Lulu has long gone,' he said, with matter-of-fact certainty.

I'd known Dan for over twenty years and I knew when he absolutely meant something he was saying. This looked pretty definite to me.

Jess's face lit up with relief. 'Thank God, because I didn't mean a word of what I just said. I'd have scorned you for life if you'd bailed on us.'

'Good to know,' Dan said, leaning back so that the waiter could put a tray of assorted starters on the burner-thingies in the middle of the table.

Jess snapped another prawn cracker. 'So how did you leave it with Lu?'

'She left, pissed off, so I'm giving her a couple of days to cool down, then I'll check on her. You know how she is: burns hard, then she'll move on to something else and in a week she'll have forgotten about it.' Even as I said it, I wasn't sure that was true this time around. Dan was Lu's Achilles Heel – and if Bobby wasn't living up to expectations, it wouldn't surprise me at all if Lulu sought out the comfort of familiarity. Much as she'd deny it until hell was one big ice cube, Lulu had an insecurity that was rooted in the confusion and lack of love in our childhoods and other than me, Dan had been her one source of stability, the man who loved her no matter what. If she was feeling lonely or lost, it made sense that she'd seek him out. None of which I said out loud because Jess would roll her eyes and Dan was king of the Sad Git parade and I didn't want to make his crown any heavier. Thankfully, Jess didn't notice that my thoughts were distracting me.

'Why don't we see if she wants to go out one night next week?' Jess suggested. 'Or maybe lunch on Sunday. The boys are coming over, so they'll keep her occupied and upbeat.'

Lulu loved Colm's boys. Like all of us, she had her faults, but she was an incredible aunt. She'd have been a great mother too, but she'd never been interested in having kids of her own – said she was worried that she'd learned to be a (hopeless, selfish) parent from her folks and wanted to break the cycle. It was both utterly selfless and acutely sad.

'Has she contacted you?' Jess asked Dan the same question I'd put to him in the cab.

'Just a brief conversation on the phone. I know this is going to sound weird, but I almost feel like she's cheating on Bobby when she calls me now. I've been on the other side of that one, so I don't want to go anywhere near it.'

He knew her too well. Over the years, Lulu's indiscretions (she admitted to two, but I knew there had been more) hadn't been a secret, but Dan had always taken her back, truly believing that the infidelity was a character flaw caused by her messed-up background. They were brief interludes that weren't deal breakers in their twenty-year, volatile, passionate marriage. I couldn't do it, but it worked for them – until Bobby.

Jess sat up a little straighter in her seat. 'Actually, that could fit in well with the second part of tonight's group work. There's a long-established tool in counselling that involves writing down what you want to say to someone and then burning the paper and letting those feelings go. I thought we could do a variation of that tonight. So Dan, what's the one thing you'd want to tell Lu if she was sitting here right now? I want you to tell us, to get it out of your mind, and then close the door on it.'

He thought about that for a moment. 'I think I'd tell her that I was happy for her. That I want her marriage to Bobby to work. That I'm glad she made the decision to go. I'd have stayed with her forever, you know? I was in it for the long haul, but looking back... hell, even at the time, I knew it wasn't healthy, but I loved her, so I tried to make it work. And I know she loved me too. She would never have stuck it out as long as she did if she didn't love me. At least I can say, I gave it twenty odd years and it's weird because I don't feel like it was wasted. The good times were worth it, but the bad times are making it easier for me to let go.'

'Bloody hell, that was profound. You should be writing those little motivational signs that are always on Instagram. Or maybe raps for Jay Z,' Jess mused. 'Can I ask you something?' she went on. 'Were you truly okay with not having children? Do you wish you could go back now and do it differently?'

'No,' he said, without having to think about it. 'I knew when we married that Lulu didn't want kids and I was fine with that. It was never a deal-breaker for me. No, if I could go back, I'd do it all the same. Although, for the sake of my dignity and my liver, I'd probably leave her the night before she met Bobby. Other than that, no regrets.'

I was so proud of him. Jess was too. 'Damn it,' she blurted, 'I feel like we should have some kind of ceremonial gesture to mark the release of emotions. If we write stuff on napkins and set it on fire, we'll get kicked out, so how about...' She scanned the table, until her eyes fell on the discarded bowl of prawn crackers. She tossed one over to Dan, then one to me and kept one for herself. 'Okay, when you're ready, you snap the prawn cracker and that signifies the ties being broken,' she declared.

'Jess, I think you've lost it, love,' I said gently, while trying to supress one of those giggles that could turn to hysteria in a split second. Her lecturers were going to be highly confused if she put this in her dissertation.

'Yeah, well, ceremonial stuff doesn't always make sense. Have you seen all that marching up and down wearing a big furry hat that goes on at Buckingham Palace? I mean... a prawn cracker is almost normal compared to that.'

Some things just couldn't be argued with.

Dan was going along with it though. I think he was a few beers in and up for anything.

He solemnly held up his pink fishy wafer and said, 'Lulu, goodbye. It was a blast. I wish you nothing but happiness with Bobby. Although...'

Oh no, he was going to backtrack on this.

'I really hope he's a crap shag.' With that, he snapped the prawn cracker and tossed it back in the bowl.

'Yasssss!' Jess said, delighted that Dan had embraced the process.

'Okay, I'll go next, because Shauna has a habit of making me cry when it comes to this stuff, and my make up is already sliding off my face.' She held a cracker aloft.

'Steve,' she said, as if her ex-husband was sitting in one of the empty chairs, 'I want to tell you that I forgive you for ending our marriage the way you did. And no, I'm not going to labour the fact that your penis found its way into your secretary. The thing is, I learned something really important from being married to you. When we met, I think that subconsciously I was searching for security. I wanted someone I could count on to be there for me, in every way: someone who would take care of me and the boys. I was hurting. It was so soon after Colm and I lost Daisy...'

Her voice thickened when she said their daughter's name. Their perfect babe, who had never taken a breath after she was born. Colm had blocked it out, pretty much pretended it never happened, because the only way he could deal with the pain was to ignore it. They'd been unable to connect, to mourn together, and Jess had been distraught. She had needed her husband and he was nowhere, had abandoned her at her darkest moment. The trauma and the aftermath, when they were both devastated by grief, had ended their marriage.

'And I just needed someone to lean on, to hold me up until I could stand on my own two feet again. Then in you swooped and you did that for me. But over the years, as I healed and learned and grew from what happened to me, I discovered that I didn't need to be saved. I saw that I could take care of myself and my boys. I don't need someone to rescue me any more because I'm pretty capable of rescuing myself. Thanks for being there when I needed you, Steve. We made each other happy for a while and I'll always be grateful that you were such a wonderful stepdad to my boys. I wish you well. And there's no hard feelings so I won't mention the penis in the secretary thing again.'

With that, she snapped the cracker and got a round of applause from her audience of two.

My turn. I really didn't want to do this. My situation was different from the others. There was no duplicitous break-up. No fault on either side. Our marriage ended because of biology, because of a bastard cancer that took my husband's life. There was no need for reproach, at least, none that I was going to talk about in the middle of a restaurant in Chiswick.

So instead of seeking some kind of justice or closure, I took another approach – I decided to articulate the thought that had been going around in my mind since the day he left us. 'Hey, Colm,' I began.

'Prawn cracker,' Jess hissed, interrupting me.

I decided to humour her. What was the harm? We were already far too close to Bizarreville to turn back now. I held up the cracker and started again.

'Hey, Colm...' In my head I could hear him reply with his usual 'Hey, m'darlin'.'

'Your ex-wife... no wonder you divorced her by the way, because she's way too bossy.' That earned a raised eyebrow of disdain from Jess, but I carried on, 'Anyway, she is making me do this thing where I have to say something to you. Thing is, if you can see me down here, then you know that I talk to you all the time. And if you can't, well, I'm not sure there's any point.'

The eyebrow was up again, so I hastily added, 'But I'm going to go along with it because she's a wonderful person who has been a great support since you... left us.' Even five years later, every time I talked about Colm dying, it still chipped off a piece of my heart.

'I guess the thing I don't understand, Colm, is why we didn't talk about the future. You know, I've never said this before, but I'm bloody furious about that. Why didn't you map out your plans and wishes for Beth, for Davie and Joe? Why didn't we talk about the mistakes we made, the things we were never brave enough to discuss, so that we could forgive each other and get closure?'

If he could hear me, he'd know what I was referring to. Across the table, Jess's pained glance told me that she did too.

I left it there and went back to my dead husband, having genuine concerns about the future viability of Jess's life coaching service. If this was an example of her process, I didn't think there were going to be queues around the block. 'Maybe it's because, right up to the end, you thought you'd still have more time, and I wasn't brave enough to make us face it. Anyway, my love, I just want you to know we're doing okay. Beth is incredible and she's so like you that it breaks my heart. I so wish I could talk to you, hear your voice. Jess and Dan want me to open myself up to the possibility of another relationship, but how can I, when I still feel married to you? I'm still Shauna O'Flynn, Colm's wife, and I don't see how that will ever change. If this is the way it always is, that's okay with me. We had everything. And I don't think anyone is lucky enough to get everything twice.'

Jess's sniff snapped me out of the place that my mind had gone to, that quiet, peaceful spot in my head where Colm and I lived, where he was still with us and I could think about him, talk to him, watch his reactions to the twists and turns of life. Damn.

One look at Jess and Dan's expressions of devastation and I felt terrible for opening up their Colm-sized wound too. I hadn't meant to do that and felt an irresistible need to lighten the mood.

I snapped my cracker. 'Oh, and by the way, Colm. I can't believe you lied to me for all those years about the king prawn curry.'

11

Right. This is probably the last of these videos that I can make before I get to the tough stuff. And I don't know how much time I have left to get them done. Every day, I'm finding it more difficult to keep my thoughts in my head for long enough to make them count. The last MRI showed that despite all the treatment, despite the fact that I'm still having this chemo pumped in to me, the brain tumour is still growing and everything is becoming... I don't know the best way to describe it. Detached.

Yeah, that works. It's like I'm half asleep and watching a movie, and it's getting more and more fuzzy round the edges. Sometimes my eyes close and I blank out altogether, then realise that I've missed something important. That happened last week when Beth was telling me about her sports day at school. My brain zoned out, I just couldn't grasp the words I was hearing, and I had no idea whether I should congratulate her on winning or commiserate her on losing. Shauna saved the day on that one. In she came with a cake, with a candle on top, right next to the medal Beth had won for the high jump. I understood it just in time to make a huge fuss of her. I hope she'll remember that day.

I press 'record' on my phone while that thought is still on my mind, and manage to get it out just before it disappears.

'Hey, m'darlin', I'm back. Listen, before I forget, remember Beth won the medal at sports day last year? I'm just thinking that she's too young to remember how proud I was of her. Truth is, I'm proud of her whether she's winning medals or not. I need her to know that, so can you show her this? Or maybe... Maybe I'll make a video for her too. Nothing too crazy. Just something that she'll have, so she's in no doubt about how I would react to the things that will come her way in the future. Yeah, that's a better idea. In fact, bugger it, I'll do it now. I'll be right back.'

I flick the camera off and lie back on my bed. It's not my own bed though. It's not even the hospital ward that I've spent so much time in over the last year. Nope, I've been moved into a hospice for a week or so, because this latest round of chemo is brutal and if the cancer doesn't slay me, the fecking chemo will do the job. I made Shauna promise that this was temporary. I'm not dying in here. I want to be home, under the same roof as my girls. Or sitting in a pub with a cold pint, preferably watching the rugby, and I'll happily keel over right after Ireland scores a try to beat whoever they're playing.

As I'm making more notes on the back of a magazine that someone has left on the bedside unit, one of the nurses, Kristen, comes in with some meds. I take so many now that I'm rattling. These are the anti-nausea ones that I take an hour before chemo. An hour. Right. Better get cracking then.

I lie on my side, too knackered to hold the phone up. Instead, I balance it against the water jug that's next to the magazine pile. I'm about to press 'play' when I stop myself.

No. This isn't what I want for Beth. She'll have this for the rest of her life, and I don't want her watching her old da' lying here like a sack of spuds.

I push myself up, grab a brush from the cabinet on the other side of the bed, and run it through my hair. I give my cheeks a bit of a slap to get some colour back in there and then I force myself out of bed and over to the chair at the window. It's a nice room, this one. Thank feck for the NHS.

Christ, I'm exhausted. Ten steps and my legs are giving out.

I make it to the seat but only just. I manage to turn myself so that the room is behind me and I'm facing the window. Lulu taught me that. She's the queen of those selfie things. 'Always have the light source in front of you,' she said, then she added some variation of, 'Although, with a face like yours, you might want to keep it in shadow.' The woman was pure cheek and she drove us all mad, but, God, no one made me laugh like Lulu did. She was the strongest of us all. Bloody bulletproof. Even when I was diagnosed and given a terminal prognosis, she didn't miss a beat. She just shows up every single day, thrashes me at cards and tells me I'm beating this, so there's no point worrying about it. I didn't think the gods would be brave enough to argue. Between Lulu's fight, my fecking optimism and my gorgeous Shauna's determination, I reckoned we still had an outside chance. I'm not so convinced now, but I'm not giving up – not while there's a breath or a bad joke in my body.

I check the screen. Okay, I don't look too bad. Decent T-shirt, bit of colour in my cheeks and I tell myself that the weight I've lost is giving me a chiselled jaw for the first time in my life. It's one of the Unintentional Consequences of A FBT (Fecking Brain Tumour) that I can live with.

I balance the phone on the windowsill and press play. I want Steven Spielberg here shouting 'action', because this might top my last performance. Best Oscar In The Category of A Dying Dad goes to...'

'Hey Bethy, how ya doing, love?' I get an image of her

watching this in one year, five years, ten years, and I have to stop because the tears are suddenly blinding me. For feck's sake.

Stop. Rewind. Dry yer eyes, ya useless lump. You've got this. It's for Beth. And for yer girl, there's nothing you can't do. Deep breath. Record.

'Hey Bethy, how're ye? I bet you're great, because you've been spectacular since the day you were born. In a way, I hope you never see this, because that means they've come up with some way of curing me, but just in case, there's a few things that I want you to know.

'Och, darlin', I don't know where to start. Okay, I've got this. The most important thing. Since the minute you were born, yer mum and I have loved you more than anything or anyone on God's earth. Don't tell your brothers I said that though,' I say with a wink. 'For a long time, me and yer mum thought we would never have children of our own, but now I know the reason we had to wait a while was because we were getting a special one. You and your brothers are the loves of my life, an' yer mum is my soulmate. That's a lot of love in that wee bubble. Don't ever forget you have that. And if you do, ask your mum about her childhood and compare the difference. Actually, if you've any questions ever, then ask your mum, because she's the smartest woman I've ever known. Right now, you look like me, but inside, you're all your mum – and I wouldn't have that any other way.

'Okay, ma love, the big stuff...

'I can't stand the thought that you'll feel a day of pain in your life, or that you'll come across people who won't treat you well, but that's life, m'darlin'. The important thing is that you spot them and ditch them and don't look back. Everyone makes mistakes, so have some forgiveness for the folk you love, but if someone doesn't see you for the incredible girl you are, and the mighty woman you'll become, then cut them loose, because that's the only way you'll find the people who deserve you.

'Can I just say here, that I'm talking about friends, because you'll not be doing any of that love stuff until yer at least forty-five. Nope, not having it, and don't argue with me, young lady.' I try to keep a straight face when I say that, but I fail and crack into a laugh.

'I want you always to be you. If you're watching this when you're still young, don't worry, you'll understand what that means when you're older. I want you to laugh every day, to seek out things that make you happy. Love whoever you choose to love, and don't let anyone tell you that you can't. But like I say, make sure that person deserves you. It'll take someone pretty special to match up to that heart of yours.

'Okay, what else? Don't drink alcohol until you're old enough that you won't do something completely stupid after a few jars. I never mastered that – yer mother will confirm that point – and if you don't believe me, you can ask yer brothers who broke the kitchen window with a football a couple of months ago.

'What else?' I think for a minute. Brain fog is closing my thoughts down. One last burst of effort required.

'Don't post anything dodgy on the internet – that stuff stays there forever. Don't take drugs, you don't need them and they're pointless, because happy comes from inside. And from Ireland winning the rugby.

'If someone wants you to do something and it doesn't feel right, then don't do it. If that person is a true friend, or a true love, they'll back off and respect your decision. If not... back to what I said earlier. Cut them loose.

'If ever you feel you need help, ask for it. You have the best people in yer world. Like I said before, your mum is the person you want by your side in your life. Your brothers would do anything for you. So would your Uncle Dan. And if something happens, or you make a mistake you don't want to share with them – and darlin', we all do it – go to your Aunt Lulu. There's nothing that could shock her, there's nothing she won't do for you and she'll keep your secrets forever. Just don't go on a night out with her, because she'll probably get you arrested.'

I'm starting to feel really crap now and it's getting harder to keep the smile on. Time to wrap this up.

'Most of all though, just remember how much I love you and know that even if I'm not there, I've got you, darlin'. I'll always have you. And you'll always have me. Just listen to your heart beating and know that I'm in there.'

With that, I wave, I blow her a kiss, and I stop the recording, then I slump in my chair. Blinding lights make me squeeze my eyes shut and I feel my chest getting so tight I can't get another breath.

That's when the world fades to black.

12

'Hey, Beth, can you tell your mum that I've left the pressie I brought her from my honeymoon over there on the kitchen work-top, next to the coffee machine?'

Over at the kitchen table, Beth giggled, then leaned forward so that her head was almost touching Lulu's. 'Auntie Lu,' she said in a stage whisper, 'she's right there. She can hear you.'

'Yeah, but I'm not talking to her. I like you much better, so I'm only talking to you.'

Over at the sink, where I was washing salad for lunch, I shook my head. My best friend was infuriating. Ridiculously petulant. Completely incorrigible. But all those things were reasons that I loved her. She was an irritating, cheeky, infuriating child, trapped in a forty-something, designer-clad, size-ten body.

Most Saturdays, Lulu would take Beth to her ballet practice in the morning, then they'd come back to our home for lunch. Of course, this was so much more straightforward when Lulu lived downstairs with Dan. Now she lived twenty minutes or so away, I wasn't sure that she'd still want to drag herself out of bed early on a weekend morning, but this morning, almost a week after she'd stormed out of my house, she showed up, right on time, just before I was about to take Beth myself. Off they went, giving me a morning of solitude.

I could have slid back into bed and had a decadent couple of hours of TV and magazines, but I'd have been restless after ten minutes, and my brain would switch on to fast-spin, running through all the things I could be doing. In truth, though, my aversion to a long lie-in was more than just my chronic inability to switch off. Weekends made Colm's absence so much more vivid. From the time we met, as long as I wasn't working, lazy Saturday mornings were one of our favourite guilty pleasures. Now, I couldn't bear to see the flat duvet and the empty pillow on his side of the bed. If I closed my eyes real tight, sometimes I could imagine that I could see him, or hear his laugh, but then came the pain of returning to reality. No. I could do without that little nugget of psychological self-mutilation, so on my rare free mornings I kept myself busy.

This morning, by the time Lulu and Beth came back from her dancing class, I'd already planned my work diary for next week, put in all my stock orders, updated the company Facebook, Twitter and Instagram pages, cleaned the house and got two lots of washing done. The phone had rung twice, and both times my heart stopped, only starting again when I heard that it was two of those spam sales pitches for windows. Not Vincent. I was doing my best to forget that he'd called. No good could come of it. None. I just wished I could stop thinking about it, stop playing the words back in my head, stop wondering what he wanted. Vincent and I were a closed chapter in a regrettable book. Yet... it was Vincent. Arrgh! The only good thing about the spat with Lulu was that it was distracting me from wondering why he'd suddenly got in touch after years of silence. I had seen him once in the last decade and that was at Colm's funeral, and I'd asked him not to contact me again. I thought he understood. Maybe not.

It was a relief when Lulu and Beth came back and distracted me.

I'd just tossed the washed lettuce in the colander, when Lulu pulled her little charade, but Beth was having none of it. 'My mum always says that the only way to solve a problem is to talk it through, Aunt Lu. She says if you care about the person, and they care about you, there will always be a way to work it out.'

Out of the corner of my eye, I saw Lulu sigh and lean over to kiss Beth's forehead. 'I hate that you're always the most mature person in the room, kiddo.'

'Yup,' Beth said nonchalantly. This wasn't news to her. She'd been told this many times before. It was incredible how balanced and secure she was given that she'd lost her dad at such a young age. We both chose to believe that Colm was with her every day though, both on the inside and on the outside. There was the unmistakable likeness, but more than that, she had his fearless spirit and easy, irrepressible joy. Something that was definitely lacking in my best mate's demeanour right now.

For the first time, Lulu glanced over in my direction. 'So are we okay or not?' This was another of Lulu's versions of an apology: an olive branch, wrapped up in about six words. She'd never been one for dragging things out. Fight. Make up. Move on. I was happy to go with it but that came with conditions.

'That depends. Are you going to charge back in and take a wrecking ball to Dan's life?'

She squirmed in her Gucci jeans. 'Noooooo.'

I didn't believe her for a second. I could see the truth written all over her stunning face. Her hand was on the lid of the cookie jar, and she was desperate to lift it off.

'Have you spoken to him?' I asked. Dan had mentioned that

she'd called, but I didn't want her to think we'd been talking about her and set her off on another defensive rant.

'Barely got two words out of him. You've clearly brainwashed him and convinced him that seeing me would be a terrible idea because I'm some kind of deranged woman who will subject him to a hostage situation until he bends to my will.'

'Think you just about summed up your marriage,' I said, plopping some plum tomatoes into the salad bowl.

That had exactly the reaction I expected. Lulu's whole face creased into a grin. 'You might have a point there.' One thing about my beloved chum – she could dish it out, and then some, but she could take it too. In fact, I think she enjoyed it.

'Do you want to be married to Uncle Dan again?' Beth asked her, picking up on the vibe of the conversation and going straight to the heart of it.

'No, honey,' Lulu said. I wasn't sure who she was trying to convince.

Two little frown lines of sincerity formed between Beth's eyebrows. 'You know, when Taylor Swift split up with her boyfriend, she wrote songs about it, and she says that you eventually find the right person. You should listen to her songs. They always cheer me up.' If she started singing 'We Are Never Ever Getting Back Together', maybe Lulu would get the message.

'Good advice. Although, I once danced to that "Shake It Off" song in a boxercise class and I pulled a hamstring. I was walking like a cowboy for a fortnight. Every time I hear her voice, I get flashbacks.'

'Well, you don't know what you're missing,' Beth told her. 'She's so smart. You could learn loads from her, Aunt Lu.'

'There you go then,' Lulu threw her hands up. 'That's where I've been going wrong. I'm more of a Nicki Minaj kinda girl.'

'That explains a lot,' Beth said, with wise nod of the head.

Thankfully she didn't dwell on it. She also had Colm's attention span. 'Right, Mum, that's the cucumber chopped. Can I go watch TV until lunch is ready?'

Trying so hard to suppress a giggle at Beth's deadpan retort and Lulu's wide-eyed speechlessness, I could only nod. As soon as my far-too-wise daughter had left the room, I dug a little deeper.

'So tell me what's happening, Lu. You only lash out like that when you're stressing.'

Her shoulders sagged. 'Yeah, sorry about that. You know I don't mean it. I was just freaking out, thinking I'd made a mistake with Bobby. To be honest, I still do.'

'Things not any better?'

She shook her head. 'Nope. But I think it's my fault too. I'm so pissed off with him for sidelining me that I'm not making any effort either. How could this happen? How could I have been so fricking stupid? Even St Taylor of the Swift would tell me I'm a daft cow for this one.'

'Yeah, well, she'd probably put it in a song, and Beth would be singing it the minute it hit iTunes.'

'Great. Global humiliation. And I don't think it would feel any worse than this.'

'What wouldn't feel any worse than this?' came a voice from the door. I hadn't heard Jess come in.

Lulu groaned. 'Here she is. President of the Secret Squirrel Club.' She clearly hadn't got over the exclusion from Jess's life-coaching sessions then, despite the fact that we all knew she'd hate what she called, 'all that introspective, touchy-feely bollocks.' 'Do you want me to leave so that you can swap confidential information about your deepest feelings?' Lulu asked, voice dripping with sarcasm.

'Aw, Lu, don't be like that. You know you love me,' Jess

crooned, coming up behind her nemesis's chair and throwing her arms around Lulu's shoulders, before leaning down and kissing Lulu's cheek repeatedly until she squealed. Jess's hair was up in a messy ponytail, her body in denim dungarees and Converse on her feet. The contrast to Lulu's designer chic and my mono-chrome blandness was striking. If we were The Spice Women, Jess would be Baby, Lulu would be Scary, and I'd be Posh, but without the glum face and with an entire wardrobe purchased in Matalan. Or rather, Jess would be Bossy Spice, Lulu would be Snappy Spice and I'd be the Spice that was too knackered for all that dancing.

'Yeah, well your appeal has faded,' Lulu bit back, but the teasing tone was there.

I exhaled a breath of relief. With Lulu, every exchange could go well or it could deteriorate rapidly – it was pretty much a crap-shoot depending on her mood. I hate that talking about her makes her sound like an awful person. She's not. Volatile and unreasonable? Definitely. But she's also the person that spent every single day sitting with Colm while I was working, enter-taining him with card games and filthy jokes. She was ride or die – as long as you didn't mind a few bumps on every road.

Jess pulled out the seat across from Lulu and plonked herself down. I poured a glass of wine for her and slid it across the table. She picked it up, took a sip, then turned her focus back to Lulu. 'Okay, get it out of your system. You've got thirty seconds to tell me how pissed off you are with me and then you have to love me again.'

Watching these two in action was an awesome spectacle. They were like rutting deer. Or French and Saunders, depending on the day. Both strong, both smart, both able to stand their ground. There was an honesty and respect there too, that came from genuine affection for each other, and our determination to make life happy for Beth. Every time I watched *Grey's Anatomy* and saw Meredith, Maggie and Amelia loving each other, despite the occasional bickers, it reminded me of us. Without the high-flying careers and the ability to transplant a kidney.

'I just don't understand why I can't join your secret society,' Lulu bit.

'Because it's for people coming to terms with losing a relationship and finding a way to move on. You don't qualify,' Jess answered calmly.

I carried on making lunch, staying right out of this one. Too many people had been taken out by crossfire.

'But I'm coming to terms with loss too. I don't have Dan any more,' Lulu replied.

Jess put her hand up and stopped her there. 'Nope, you don't get to play that card. You didn't lose anything, Lu – you gave it away because you thought you'd found something better. That's a whole different set of circumstances. The three of us – Dan, Shauna and me – weren't the ones who made the choice to go or to end our marriages. That choice was taken out of our hands, so that makes it so much harder to process.'

'Urgh, I hate it when you're logical and make sense,' Lulu groaned. 'I've no idea why we're friends. I much prefer neurotic and irrational.'

'Thanks,' I piped up, as I carried a laden tray over to the table. Salad. French bread. A bowl of Cajun chicken strips. The smell was making my stomach gurgle.

Jess had her mind on other things. 'I take it that if you're suddenly feeling the loss of Dan, then all isn't happy families over at Rod Stewart Towers?'

Lulu ignored the provocation and I wondered how this would play out. She rarely kept secrets from me, and if she did, it was only until she'd worked the situation out for herself and then she'd tell me afterwards. She was far more guarded around just about everyone else on earth, Jess included.

'No, it's all going great,' Lulu argued.

I didn't utter a word, already feeling guilty that I'd said anything to Jess and Dan. Was Lulu really going to keep this to herself? We were all huge parts of each others' lives – being in an unhappy relationship was going to be a tough secret to keep.

Lulu must have realised the same, because she made a swift U-turn. 'Okay, it's not,' she conceded, reaching for the bread.

Jess's eyes widened. 'Holy shit, it must be really serious if you're eating carbs.'

'I've made a mistake in marrying Bobby,' Lulu admitted.

I felt an overwhelming wave of relief. That's as much as I'd told Jess and Dan the week before, so now that Lulu was being open about it, I didn't feel like I'd overshared.

Jess had the decency to act like this was the first time she'd heard this.

'Oh, God. Are you sure it's not just that anticlimactic thing that all brides get after the wedding? Especially a wedding like yours. I mean, that was extra.'

I was back at the table again with plates and cutlery. 'Doesn't everyone have a diamond-themed wedding at Clivedon House, with several high-profile celebrities and at least three people who sang at Band Aid?' I teased.

'Still can't believe that Bananarama wouldn't let me sing with them,' Lulu pouted. 'Total dream crushers.'

"Beth, lunch is ready,' I yelled, before taking a seat at the table. 'We really need to get a butler. Can't believe you never bought me one from Clivedon. Isn't that the kind of stuff you rich people buy their matron of honour? Especially since I've done it twice now.'

Beth came in, singing along with the song on her phone.

Naturally it was Taylor Swift, and I recognised the tune. 'Lover'. Not exactly appropriate for an eleven-year-old, but I was pretty sure it wasn't going to lead her astray.

'Mum, can I please, please, please take my lunch into the living room. I want to chat to Marcy on FaceTime. She downloaded a Little Mix concert last night and I want to know what Jade was wearing. She's my favourite,' she declared to the others.

'Mine too,' Lulu agreed.

'And mine,' chimed Jess.

I didn't point out that neither of them would recognise any of the members of Little Mix if they strolled in here and pulled up a chair.

I was torn on the answer to Beth's question. I usually insisted that we eat together, but Little Mix and my best mate's potentially life-changing crisis swayed me.

'Go on then. As long as you eat all your salad.'

'Toss it out the window. I'll hide the evidence later,' Lulu hissed to her.

Beth giggled, then kissed me on the cheek. 'Thanks, Mum. You're the best.' She loaded up her plate and off she went.

We mentally rewound to where the conversation was going before Beth came in. Lulu got there first.

'To answer your question, no. It's not just the anticlimax. It's more that I had a couple of realisations while I was on honeymoon.'

'Such as?' Jess asked, genuinely interested.

Lulu glanced at me. 'You didn't tell her?'

'Of course not. It wasn't my place to say anything,' I replied. It was a half-truth, but I wasn't going to elaborate.

Unfortunately, Jess chose that moment to take a chug of her wine, which she almost choked on when Lu said, 'I realised that I made a mistake leaving Dan.'

Cue vociferous coughing from Jess. It took a few moments for her to regain her power of speech and when she did, it was to blurt, 'You're a fricking nightmare.'

'So I've been told,' Lulu admitted, dipping a piece of chicken into a large dollop of honey mustard salad dressing on her plate.

'I've already told her she can't storm in and mess his life up again,' I said.

'But who says I'd mess up his life?' Lulu argued. 'Maybe he's miserable without me. I mean, why else would he be doing that stupid life-coaching thing with you two. It must be because he's struggling to move on. By the way, I don't believe for a minute that he was out with that Stephanie chick from Bracal Tech. She's totally not his type. Way too high maintenance.'

It would have been easy to point out the obvious, but we didn't.

Instead, Jess tried to bring some sense to the situation.

'For the benefit of staying on track with this conversation, I'm going to overlook the fact that you just called my career "stupid", and stick to the main issue. Maybe Dan's not struggling to move on,' she said. 'Maybe he just wants to learn new behaviours so that he doesn't repeat past destructive patterns and make bad decisions.'

This time, Lulu's glass of wine got stuck in mid-air, as she responded to the inferred dig, aping Jess's language. 'For the benefit of staying on track with this conversation, I'm going to ignore the fact that you just implied I was destructive and one of his "bad decisions".'

'No jury would disagree,' Jess blurted. This wasn't helping. Lulu's claws were coming out and Jess was getting exasperated, whereas I'd heard all this before, so I just wanted to go lie on the couch with Beth and watch romcoms.

I sent a silent prayer up to Colm. *Babe, if you're up there and you can hear me, make this end, before these two kill each other. Thank you. Love you. And if you could land me a couple of new catering contracts, and fix the leak under the sink, that would be dandy too.*

I left the afterlife and came back to my kitchen, where Lulu was now in full flow.

'Who made you the authority on my relationship with Dan? How do you know what he wants? Maybe he's been waiting for me to come to my senses. Maybe he wants me back too.'

Barely a second passed before a voice at the door said, 'No I don't.'

13

'Sorry, Shauna, didn't mean to gatecrash. Beth let me in. Just wanted to fix that leak under your sink.'

I raised my eyes heavenward. *Colm O'Flynn, you have a wicked sense of humour.*

Strangely, Dan wasn't even looking at Lulu. It was as if he hadn't heard her, hadn't responded, hadn't just summed up over twenty years of love and heartache in a single exchange.

'Maybe he wants me back.'

'No, I don't.'

Ouch.

Now Lulu was staring at Dan, who was making his way over to the sink. He was avoiding eye contact with everyone. Jess and I were both wide-eyed, looking helplessly at each other, completely stumped as to how we should handle this.

Bugger. Was there a Taylor Swift song that covered this level of romantic complexity? If so, we could really do with her words of wisdom.

'Obviously you weren't meant to hear that like that,' Lulu said and I struggled to think of another time that I'd ever seen her look visibly embarrassed.

'Yeah, I guessed that. No sweat. Shauna, do you know where the wrench is that I left up here last time I fixed this?' And the top prize for staying cool in an awkward situation goes to Dan Channing. He was acting like Lulu was talking to him about the weather.

'Yeah, it's just behind the Flash mop in the corner cupboard.'

He reached in and pulled it out, then opened the under-sink cabinet. The top half of his body disappeared into the void, leaving only his jean-clad legs sticking out.

Lulu pushed her plate away and stood up. 'I'm going to go.'

'Lu, don't...' I began, but I knew it was hopeless. No one could change Lulu's mind about anything, and especially not when her face was burning with humiliation.

She left without saying another word to us, but she must have popped her head into the lounge to say goodbye to Beth, because we heard a cheery, 'Bye, Auntie Lu – love you too.'

When the door banged, Dan curled his way out of the cupboard. 'I'm pretty sure a showdown with the ex-wife isn't in the job description for a plumber.' He was trying to brush it off, but I knew that inside he must be so conflicted. He'd loved her for so long, and she'd almost wrecked him, but now she wanted him back.

'Are you okay?' Jess asked him, needlessly. We both knew he wasn't.

'Yeah, I'm just going to nip downstairs and get a washer for this, Shauna. I'll be back up in a tick.'

'Sure, no worries,' I said, uneasily. I wanted to sit him down, tell him not to move until Lulu had definitely cleared the building, but hey... He was a grown man. It was up to him. And I loved him enough to let him make his own decisions. Dan and I had been through the wars, gone to hell and back, and we'd survived because we gave each other space and respect. I wasn't going to change that now.

Jess and I sat in silence until we heard the door close after him.

'Do you think he's gone to chase after her?' Jess asked, and I noticed the veins in the side of her neck were popping with tension. Strange.

I shrugged. 'I don't know. Maybe. Or maybe she's already gone and he really is just going to get a washer.'

Jess got up and went over to the window, peering out, scanning the street below. 'I can't see her car,' she said, and I could hear a twinge of relief in her voice.

I began clearing away the plates. 'She's probably still parking in the alley at the side.'

'Shit.' Jess came back, sat down at the table, picked up her mug. 'He's such an idiot.'

'Eh, you're taking this life coach thing a bit seriously here, Jess,' I told her. 'He'll work it all out for himself. Don't worry. And if he doesn't, you'll still have a client to sort out and put back together again.'

She didn't respond. And those veins were still popping. What was going on here? I knew she was super-protective of Dan – we both were – but we could only give them our opinions and then be there for them when they needed us. Jess was acting as if... as if...

It took me a moment to compute.

My stomach plummeted.

Oh no.

'Jess, what's going on?'

'What do you mean? Nothing is going on.'

That was feigned innocence, with a touch of defensiveness and a flush that was creeping up from her neck.

Again, oh no.

'Jess...?' I drawled, refusing to let this go. I was sitting back at the table now, directly across from her, and I knew my expression was making it clear that I was refusing to let this drop.

'It's nothing. It's just...' she paused. It was like that moment in every crime show where the suspect was trying to decide whether to maintain his innocence or crumble under the weight of the interrogation and spill the truth in the hope of negotiating a decent plea deal. 'Okay, so you know how you and I have kept each other's biggest secrets over the years...?'

The suspect was crumbling. The only problem was, she had the ammunition to take the interrogator down with her. The secret that Jess had kept for me was one that I never wanted to think about again. Even referring to it made my skin crawl.

A tight 'Yes' was all I could manage.

'Well, I'm about to add another one to the list.'

No. It couldn't be. Surely I was misreading this. 'Dan?'

She nodded slowly, her mouth a thin line of apprehension and resignation.

'You've been seeing him?' How could I have missed this? How long had it been going on? Why hadn't anyone cracked a fricking light in my direction?

'No!' she blurted. 'I'd never have done that to Lu. Never.'

'Tell me,' I coaxed her. 'You know I won't judge you. Although I can't promise I won't put my head on the table and weep,' I added, trying to lighten the mood and give her the confidence to share.

I could see she wanted to. We were now at that bit in the criminal interrogation where the perpetrator begins to confess his crimes and feels the burden ease as he finally shares his truth. I'd seen this so many times on *Line Of Duty*.

'I love him,' she said simply.

My mouth dropped. 'Like, love love? Or sisterly type love?'

'Definitely love love,' she confirmed, making my heart clench in my chest. This wasn't good. I'd had the information for about two seconds and I could already see that this had horrible consequences for everyone involved.

Shit, Lulu would self-combust.

I was going to need more coffee for this one. I got up and filled both our mugs, then slid hers back in front of her. Poor Jess. She was a slumped, drawn, picture of dejection and woe.

'Okay, I think we need to rewind. Since when have you been in love with him?'

She shrugged. 'To be honest, I'm not entirely sure. For a long, long time, it was the whole sisterly love thing. My heart was broken for both of you when Colm died – and I just wanted to be there for you and Dan too. Then, over the next couple of years, we got closer and just kind of slotted into a friendship that was another level to the one we'd had back in the days when Colm and I were still married.'

'I get that. I think grief takes friendships to a deeper place – or destroys them altogether,' I said, trying to show her I was empathetic to how she'd got here. I refrained from pointing out that Lulu would destroy her altogether if she caught wind of this.

'I think I pushed how I felt to one side, because we were friends... I don't have to tell you how that goes,' she added, and my jaw clenched again.

Yep, I knew all about that. I also knew the consequences of dropping that restraint. Yet again, I shut down the memory and moved my focus back to Jess.

'No, you don't have to explain that one to me,' I conceded, then switched the focus back to the present. 'So does he know?'

She shook her head. 'I only really knew myself in the last few months. I think when he split with Lu, it gave something inside me permission to admit to myself how I felt about him. I love him, Shauna. And I thought that... Ugh, I can't even say it.'

She didn't need to spell it out. I had a growing sense of stomach-clenching clarity as to where she was going with this.

'You thought that when Lulu remarried, that it left Dan free and you thought that the two of you might get together?'

'I really hate it when you know what I'm thinking,' she said, through pursed lips.

Bingo.

Or as Colm would say, 'Ah, bollocks'.

I pushed a packet of KitKats in her direction. I'd been saving them for a movie afternoon with Beth, but they were required right now for medicinal purposes. My gran Annie used to tell me that tea, caramel wafers and a shoulder to cry on could make any situation feel a whole lot better. She was always my shoulder. I just wished she was here now for Jess. 'Och, sweetheart,' she'd say in the broad Glasgow accent that had stayed with her until the day she died, despite leaving Scotland when she was in her early twenties. 'Dry yer eyes now. Aye, he's a good-looking man, and I wouldn't kick him out of bed for making crumbs with his crackers, but weeping gives you wrinkles and no man is worth that. Not when you've got yer pals.'

'I still don't understand why you didn't tell him. Lulu left a year ago and she's remarried. What were you waiting for?'

She threw up her hands in frustration. 'This! This is exactly what I was waiting for. I had a horrible feeling she'd bail on her marriage to Bobby – come on, Lulu is far too shallow to maintain an attraction to a man with highlights who's not far off his bus pass. Money can only turn you on for so long, then you realise that you had nothing in common except rank materialism. She's his trophy, and he's her unlimited bank account and her entry into the kind of life that comes with a personal shopper and a walk-in wardrobe.'

Again, I couldn't argue. Those had been Lulu's first two acquisitions after Bobby had given her a Platinum Amex card.

'You want to hear something even more pathetic?' she asked hesitantly.

'Go on. It'll take my mind off my sad, lonely life,' I replied, trying again to lift her spirits a little.

'That's the reason I suggested the whole "moving on" life-coaching programme. Two birds with one stone. Gets my dissertation done, while trying to get Dan to a stage where he's truly come to terms with his divorce. When he moved to an emotional place where he was ready for another relationship, that's when I was going to tell him. God, if there was an ethics board for life coaches, I'd be getting struck off right now.'

I shook my head, heart aching for her. 'Oh, I don't know. I think it's pretty creative. And you'd certainly be making his life better. I think you'd deserve a commission for that.'

'Anyone who could make Dan break ties with Lulu deserves a fricking medal,' she countered. 'I was just weeks away from telling him. Weeks. And there she comes, that crazy bint, riding in to snap him back up. Part of me always knew that she wouldn't let him go. She hasn't got it in her. She thrives on the challenge, on the feeling that she's adored, and I had a horrible suspicion that the first sign of irritation with Bobby would bring her running back to Dan to have her ego stroked. And he falls for it, every time.'

I tried to be the voice of reason. 'You don't know that he will this time.'

Her gaze met mine and all I saw was cynicism. 'Come on, Shauna. All the times she's been unfaithful, let him down, made unreasonable demands, and he always forgave her. She's his addiction. Maybe he doesn't want to give it up.'

I sat back in my chair, took a sip of coffee. 'Maybe he doesn't realise that there's something worth giving her up for.'

'Yeah, well, he's not going to hear it from me.' She stretched up, went over, peered out of the window again. Her silence said there was still no sign of Lulu, her car or Dan.

'So what's your plan, Mrs Life Coach?' I asked her. 'Aren't you the one who encourages people to go after what they want and stop at nothing until they get it?'

'Mmmm. I'm thinking it might not be too late to retrain in another field. I'm thinking lollipop lady. Maybe a tour guide. "Here on the left is where my first husband bailed on me. On the right, you'll see the place where my second husband put his penis in his secretary. And just along there... well, that's the spot where I fell in love with my friend and was then murdered in cold blood by the ex-wife who wanted him back."'

Despite the circumstances, I was actually laughing now. 'And we always thought Lu was the dramatic one,' I chided her. 'You're supposed to be the oracle of calm reasoning and common sense.'

'Those traits have definitely deserted me recently. Do you think it's a menopause thing? My hormones are fecked, so they're making me eat more, sweat at night, and fall in love with my pal's ex-husband?'

'I'm fairly sure those are the exact symptoms. They talked about it on *Loose Women*. Anyway,' I said, 'what happens next?'

She shook her head. 'Nothing. I just need to let it play out and see if they get back together. And I need to hope that they don't. If there's one woman who doesn't need a life coach, it's Lulu. So I just need to wait and see if she goes after what she wants and if she gets it.'

'And if she doesn't? If Dan doesn't take her back, are you going to admit how you feel about him?' I asked, fearing the answer.

A long, deep sigh came before her words. 'I guess that's when I'll have to choose... who do I want in my life more? The guy I'm in love with, or my friend who is in love with him too?'

14

SHAUNA

Beth and I were cuddled up on the couch together, her favourite blue furry blanket over us, when the doorbell went. It made a refreshing change that someone actually rang a bell before wandering on into my home. That said, it could only be Dan, Lulu or Jess, because no one else could get past the main door of the building without buzzing up first.

Actually, forget that. Lu or Jess would have used their keys to come in, so it could only be Dan. I hadn't heard from him since he'd left earlier to go and find a washer. That was hours ago, so it was clearly proving elusive. Or perhaps he was searching for it somewhere around Lulu's tonsils.

As I eased my arm out from under Beth's head, I realised she'd dozed off. My beautiful, sleeping girl. She always looked like Colm, but even more so when she was asleep.

Performing gymnastic moves that would make Simone Biles proud, I managed to get up and over Beth without waking her, then quietly closed the door behind me. I could see Dan's outline in the glass, leaning against the frame of the wood. When I opened it, he didn't move. Only his eyes flicked towards me.

'Stop me doing something incredibly stupid,' he said, his voice oozing weariness, his whole body slumped.

'Certainly,' I chirped. 'This is the Stupid Prevention Centre. We're great at that shit. Come on in.'

He followed me as I padded through to the kitchen, my woolly socks silent on the wooden floors.

'You realise we live our whole lives sitting round tables trying to sort relationship stuff out? I always thought we'd be accomplished and organised grown-ups by now, but I think we're regressing. Beer or coffee?' I wittered.

'Beer. Definitely beer.'

I pulled two Buds out of the fridge and joined him at the breakfast bar.

I opened with, 'I'm scared to ask what happened...'

'Nothing,' he said quickly, and the relief made my shoulders drop a couple of inches. 'Thing is, for a moment I wanted it to.'

Shoulders back up.

'She was downstairs, sitting on the stair outside our door when I got there. I knew she would be, and I think that's why I went. It was nothing to do with a washer...'

'I'm never getting that leak fixed, am I?' I chided playfully, trying to make him smile. He still looked like the weight of the world was crushing him.

'Only if you call a real plumber,' he quipped back with a cheeky grin, normal service resumed for just a second.

'God, my landlord is crap,' I chided dramatically. 'Fixes nothing and brings all his drama to my door.'

'Yeah, you should definitely move out.' A pause. 'Wait, we're still joking, right? Because if you move out, I swear it's over. I'm selling up and going to live in a beach hut somewhere.'

'Lu would still find you.'

'I know. I'm sure she's got me chipped.'

I didn't admit that wouldn't surprise me in the least.

'Anyway, so the pamphlet version of the last few hours is that she's miserable with Bobby, after a whole month of marriage, and she wants to rewind and come home... I mean, come back to my house. I've got a feeling that the only reason she isn't there already is because I changed the lock.'

I stretched up, still trying to shake off my afternoon laziness. I didn't tell him that I knew all this already. Being Switzerland between those two required ultimate tact and discretion.

'And how do you feel. Do you want her back? If you've spent the last couple of hours doing naked bendy things, I really don't want to know.'

'No! I swear. Everything fully clothed. We just talked. But the thing is, a couple of times I was tempted to just toss the barriers and give in to her.'

'But you didn't?'

'No. I told her I needed to think about it. Do I though? Any other sane bloke would have canned this by now. Why am I even leaving a crack in the door? I should have slammed it shut by this point. Christ, I'm pathetic. If Colm was still here, he'd have me locked up to save me from myself.'

His words lit a tiny flame of warmth in my gut. Yes, he would have. Much as Colm loved Lulu, he'd been warning Dan about her for the last two decades.

Switzerland took a more diplomatic approach.

'Why can't you shut her off? Is it because you're still in love with her?'

He shrugged. 'I honestly don't know. I think... I think it's habit too. My muscle memory has always kicked in when it came to Lu, and I just repeated the same crazy shit every time. She'd mess up, I'd take her back, we'd be happy for a while, sometimes years, until it happened again. I was no angel either though, Shauna. You know that.'

I nodded. I did. During one of their splits, Dan had a brief fling too. Although, in his defence, it was after Lulu had thrown yet another infidelity bomb into their lives.

'No one has ever made me feel as great as Lu does. Or as shit. Either way, that's hard to forget.'

I thought about that for a moment. 'But you didn't give in to her today. You've still got your clothes on and you're here. What's different?'

'I'm just sick of the lies and the cheating. Done with it. I don't know how I got myself into a place where that was something I could come back from.'

I gave his shoulder a soft punch. 'Wow, personal growth! Go you.' I wasn't sure why, but he didn't seem to be viewing this with the same excitement.

'Can't believe I'm having this conversation. You know I don't do all this feely, emotional stuff. Colm would have told me to get a grip and suggested we go play snooker by now.'

'Maybe that's the problem, though.' I gazed upwards for a second. 'Sorry, Colm, but it's true.' Back to Dan. 'Talking helps. The dearly departed love of my life just never quite got that. As far as he was concerned, talking about stuff just prolonged the agony. Far better to ignore the problem, and hope it miraculously disappeared.'

'It was part of his charm,' Dan said, a genuine smile for the first time since he arrived.

'I'm missing him today, Shauna. I never say that to you because I know you've got it so much worse.'

The sentiment was thoughtful but misplaced. Colm and Dan were best mates long before I met them. 'Doesn't mean that you can't miss him too though. Just like it's understandable that you miss Lu.'

He sat with that for a heartbeat. 'Problem is, there's a part of me that still loves her. What if she is the only woman I'll ever truly love? You've never wanted anyone else since the day you met Colm...'

Another creeping rash of shame began to creep up from my chest. That wasn't true, but I couldn't admit that to him. I clenched my teeth shut.

'So what if Lu is the only woman who'll ever love me? Do I really want to go the rest of my life without feeling that again? And how do I force myself to take that chance?'

I shrugged helplessly, fearing that there was only one answer, and it came with a whole crap load of potential issues. 'I honestly don't know, Dan. But maybe that's a question for your personal life coach. Why don't you ask her?'

15

SHAUNA

'The gist of it is then, Gran, that Lulu has married Bobby, but she thinks she's still in love with Dan. I'm not sure she is, though – I think she might just be panicking and going back to her safe place. Dan doesn't want to take her back, but there's part of him that's too scared not to in case he never finds love again. Meanwhile, Jess has decided that she's in love with Dan, but she won't tell him because if he's not open to the possibility of adding nudity to their relationship then it could ruin their friendship. And no, I still haven't had sex, or met anyone else, because I'm an emotional cripple who still can't come to terms with the fact that her husband died, and I'm still too wrapped up in that to even muster an iota of interest in finding someone else. Ah, it must be killing you listening to all this and not being able to give your opinion. If you weren't, erm, dead already.'

In my head, I heard her uproarious cackle when I said that. Annie always liked a bit of gallows humour.

If anyone could see me, they'd be absolutely one hundred per cent sure that I'd lost my faculties, but I didn't care. I'd had a chair installed just in front of Annie's grave, and once a month or so I'd come and sit on the deep mahogany wood and update her on everything that was going on. When she was alive, she always loved to be fully appraised of all gossip and I had no reason to believe that had changed, so now, a couple of weeks after Lulu and I had kissed and made up, I was sitting in the cemetery on a chilly August morning chatting to my dearly departed grandmother.

'You know, I spend way too much time speaking to dead people, Gran. If it's not you, it's Colm. I'm going over to see him in a minute. If you hear a spinning noise, it's him after I've told him Lulu wants Dan back.'

I'd already filled her in on all Beth's news, so I was almost done and ready to move on to my next headstone. There was a chair at Colm's grave too. I think I knew right from the start that I'd spend a lot of time here. The only other person I'd lost in my life was my dad, but I rarely visited his resting place. We barely had a relationship when he was alive, so I thought it would be hypocritical to have one when he was dead.

'Anyway, Gran, who's been bringing you these flowers then?' I asked, gesturing to the big bunch of sunflowers that had been placed in front of her stone. Maybe one of the women from her line dancing group. That thought sparked another one...

'Oh, and, Gran, Vincent called. Left a message on my answering machine. You know, I can almost hear you saying that he was the sexiest man you ever met, and you wished you were fifty years younger every time you clapped eyes on him.'

I'd heard that so many times over the years. My gran and my former friend and business partner, Vincent, had been the best of buddies, an unlikely pairing who revelled in each other's company.

I closed my eyes and rewound to the start of one of the best and worst days in my life. I could still see every moment in vivid

technicolour. I'd called my gran to let her know that I was planning to visit her that evening, after Vincent and I had catered an
event near her home. When she told me she'd be out, I asked
where she was going.

'Line dancing.'

'What?'

'I'll be at line dancing, my lovely, but you're welcome to come
with me.'

I tried to keep the hilarity out of my voice. Class. Sheer class.

'Gran, when did you take up line dancing?'

'When I got bored rigid at Pilates. There's no point to it at all. I fell
asleep last time I was there, and some strange and very flexible
gentleman with his hair in a bun wasn't best pleased.'

Hilarity won, as I exploded into giggles.

'There are no words to express how much I frigging love you, Gran.'

'Try, dear. I need the ego boost,' she cackled.

'So, line dancing it is. What time do I need to be there?'

'Eight o'clock.'

'Okay, I should be done around seven, so I'll pick you up on the
way.'

'Lovely. Oh, and you need to bring cowboy boots. And a Stetson.
And Vincent.'

She was still chuckling when she hung up. After work, when
Vincent dropped me at Annie's house, he tried to resist, but she was
having none of it.

'Vincent, you have to come. I swear it'll be the biggest thrill those
ladies have had since before the menopause.'

'I don't have a hat,' he argued weakly.

She took hers off and plumped it on his head. 'You do now, son.'

He was powerless to resist the passive-aggressive demands of my
seventy-something Glaswegian powerhouse granny. It wasn't a
surprise. I'd never yet met anyone who could.

A few hours and a whole lot of heel-tapping later, 'Achy Breaky Heart', 'Boot Scootin' Boogie', and my personal favourite, 'Honky Tonk Badonkadonk', were just a few of the tunes that stuck in my mind. Annie knew every step, every turn, every holler, while Vincent and I tried desperately to follow, like the two new kids on the yee-hah block who didn't have a clue what was going on. We were hopeless. Embarrassing. Yet, it was the most fun I'd had in as long as I could remember.

'Gran, you totally put us to shame,' I told her on the way back to her house.

'Aye, there's life in me yet, love,' she preened. 'The day I can't spin around a dance floor you can shoot me.'

'Gran! Don't say that. Anyway, you can't pop your cowboy boots until you've taught us how to do those bloody dances. Vincent, we were officially rubbish.'

Annie sighed. 'Aye, thank god you're good-looking, son, because you're never going to get a woman with those dancing skills.'

Vincent could only laugh. Sometimes there was really no answer to my gran.

At the house, she persuaded him to come in for a nightcap. The woman was incorrigible. It was near midnight and she still wanted to keep the party going.

Inside, she went to take her coat and boots off, while Vincent and I went to the kitchen to make tea.

'So, not exactly how I anticipated tonight unfolding,' he said, deadpan. 'Kidnapped by Annie, forced to dance for my life, scarred by my inability to co-ordinate my arms and legs.'

I plopped two sugars in my gran's tea and poured her two fingers of her beloved MacCallan nightcap. 'Are you traumatised?'

'Absolutely. But I don't think I've ever laughed more. You're some team, you two.'

I took that as a compliment.

Picking up the tray, I headed to the lounge, Vincent at my back. I'd only taken a few steps in, when I stopped, forcing him to crash into the back of me.

'She's sleeping,' I whispered, nodding to Annie, in her favourite chair, eyes closed, a hint of a smile on her lips...

I paused the movie in my mind, swallowing the boulder that was now blocking my throat. It turned out that she wasn't sleeping. Just seconds before, Annie Williams had suffered a massive stroke and died instantly, in her favourite chair, after a fabulous night out with a good-looking man and the granddaughter that she loved more than words.

Part of my heart snapped off that night and I'd never been able to glue it back together.

That's why, whenever anything happened in life, I came to the cemetery and chatted to her. This morning, I knew she'd want to hear all the Vincent news.

'Anyway,' I told her, 'He says he's back – must be on holiday here – and he wants to talk. And don't get your immortal knickers in a twist, but I deleted the message. There's no point in seeing him. Too much water under that bridge.'

My mobile buzzed and I checked the screen.

'Hang on, Gran, it's Beth,' I said, as if Annie Williams was sitting right in front of me with a cup of Tetley and a caramel wafer.

'Hey, honey, how are you doing? How's your gran?' I asked.

Beth was spending the weekend with my mum and they were probably in some swanky spa with cucumbers over their eyes, having their feet rubbed. My mother's view of suitable pastimes when spending time with her eleven-year-old granddaughter was definitely outside normal granny territory. If anyone suggested trips to parks or maybe a wander round H&M, my mother would need smelling salts.

'We're good, Mum. I had a gold leaf facial this morning.'

When Beth was with her gran, nothing surprised me. I mean, seriously – who got an eleven year old a gold leaf facial? My mother, ladies and gentlemen. 'Was it any good?'

'It was supposed to be relaxing. I just kept wondering when it would be done so we could go for lunch, and then lunch was all green stuff. I think Gran is starving me. The snacks you sneaked into my bag are the only thing keeping me alive.'

She definitely got her sense of drama and her storytelling from her father. And I loved her for it.

'I'll get the fridge stocked up for you coming home, my love, don't worry.'

'If I don't make it till then, could you give all my Taylor Swift and Little Mix merch to Marcy?'

'I sure will,' I agreed, chuckling. This was the most bizarre conversation ever to be having in a cemetery. Even more bizarre, it was amusing me no end.

'Is that why you called? Or was it to tell me you loved me and were counting the minutes until you saw me again?' I teased her.

'Yeah, both of those things. But something else too, and please, please, please think about this before you say no.'

I had a feeling of foreboding. Beth was usually pretty low maintenance and laid-back, so if she was going for three 'pleases' in one sentence, it was either really important to her, or really unlikely that I'd agree.

'Okaaaay.'

'The thing is, I think Gran is lonely,' she began and my heart swelled. How sweet my girl was. How sensitive to other people. Sometimes she showed a maturity that was way beyond her years and made me swell with pride. I don't think there was anything I could refuse her right there in that moment.

'You know how we're all going up to Scotland next weekend... could Gran could come with us?'

Oh hell no. Nope. No way. Turns out there was something I could refuse her after all.

We were going up to Glasgow for my Aunt Flora's birthday party. Flora was Annie's sister, although they hadn't seen each other for the last fifty years of their lives. In fact, I hadn't even known that my gran still had family back in Scotland. It was only when I was clearing out her house after she died, that I found letters from her brother and sister. Turns out there had been a family rift when Annie was young, and she'd hotfooted it to London, and never gone back. A few years ago, Lulu and I had headed north one weekend, curious to see if we could solve the mystery, and we'd tracked down, not just my gran's siblings, but some lovely cousins too. We'd stayed in touch ever since and visited each other a couple of times a year.

I'd been so looking forward to the trip, but now, the prospect of spending a weekend with my mother had definitely zapped my excitement. This was the woman who had pretty much disapproved of me since the moment I was born. The mother who took disinterest in her offspring to a stratospheric level. The mother of the bride who wasn't sure if she'd have time between golf jollies to attend her daughter's wedding. There was no denying that she was a half-decent grandmother to Beth, but I suspected that was only because she was running out of people in her life to pass the time with now that my dad was gone, Lulu's parents had moved full time to Marbella, and she wasn't picking up the same amount of interest from the opposite sex.

'I know you're about to say "no", but please don't. Come on, Mum, you're always telling me I have to be kind to people, especially those people who are sad or who need a friend. Well, I think Gran is sad and I think if she came away with us, it would really cheer her up. Say yes, Mum, pulllleeeeeeeeeze.'

Urgh. Save us from children who use our own values against us and force us to practise what we preach, dammit.

I sighed. 'Okay, put her on and I'll talk to her about it,' I said.

'Yaaaasssss! Mum, you're the best. I love you. Gran is having her gold leaf facial right now, but she'll be finished in a minute. I'll get her to call you back. Love you, Mum.'

And then she was gone.

I let my head flop onto my chest, then resumed my conversation with Annie. 'You're going to love this, Gran. Beth has invited Cruella to go away with us next weekend. I think I'd rather have my toenails trimmed by a chainsaw.'

Cruella was Annie's nickname for my mother, a woman she barely tolerated in life. In fact, Annie wasn't too keen on my dad either, and she'd given birth to him. Underneath her brutally honest exterior, she was the most kind-hearted, loving woman who ever lived, so it had never failed to disappoint her that my parents were two such self-centred, reprehensible human beings, who didn't give a damn about anyone.

'Honest to God, I don't think he's mine,' she'd say about my dad, her Glasgow accent even thicker when she was riled. 'The wean that shot out of my vagina was a lovely wee thing. There's no way he grew up to be that gutless oaf. And don't get me started on her. Cold, feckless tart. They deserve each other, they really do.'

There was a rumbling in the cloud above me. I was pretty sure it was Annie laughing her ass off at my misfortune.

Before I could comment, my phone rang again and Beth's name flashed up. Hopefully she'd either changed her mind about inviting my mother, or Cruella had refused to accompany us because she had a better offer.

'Hey, honey,' I began.

'Shauna, it's your mother.'

Another rumble from the clouds. Annie was loving this.

'Hello, Mum,' I replied, with as much niceness as I could muster.

She got straight to the point. 'Beth says you want me to come on this trip with you next weekend.'

I made a mental note to ground Beth until she was at least forty-five for bending the truth with this one. I had no choice but to go along now.

'Yes, Mum. That would be nice. But, of course, I totally understand if you've got other plans. It's such short notice, so it's fine if you can't make it.'

Silence.

Say you're not coming. Please refuse.

I looked heavenward. *For the name of God, Annie, help me out here.*

'I just think you've got an absolute cheek,' she spat, shocking me senseless. 'I know you're only asking me because I'm your unpaid babysitter, and you want me to look after Beth while you go gallivanting round Glasgow.'

No words.

'You've got such a nerve, Shauna, you really have. I'm appalled.'

There was no point trying to explain the truth. Debbie in full force was like a cruise missile and it was only going to stop after she'd wreaked doom and destruction on her target. Lucky old me. Beth was now grounded until she was fifty.

'That was never the intention, Mum—'

She cut me off. 'Of course it was.'

Only a mental picture of Beth's pleading face, and the fact that my daughter genuinely loved her grandmother, stopped me from blurting out the whole story.

'It wasn't. But it's absolutely fine, it was just an idea. We'll leave it.'

'No, I won't let Beth suffer just because of your ulterior motives. I'll come, but for once you can pay for my services. Maybe then you'll appreciate everything I do for that girl.'

I'd never wanted to scream more. It was such a distortion of reality. The truth was that I encouraged a relationship between Beth and my mother because I thought it was good for them both: it gave Beth a grandparent figure in her life who could teach her new things: mostly about social snobbery and gold leaf facials, but that was beside the point. Colm's parents were dead, as was my father, so my mother was the only grandparent Beth had left. No matter what my mother's failings were, Beth could learn from her. Right now, she was learning what a deluded, unreasonable, stuck-up, impossible woman sounded like. And as for my mother, I thought that Beth would give her a bit of a purpose in a life that was pretty much devoid of love and affection.

Clearly, my motivations were lost in translation somewhere.

'Now where are we going and I hope we're flying, because you know I don't do public transport. The last time I was on a train, I had labyrinthitis for a week.'

Shoot me. Shoot me now.

'I'll email you all the details, Mum. Yes, we're flying. And I've rented a house in the west end of Glasgow.'

We had other accommodation options, but renting a house seemed like the best idea because there were so many of us. Beth and I were going. So were Jess, Davie and Joe. Definitely Dan. Possibly Lulu. Seven people, and that was before Cruella joined the party.

My lovely, chilled-out trip north had suddenly become a prospective battle ground and I didn't relish hearing her opinion on every single thing that we did. I was going to have to call my cousin, Tom, and my Aunt Flora and warn them what was coming. It was strange, but I felt just as at home in Glasgow, a city I'd never even visited until I was in my forties, as I did in London. I felt closer to my family there than I did to my own mother. I suspect that was all down to Annie's DNA and her heavenly influence.

My mother was still wittering on. 'Right, well, I suppose I can just about tolerate it for a few days, for Beth's sake. But I'm not looking forward to it. I've always avoided Scotland. They fry all their food there.'

My mother's negativity was already making me regret buckling to my daughter's request. Beth's grounding just stretched to sixty.

'Actually, Mum, that's just a myth. They don't fry all their food at all.'

'That's not what I heard. And the accents... I didn't understand a word your grandmother said for the first ten years I knew her.'

That actually made me smile. Annie had told me she deliberately made her accent thicker when she spoke to my mother because she couldn't bear her and just wanted to do as much as possible to irritate her. It was a subtle act of rebellion, but it kept Annie amused.

I couldn't help going back with a breezy, 'Really? I always found Gran so easy to understand.'

My mother harrumphed, which was something that I didn't think people actually did outside bad sitcoms.

'Yes, well, I don't think I missed anything. It wasn't as if she ever said anything interesting. Your father used to cringe when she told those vulgar jokes.'

Again, a deliberate ploy on Annie's behalf, to rile my parents.

She once went off on a rhyme about a young man from Hunt at a dinner with my dad's entire board of directors. My mother pressed the fire alarm because it was the only way she could head off the punchline.

'That's why we all loved Annie so much, Mum. She was one of a kind. I miss her every single day.'

'More fool you,' came the reply. There was the paradox with my darling mama. She was utterly disinterested in me, and completely disdainful of everything I did. But for as long as I can remember, my love for Annie, the mother-in-law she loathed, made her bristle with what I could only describe as jealousy. She didn't want my love, but she couldn't stand the fact that I adored someone else.

My phone began to beep.

'Mum, I have to go, I have another call coming in. Tell Beth I'll see her when she gets home tomorrow.'

And that she's now grounded until she's sixty-five. I didn't say that last bit out loud.

I pressed END, and switched to the other call. At this rate, I'd be on this bench in the cemetery all day.

'It's me,' Jess said breathlessly.

'Are you exercising or being chased by a mugger?' I asked.

'Boxercise. I'm trying to get my frustrations out.'

'Is it working?'

'Nope,' she panted. 'But I've been thinking. You're right.'

'I like the sound of that, but I've no idea what you're talking about.'

'You were right about me being a life coach and practising what I preach. So I've decided that at the meeting tonight...'

The line went crackly just as a feeling of impending doom gripped my stomach.

'You've been thinking what?'

'That I have to be authentic in my actions.'

'I have no idea what that means, Jess,' I responded, trying to detangle the psycho-speak.

'Basically, it means I'm going to go for what I want in life. Tonight, I'm going to tell Dan how I feel about him.

That's when the heavens opened and the rain began to pour.

'Eh, I don't want to rain on anyone's parade, but what are we doing here?' Dan asked me, glancing around at the crowded bar. It wasn't exactly the obvious place for a life coaching session, but then, I had the feeling nothing about tonight was going to be predictable.

'Don't do it, Jess,' I'd blurted, when she'd told me her plan on the phone earlier.

'Why?'

I admit that panic and my location at that moment influenced my response. 'Because, because... because Lulu will have a hit out on you by the end of the day, and I'd miss you. I already visit too many people I love at the cemetery.'

'I'm going to ignore that you just said that,' she'd retorted, in the kind of tone that you used with a child when you were indulging their tall tales. 'Do you have an intelligent, logical reason that I shouldn't do it?'

That gave me time to think. 'Because he's in a mess and he's confused. He needs to get over Lu before he even thinks about seeing anyone else.'

'We've covered this already. What if he's so blinded by the thought that he'll never love again that he takes Lu back? Devil. Deep blue sea. At least with me he'll be swimming in waters that don't have sharks.'

I'm not sure if it was the corny line or the cold that made me shiver. 'Did you spend all day thinking that line up?'

A throaty laugh came down the line. 'Sure did. Too much?'

If Annie was listening in on this she'd be floating on a celestial cloud. This was the kind of gossip she'd lived for. 'Definitely. But I see your point about the timing. You know what? You do whatever you feel is right. What the hell do I know? I'm an emotionally stunted widow who couldn't build a healthy relationship with the plant in my kitchen.'

A few minutes later the text came in to our 'Life Coaching by Jess' WhatsApp group. I wanted to change the name of the group to Sad Gits by Jess, but I wasn't brave enough.

Hey chaps, change of plan for tonight. Let's get out and about. Meet in Graca House at 8 p.m.

So here we were. Dan and I had just walked the ten-minute stroll from our building and now we were in a very chic, trendy, busy bar, with absolutely no idea why we were there. We were in July, so even at this time in the evening, it was still light outside.

'I feel like coming here is one of those decisions that we'll have to explain to a *Crimewatch* team later,' I muttered, suspecting there might be a grain of truth in there.

Dan, meanwhile, was loosening his tie and visibly perking up. 'Shit, I'd forgotten what it was like to be out and about,' he told me. 'With all the stuff going on with Lu, I've been a hermit for months. What do you want to drink?'

'Gin. Make it a bottle. With a straw.' Thankfully he knew I was almost one hundred per cent joking and ordered me a standard gin and tonic.

Jess strolled in five minutes later, just as we were about to swallow dive onto a table as the previous occupants were leaving, potentially pissing off a group of suited blokes who were eying it up. Tough. I hadn't been in a bar like this for years – I was out of practice at standing in one place being jostled by strangers on their way to the loo.

Luckily for the suits, Jess's appearance distracted us. She'd clearly made an effort for tonight. Her yoga-toned legs were encased in inky skinny jeans, below a white top and beautifully cut black tuxedo jacket. Her brunette hair, usually styled in a chin-length bob, was slicked back behind her ears. If she'd been six inches taller, I'd have said she was a former model, who hadn't lost her sense of style or her cheekbones.

'Wow, you look fantastic,' Dan whistled, kissing her on both cheeks.

The corners of my mouth turned up as she hugged me and I whispered, 'Nicely played, you goddess,' into her ear. She winked as she released me. I then kissed her other cheek and whispered, 'But if you say anything to him, I'm feigning a heart attack.'

'I've booked a table for us on the roof terrace,' she announced. 'It's quieter up there, so we can talk, and it's heated too, so we won't freeze our buttocks off.'

Dan was up for it. 'Good idea. I haven't been here for ages. Colm and I used to stop in for a pint after work.'

Jess's nod told me that she already knew that. She ordered a gin and tonic from the waitress who showed us to our table, a black granite square with cream leather chairs at the edge of the terrace, lit by thousands of fairy lights twinkling above us.

For the first hour or so, we ate the platter of nachos that we'd ordered for the table while we chatted about everything and nothing: work, Beth, the bar, and there was a five-minute mutual consultation about whether the bloke in the corner was the guitarist in McFly. I was pretty sure he wasn't. Unless he stood up and sang 'All About You', I wasn't buying it.

I was on my third gin and tonic when I finally began to relax. Jess must have changed her mind about sharing her feelings with Dan. She might not even have been serious about it in the first place. Perhaps it was just a joke, a wind-up to get a rise out of me. Yep, that was it.

'Right, my two fellow saddos, let's get tonight's meeting of the Sad Gits' Recovery Club in session,' Jess declared.

As my dearly departed husband would say, 'Ah, bollocks.'

'Tonight I want to talk about moving on and making sure we don't slip back into unhealthy relationships just because it's the easy choice.'

I wondered if I should clutch my chest now or leave it a few more minutes. This was up there with Rachel deciding she wanted Joey instead of Ross in *Friends*. But without the huge salaries and the iconic hair. In my head, I called in the celestial cavalry.

Colm, can you see this? Your ex-wife is about to proposition your best friend. This will cause chaos in our group because if Dan is into it, then Lulu will FREAK THE FECK OUT, or if he isn't, it's going to make things mighty uncomfortable for these two. Feel free to intervene. I was thinking fake heart attack, but if you want to go with a fire alarm or sudden bolt of lightning, I'm good with that. Oh, and I love you. I'd give anything on earth to have you here.

Jess set her sights on Dan. In more ways than one.

'How are things going with Lulu after you saw her last weekend?'

Ouch, straight for the kill.

Dan shrugged, seeming fairly relaxed compared to the stressfest he'd been in for the last couple of weeks. Being back in the kind of environment he enjoyed was obviously good for him. The four women at the next table clearly thought so because they seemed to be unable to stop glancing over at him. If Jess wanted to boost his ego, she'd picked the right place. Maybe she knew what she was doing with this life-coaching lark after all.

'You know, when I went back up to speak to Shauna later that night, I was rattled, I admit it. Took me a few days to process everything and get a grip of myself, but then... I don't know how to explain it. I woke up on Wednesday morning and just thought, "Fuck it. I'm done." It was like I could hear Colm's voice in my ear again. Sorry, Shauna, hope that's okay to say...'

'Of course it is! I love that you still feel him around. If you're having a chat to him anytime soon, can you ask him to pay more attention to me, because I've sent him a couple of requests that he doesn't seem to have sorted out.'

I threw a pointed stare at Jess, and got an eye roll in return.

The last nacho on the plate shouted to me, so I picked it up to prevent my gob from butting in. Surely she wouldn't say anything in front of me? The conversation she wanted to have with him had to be a private one. *Come on, Colm, there's still time to stop this.*

Dan realised that Jess was looking at him expectantly, waiting for more.

'Aw crap, this is where I have to talk about my feelings, isn't it? If I was having this discussion with Colm, we'd already have wrapped it up, and be on the way to the bar for another pint.'

I swallowed the nacho, as the picture Dan painted made me smile. 'Welcome to the adults' world. Colm hated it here too.'

His chuckle made the four women at the next table flick their eyes over again. I could see the appeal. With his swept back black hair, *GQ* cover jawline, and shoulders like a linebacker, he definitely still had the whole forty-something, sexy thing going on.

Jess took control again. 'So you're definitely done? No going back?'

'I think I've done that too many times already. You know, every time, I thought it would work out. I just always figured that despite the craziness, Lu and I were forever. Now I know we're not. And if I were to give it another chance, I think it would be half-hearted, because I'd always be waiting for her to leave me as soon as someone she thought was better came along. I don't want to live with the fear.'

Impressed, I tried to give him some encouragement. 'For someone who hates talking about their feelings, you're doing good, rookie.'

'Are we done now? Can we go play snooker or discuss Chelsea's chances in the cup?'

'Eh, we're still in session,' Jess chided him playfully. 'And we're only just getting started.'

Dan yawned. 'How do you lot do this? Tearing out your soul is exhausting. Why would you subject yourself to this?'

'Prepares us for period pains, pregnancy and menopause,' I offered.

Jess reined us in, directing her words to Dan. 'Do you think you could start thinking about a relationship with someone else now?'

Aw, Jeezus.

Dan shook his head. 'Doubt it. I know Lulu loved me, but she still cheated and lied. The thing with her was, I knew her so well I could usually tell when something was going on. But if I met someone new, how would I know if I could trust them? How would I know if they were lying to me? I'm just not ready to take the chance.'

'Go with me here. What about if you absolutely knew this

person wouldn't lie to you?' Jess probed, and I could see where she was going with this.

'Do you think that kind of certainty exists? I want no secrets. Zero. Full disclosure about everything. No lies whatsoever. And someone who is absolutely, completely, one hundred per cent monogamous. Someone who would never dream of cheating. How can I ever be sure I've found that?'

'What if it was someone you knew? Someone you trusted? Someone you love spending time with?'

Bait on hook. Cast out. Waiting for bite. I could see what was hurling towards us and I wanted to adopt the brace position. Dan, on the other hand, was still oblivious.

'That would just be too good to be true.'

Bite.

Jess and I locked gazes again and I could see questions in her expression. Should I do this? Now's my chance, but would it be a mistake?

I answered with an affectionate shrug. Perhaps my objections were selfish. Who was I to interfere with two people I adored finding love with each other? There had to be a way to deal with Lulu and her inevitable fury about this. Maybe Dan could take out the second bedroom and put a panic room in instead.

'Dan, what if it wasn't too good to be true. What if there was actually someone who met all those criteria?'

He picked up his beer. 'There isn't,' he laughed. 'I'm pretty sure I'd have spotted them by now.'

A shadow of anxiety flicked across Jess's face.

I didn't know if I was terrified or excited that she was actually going to do this. She was. I could see it.

She put both hands on the table, her usual pose when she was about to say something important.

Colm O'Flynn, I hope you're watching this and ready to intervene with that fire alarm or a bolt of lightning if it all goes wrong.

'Dan, the next five minutes might be a bit of a surprise, but I want you to stick with me.'

'Sure...' he drawled hesitantly, in a tone that suggested he was anything but sure.

'When we formed this group, we made some promises. We were going to be honest. We were going to share our feelings. We were going to look out for each other and we were going to start taking positive steps towards recovering from the way our last relationships ended. We said we were going to have balls of steel...'

'Don't think I said that,' I interjected. Jess carried on speaking as if she hadn't heard me.

'And be brave and do what we needed to do to be happy, even if it came with risks and vulnerability.'

'Don't think I said that,' Dan aped my response, obviously not taking this seriously. Again, she kept going.

'If I'm going to be a half-decent life coach, then I'm going to have to woman up and show I can do that, prove I can practise what I preach. I need to demonstrate the strength to go after what I think would make my life happy and complete, and let nothing stand in my way.'

I could see from Dan's expression that he still had absolutely no idea what was coming. He was just doing what he always did when anyone was speaking in emotional psychobabble: tuning it out and thinking about whether or not he felt like ordering a pudding.

'Excuse me,' he said to our waitress, just as she walked by. 'Can I have the dessert menu?'

I knew him too well.

'Dan, I think that maybe we should explore the possibility of a relationship.'

'With who?'

Poor bloke. There he was, only half paying attention, about to be blindsided while trying to decide between a sticky toffee pudding and a tiramisu.

Maybe Jess would realise she'd lost her audience. Maybe she'd change her mind. Back out.

Or not.

'With each other,' she blurted.

17

SHAUNA

'Oh my God, I can't believe you let me do that,' Jess groaned, although the words were muffled because she was on my sofa and holding a cushion against her face.

'If you're going to suffocate yourself, can you use the other cushion because that one is Beth's favourite. Also, you've got your face in One Direction. It's not right,' I said, trying not to spill the two large gin and tonics I was carrying from my kitchen area over to the sofa.

After a couple more wails, she put the cushion down and took the drink, knocking back a good third of it in one go.

'Was it as bad as I think it was? No. It couldn't have been. Was it?'

Truth or lie? Truth. Wasn't that what got us here in the first place though?

Aw, feck it...

'Do you think it was completely excruciating and did it make you want to slide under the table and stay there until the end of time?'

'Yeeessssss,' she wailed again.

'Then yep, I think you pretty much have an accurate memory of it.'

On a mortification scale of one to ten, it had been a solid twelve.

Dan had been thoroughly confused. 'Jess, what are you talking about? Is this some mad experiment for your life-coaching gig?'

Why, oh why, had she done this while I was with them?

'No,' she'd blurted, and I could already see that she'd do anything to take it back. This definitely wasn't the reaction that she'd expected or hoped for.

'What do you mean, then?' he'd continued. With this level of emotional intelligence, it was, quite frankly, a miracle he'd ever managed to form a relationship. My stomach was churning for Jess.

But again, why, oh why, had she done this while I was with them?

She'd decided to spell it out for him. 'Ok, so here's the thing... You and I have known each other for what, twenty-five years? And we've been mates the whole time. You know me. I'm honest, I'm trustworthy, I'm monogamous...'

She was selling it well so far.

'And we're both at the age in our lives where we're not going to meet someone in a club, and we're far too technophobic and weirdo-averse to do the dating app stuff.'

Making sense. Definitely putting out some good points.

'Also, we're already entwined in each other's lives and spend loads of time together. We like the same things, the same people...'

'And physically, you're definitely both tens,' I'd piped in, trying to help the case and boost their egos at the same time. Trite and superficial, but I was cringing and my mind was blank and out of other options.

'Yeah, that,' Jess had agreed awkwardly. 'And on top of all of those practical things, since you split with Lu, I've discovered I have feelings for you. Like, not just the best pal, brotherly kind of feelings.'

'Naked feelings,' my mouth had chimed in, without consulting my brain first. Feck.

Aghast. That was the only word I could use to describe the expression on Dan's face.

'Yeah, that too,' Jess had repeated, with a noticeable wince. 'What do you think?'

Tumbleweed. He'd just stared at her for about an hour and a half in total silence. At least, that was how it felt. It was probably ten seconds or so.

When he'd finally regained his motor skills, he'd managed a strained, 'Okay, so if this isn't a mad exercise for your work, it must be a prank?'

'Erm...' Jess had played for time, and I could see that she was trying to decide whether to take the out he'd just handed her. She could say yes, and have a good old giggle and a slap of the thighs at his reaction. Or she could decide that she was so far in, there was no going back.

If she had the power to pick up paranormal messages, she'd have been able to hear me say, 'Take the out. Dear God, take it and run.'

Instead, she'd deflated, crumbled, exhaled like she'd been holding her breath for the last five minutes.

'I know it sounds crazy, Dan, and I promise it took me by surprise too, but I honestly think, that if you've got any kind of romantic feelings for me at all...'

'I haven't, Jess,' he'd winced. 'I've just... I've just never thought of you in that way. You were Colm's wife, and then you were his ex-wife. I've always thought of you as his. No offence. I don't mean it literally. It's just that whole guy code thing. It's bred into us. You don't go near you mate's partner, ex-partner, or anyone he's interested in. So I've just always thought of you as my mate.'

'Ok,' Jess had snapped, but not in an aggressive way. More of a clipped, 'Right then, let's move on, shall we?' type of deal.

I'd pondered whether closing my eyes would allow me to transport myself to my happy place. Which was anywhere that one of my closest friends wasn't hitting on the other. Right then, I'd have chosen sitting between Lulu and Bobby on a sofa watching *Love Island* rather than this situation right here.

For the third time, why, oh why, had she done this while I was with them?

And was it my imagination, or were the four women at the next table straining to listen to the conversation? Had they heard Jess's words? Were they intoxicated by the drama?

'Jess, no,' Dan had said softly, reaching over and taking her hand. 'Please don't be annoyed.'

She'd shrugged it off. 'I'm not annoyed, I'm just... embarrassed. This had all seemed like such a good idea in my head. Maybe my hormones got the better of me. Or my boiler! Yeah, maybe my boiler is letting off some weird gas and I'm giddy with it. I'm sure that happened in a programme I watched.'

Oh my God, this was excruciating. I had a silent exchange with the missing-in-action cavalry.

Colm, I swear if you don't send down a bolt of lightning, I'll never forgive you.

Nothing. Not even a minor interruption, like a passing waiter or an argument at another table.

'Look, Jess, I'm flattered. I really am,' Dan had blustered.

'Oh no, this is bad enough. Please don't give me the "I'm flattered but" conversation,' she pleaded.

More silence.

'That was all you had, wasn't it?' she'd asked, realisation dawning.

He'd nodded. 'I love you. I really do. But I just don't see us that way. To be honest, after Lulu I don't see myself that way with anyone. Maybe I just need time to process everything. To let all the old stuff go and see everything in a different light.'

Jess had seemed agreeable to that. 'Good idea. It takes time. Like, you have to give yourself permission to say goodbye to your old hopes and wishes. I can't tell you how much I wish I'd got hit by a truck on the way here.'

In some twisted way, Jess's attempts to smooth things over with humour was making it all even worse. I had to jump in to help.

'Please don't let this become a problem between you,' I'd begged. 'Dan, I get that it was a surprise. To be honest, I was pretty surprised when Jess told me too.'

'You knew about this? And you didn't say anything?'

Oh God, I was making this worse. I knew it was coming from a place of embarrassment, but now he was pissed off with me too.

I swear to God, Colm O'Flynn, if you don't show up soon...

'Yeah, but I, I...' Stuttering for time didn't help, in the end all I came up with was a weak, 'I... I'm Switzerland. Anyway, it's been an emotional couple of months, with so much change. I know the whole point of all this was to find a way to move on and find new love, and build new relationships, but that isn't going to happen overnight. Just take some time. Think about everything. No pressure. Now you know how Jess feels, but it doesn't have to be an issue between you – we can all just carry on the way we were before.'

I knew that was wishful thinking, but I was just throwing everything at the cringe-fest wall and hoping something would stick.

'Yeah, okay. Jess, I feel like I've totally hurt your feelings...'

'No, not at all,' she'd argued, when she actually meant, 'You absolutely have.'

'I'm so sorry. This has just been... a lot. I thought we were having a bit of dinner and then Shauna and I would pretend that we were going to embrace the process and that we thought it would work.'

I'd groaned on the inside. Now he was making it worse with bad humour attempts too. The thing was, that's exactly the type of cheeky comment that Dan would have come out with to Jess on any occasion before now, and she'd laugh and come back with some deadly one-liner that would slay him. Then we'd all chuckle and think how lucky we were that taking the piss was one of the foundations of our relationships.

Now, Dan's jokey comment landed somewhere between mean and misguided.

I couldn't remember a worse night out in my life. And I'd once got stuck in a nightclub cupboard when I'd gone through the door thinking it was a loo and realised it wasn't just as the door clicked shut behind me. It was pitch dark, and alcohol had been taken, so I couldn't work out how to get it open. I was only saved when Colm came looking for me after an hour and a half and heard me banging on the door. Yes, I was only replaying that in my head because it took my mind off what was going on at the table.

'Anyway,' Jess had said, with breeziness so fake it had Kardashian written all over it. 'Tonight's session of the Sad Gits Recovery Club is now at a close. Good work, people. I think we broke uncharted ground and made real progress here.' Her words had been loaded with irony. 'I'm ready to head home, if that's okay with everyone?'

'Yep, of course,' I agreed, lifting my bag from the back of the chair. At that point I'd have done anything to get away from there. The three of us still had to walk home to the same building, as Jess had already said she'd stay at my place. I think she was hoping she'd have wrangled an invitation to sleep over with Dan. The awkwardness made it clear that wasn't happening, but I'd stood up, reasoning that at least when we were moving along the streets, we weren't all sitting staring at each other.

Dan had hesitated uneasily. 'I think I'm going to hang out here for a bit longer. You guys go on ahead. I'll finish my beer and get the bill.'

I'd pulled on my jacket. 'Are you sure? We're happy to split the bill.'

'No, no,' he'd waved my offer away. Dan was unfailingly generous, so that wasn't unusual, but somehow it had seemed like he was doing it out of pity. My cheeks were burning and it wasn't even me who'd propositioned him.

Outside, I'd taken Jess's arm, more so that if one of us got our heels stuck in the cobbled street, we were both going down.

'Don't say a word, because if you do, I'll cry,' she'd warned me. Jess's habit of crying at every event, both good and bad, never failed to impress me. I was all uptight repression, whereas she just let her feelings flow.

I'd squeezed her arm as we walked. 'You're going to cry anyway, aren't you?'

'Most definitely,' she'd sniffed. And sniffed again. Then sniffed all the way back to my home.

Now, under the watchful comfort of Harry Styles on the One Direction cushion, she'd stopped sobbing and settled into the kind of sound that generally came from a wounded animal on *Hidden Planet*.

'I. Am. Such. A. Tit,' she moaned. 'What was I thinking? I mean, I'm an intelligent woman – where the fuck was my common sense and my self-preservation?'

I shook my head. 'No idea. If I knew where they were I'd have sneaked them into your bag on the way out tonight so that you would have changed your mind about doing the whole revelation thing. Oh, Jess – if it's any consolation, I love you.'

'It isn't,' she replied sadly, but there was a hint of a smile. 'I love you too, Shauna. Lesbians. Let's become lesbians. I'm up for experimenting if you are.'

That made me chuckle. 'Are you trying to hit on everyone in our friendship group tonight? You may as well, then you can just blame your boiler for the whole lot.'

The bang made me jump as the front door slammed shut. In our altered and emotional state, had we forgotten to close it? Had the wind blown it over? Had Beth taken ill and come home from Marcy's? No, she would definitely have phoned first. Was Colm finally making his presence felt?

'Is it Dan?' Jess whispered, eyes wide with hope.

I concede he should probably have been the first person I thought of.

Fantastic! If Dan was here, that could only mean one thing: he'd thought it through and saw how much sense it would make. He knew Jess was staying here tonight, so he'd decided to come by, declare his mutual affection, then pick her up in the manner of Richard Gere in *An Officer and A Gentleman* and carry her off downstairs to his own place, where they'd ravish each other until dawn. Which would, as a bonus, give me time to watch a couple of old *Prime Suspect* reruns before turning in and dreaming that I was Helen Mirren chasing some bad guys.

Jess and I both had our stare fixed on the hallway door, as it slowly opened. A boot. On a foot. A leg with jeans on in. Skinny hips and...

Not Dan. Definitely not Dan.

'Lu!'

'Am I interrupting something?' she asked, taking in the dim lighting and the fact that Jess and I were cuddled on the sofa.

'No, of course not,' I countered, stretching up.

Beside me, Jess wiped her cheeks with the palms of her hands. Lulu spotted this.

'What's wrong then? Why are you crying? I mean, you cry at everything, so it's not exactly a shock, but what minor niggle has set you off now?'

Like I said, mocking each other was a foundation of our relationships.

'Nothing,' Jess recovered quickly. 'I was just telling Shauna about *24 hours in A&E* and this old lady died alone because she was a complete bitch to her friends. There was something so sad, yet so familiar about it.'

Ouch, Jess was back.

For the second time tonight, I jumped in and intervened.

'Are you okay, Lu? What are you doing here at this time?' I really, REALLY had to stop giving out keys for my flat to my friends.

Her shoulders slumped, her chin went down, as she reached behind her and pulled a Gucci trolley case through the door.

'Sorry to land on you like this, babe, but...'

Oh no. Don't make this be happening.

I felt Jess tense up beside me, as she sussed out what was coming at exactly the same moment as me.

'I realised I was never going to get Dan back if I stayed with Bobby, so I've left him. Not that he actually knows that. I've told him my mother is ill, and I'm staying with her until she's better. Don't want to burn my bridges just yet, especially when he'll barely notice I'm gone. He's been at the office pretty much permanently since we got back from honeymoon. Anyway, I know it's a big ask, but can I move in here until I get everything sorted out with Dan and move back in there?'

For about the tenth time tonight, the only person I wanted to speak to was my late husband.

Colm O'Flynn, if this is your idea of a joke, you're in so much trouble when I get up there.

18

My hands are shaking as I try to prop the phone up against my water jug on the table that stretches across my bed. Actually, it's not always water. Sometimes, Lulu slips in a touch of vodka to change it up a bit. What's the worst it can do? I already feel shite, I have a brain tumour and my head has been fried by my treatments. A dash of vodka in my afternoon beverage, while we play cards and binge watch *The Sopranos* on Lulu's iPad isn't going to kill me and it might just get me through the day.

That's pretty much the routine we're in now. Lu comes and leads me astray while Shauna's at work, then Shauna comes before or after her catering gigs. She's working her ass off and I can't tell you the guilt that's shovelling onto my soul. There are so many ifs and buts. If we hadn't bought that house at the peak of the market, only to watch the value plummet in the global crash, then we wouldn't be lumbered with the huge mortgage that she's working round the clock to pay. If Dan and I hadn't quit our jobs and set up on our own just a few years before I got diagnosed, then we'd have a steady income and sick pay and life insurance. But no. The fecking Gods of Bastard Bad Luck were shining down on us. Shauna and I agreed she would support us while I got the business off the ground and then I'd take over the bulk of the financial responsibility when the company moved into the black. Didn't happen. So now everything, including a husband in a hospice bed, is on Shauna's shoulders. And you know what kills me most? She just does it. Takes care of everything. Never moans or falls apart – or, if she does, it's not when she's with me. She breezes in here every day, sometimes with Beth, and she's got a smile on her face and some chat that makes me laugh.

Dan mentioned the other day that if we ever sell the house, we could move into his building because his tenants are moving out. It's a cracking flat, more space than the house we're in now, and right on Richmond Green, so it's not a bad idea at all. Bit of a turn of luck inheriting it from his uncle. Not that I'm bitter because he's my best mate and I just want good things for him – especially if he lets us in on the luck by renting us the flat at mates' rates. I just hope I get enough time to move there, or if not, that Shauna does it after I'm gone. It would be good for them all. Shauna would have support and help right there, Beth would grow up in a family atmosphere and Dan and Lulu would have a distraction that will leave less time for them to kill each other.

I'll feel better if I know there are more people looking out for Beth. Dear God, that video I made for her last week was nearly the death of me. I barely made it to the end before I keeled over. And that was without a few shots of vodka in ma water jug. No more wanders over to the seat at the window for me. The nurses weren't happy. Apparently, they'd told me I couldn't get out of bed without a nurse on standby, but I swear to God, I've no memory of that. I hate to point out the obvious, but is telling a bloke with memory loss what he can and can't do really going to work? I've forgotten everything they've told me by the time they get to the door. Anyway, they've stuck it on a poster on the wall now so I can't miss it.

Colm O'Flynn.
   Stay in yer fecking bed, ya eejit.

I dictated that to Mike, the nurse on night shift, and he wrote it up for me. He says if anyone asks me, I've to deny it was him. That's not such a tough ask – I forget who did it at least half a dozen times a day.

That thought ends and it takes me a moment to get to the next one. The gaps are the worst bit, because sometimes I get the fear that another one won't come. That's why I have to get these videos finished. Don't get me wrong – I'm not giving up. They can tell me I'm a dying man all they like, but I still think the treatment will work, it'll buy me some time and then someone, somewhere will come up with an even better treatment or cure for this thing. It's got to happen because I'm not ready to go yet. Nope, not at all.

But just in case…

I run my fingers through what's left of my hair – it feels thinner, but, Jeysus, I'm still a good-looking bastard. I should write that on the wall too. Colm O'Flynn. Jeysus, yer a good-looking bastard. I'll speak to Mike when he comes on shift.

Right, let's do this. The last video was for my girl, so I need to do one for my boys. I have to get my very best dad demeanour on for this one. The boys are not far off twenty now, and they can read me like a really depressing book. They're smart guys and I can't fudge the truth about what's happening, but I can at least leave them with the knowledge that their old da' went out with a laugh.

I reach over and press 'record.'

'Hey, m'darlin's, how are we all today? This is the O'Flynn News Channel with a special broadcast.'

I try my damndest to get some energy and humour in my voice because the truth is, I just want to sleep. These drugs they've got me on are kicking my arse, but I can't give up.

Okay, back to the screen. I always fancied myself on the telly, but this wasn't how I thought I'd get there...

...

...

Shit, lost my train again there.

Video. Okay. Go.

'The other day I made one of these film things for Beth and I hope with all my heart that she sees it one day. Actually, I hope with all my heart that some bugger will find a cure for this bastard tumour in the next few weeks but I reckon my odds are pretty low.' I tried to laugh, but I wasn't sure I was convincing anyone, least of all me, so I reverted to the point of this. 'Anyway, love, today, if you'll indulge me, I want to talk to my lads.'

Just like the other day, the mention of my kids catches in my throat.

Come on, O'Flynn, get yerself together.

'Davie, Joe, yer old man has some things I want to tell you, just in case... well, just in case I don't get out of this. If yer watching this, then I guess I didn't.

'If that's the case, lads, I can honestly say that if you put the whole brain tumour, early-death situation to one side, I've been a lucky man because I've had you two since I wasn't much more than a kid myself. Twins. I just about fainted when I found that out. It wasn't till you were born that I realised what that means is you get to give twice the love and have twice the laughs... And half the sleep, but I don't bear a grudge.'

I start to laugh when I say that, but it turns into a cough. I reach for some water, but lift the vodka instead and line my throat with fire, making me splutter again. My death certificate is going to say death by Lulu. I can't even laugh at that thought in case it sets off more coughing. Christ, my body's not ma own any more. I just want to sleep, or drink, or scream, but I want to do this video more, so I carry on.

'Almost nineteen years of being yer da' has been... what is it you lot say now? Epic. Yeah, definitely epic. Your mum... well, you know this already, but she's a special lady. Take care of her. Not that you'll need to, because she's as strong as they come, but don't ever be the kind of blokes who forget to be grateful for all she's done for you.

'You know I'm not one to dish out the lectures, because, God knows, half the time the three of us have ended up in trouble, it's been my fault. Your mother still hasn't forgiven me for wrecking the grass when I spray-painted it with white and gold stripes for St Paddy's Day. Or for buying you those go-carts. I admit crashing one into your mum's car wasn't the best move. Davie, son, thanks for taking the heat for that one. Although, I can't believe I had to bribe you with a Scalextric. And Joe, same goes for the time I smashed the bathroom window. That bulk box of Yorkies for you to take the blame was worth every penny.

'Like I said, given my occasional divergence from the truth, I've no place giving either of you advice, but, well, I'm going to anyway.

'There's all the stuff I tell you every time you leave the house to go to a party. Don't drink too much, because nobody loves cleaning up after someone has lost their guts. And no decision that's made when yer mangled on drink is going to be one of your best. Be respectful to the girls you meet, and never, ever let things get intimate with a lass – or a lad if that's yer thing – who's over-done the drinking. Take them home, make sure they're safe and then check on them the next day. If they're worth getting to know, it's better to do it when they're sober. I say that from experience. When I've overindulged, all I want to do is arm-wrestle your Uncle Dan and sing George Michael songs on the karaoke. It's not pretty.

'Right, what else? Okay, this is the big one, lads. Be there for the people that you fall in love with. Let me tell you something. Yer mum and I, well, I know she was always gracious enough to go with the line that we just grew apart, but that's not the whole story. I always planned to tell you the truth one day, but just in case we don't get to that, you need to know it was my fault. All mine.

'I've never been much good at all the deep and important stuff. I know that won't be a newsflash. After your little sister, Daisy, was born sleeping, well, the truth is, I checked out.'

I pause. I realise that might be news to Shauna. I've never told her about Daisy. Couldn't say the words. I think about stopping, rewinding, doing this again, but I don't have the energy. I'll do it later.

Instead, I plough on, 'Turns out that the other thing I'm not good at dealing with is pain – mine or anyone else's. I should have been there for your mum, but I wasn't. I blocked it out, refused to talk about it, shut out your mum, and what makes it even worse is that I did it when she needed me most. It's one of my biggest regrets in life, and I'd love to say I learned from it, but I didn't. In fact, I did exactly the same thing to Shauna years later when she lost someone she loved. Another regret. It was a miracle I didn't lose her too – I definitely deserved to. So I guess what I'm saying is that I really hope you've got enough of your mother in you to handle the hard stuff so much better than I did. The thing is, caring about someone isn't the same as caring *for* them. Maybe if I'd lived longer, I'd have grown enough to deal with that kind of stuff instead of burying my head in the sand and avoiding tough situations. I know you'll do so much better. You two are the most loving, caring, special guys a dad could ever have, and I couldn't be more proud of you.

'Joe, my trilingual brainbox, you're smarter than all of us. I know you're going to have a brilliant career and a brilliant life. Davie, keep in with the rugby, son. Standing on the touchlines watching you play has been one of the joys of my life. I can't tell you how much it breaks my heart that one day you'll run on a pitch and I won't be there to see it and make an eejit of myself. Just know I'll be watching from somewhere. You can count on it, son.

'Ok, what else should I tell ya? Ah, yes. Pick strong, caring women – or blokes – who love you, and love them back when life's good and even more when it's not. I wish I'd done that with your mum and Shauna – the only consolation is knowing that my hopelessness as a husband to your mum ended up giving you two great women in your lives. Be good to them. Make sure you see them often, drop in regularly, and I know it's not fashionable these days, but open doors for them, remember birthdays, Mother's Day, treat them with chivalry and care.

'And look out for your sister too. I need you guys to be my stunt doubles and love and protect her.

'Growing up, you two have been amazing lads. Now go and be good men.'

The catch in my words tells me that I'm starting to lose it and I know I need to wrap this up before I fall apart.

'Davie, Joe... I love you. You'll always have yer mum, you'll always have Shauna and Beth, you'll always have each other, and you'll always have me.

'And remember, you two might be big strapping lads with all the advantages of youth. But you'll never beat yer da' at footie.'

I switch it off just in time, before the waterworks start again.

Christ on a bike, this is brutal. Why the fuck am I subjecting myself to this? And why am I falling apart? I'm going to beat this fecking disease. I am. And then Dan and I will take Davie and Joe down the pub, and we'll laugh when I tell them what I said to them in this video and they'll slag me off for being a sentimental fool.

I'd be as well deleting all these recordings now, because I'm never going to need them. I've got this. I'm not giving in to it.

But... just in case, I'll crack on with the others. Two more to do. Only two.

And I know I'm leaving them until last because I'm not sure I've got the strength or the bottle to say what needs to be said.

19

A feeling of impending doom was gnawing at me.

As far as trips go, the line-up was definitely eclectic.

A widow. Her dead husband's ex-wife. The bloke who rejected the dead husband's ex-wife last week. That guy's ex-wife, who's on a mission to win him back. My high-maintenance mother who doesn't want to be there. The dead bloke's twenty-five-year-old twin sons and an eleven-year-old who thinks she's Taylor Swift.

Hi-de-hi and happy holidays.

I'd cleared my diary, already sparse because I cut my work down to the bare minimum during the summer school holidays so that I could be with Beth. She'd be going back to school soon, so I wanted to add a bit of fun with this trip.

Family trips with Jess, the boys, Beth and me were precious to us all. Now that the boys were in their mid-twenties, it wasn't always easy for them to get away from work, but we tried to do something together every month or so. Sometimes it was a weekend away, other times just a day trip. This was somewhere in the middle, with extra people tagging along for the ride.

We'd flown up Saturday morning for my Aunt Flora's eighty-fifth birthday party that night. Flora had never forgiven herself for the rift that caused Annie to leave Scotland when she was twenty-four and Flora was twenty-one. It was a long story, but the pamphlet edition was that Flora took Annie's boyfriend and they never spoke again. It was Flora and her brother George's biggest sorrow and they'd lived their whole lives addled with regret.

After I'd discovered my Glasgow family, we'd become firm features in each others' lives and I was so grateful to have them. The family was small, but there was a whole lot of love. Maybe that's why, a few weeks ago, I'd invited Dan to come with us. I thought he could do with a change of scenery and a reminder that life goes on and there's a big world out there. Of course, that was before the whole triangle with Jess and Lulu had popped up. Lulu had invited herself along, keen to see my aunt, whom she adored, and perhaps even more keen to get some time alone with Dan. I didn't even want to let my mind go there. This had so much potential for a bad outcome, and that was before we threw my mother, Saint Debbie of the Eternal Disapproval, into the mix.

We landed at Glasgow and the minibus I'd hired to collect us was waiting.

'Shauna, we'll help the driver load the luggage. You go on inside,' Davie offered.

'I should think so, young lads like that. It's the least they can do.'

Yep, my mother. Her ice blonde bob staying perfectly still as she teetered along in her 'casual' outfit of black tailored trousers, Gucci loafers and a pale grey Chanel jacket.

Davie didn't rise to it. He'd known my mother for long enough to be aware of her quirks. And by 'quirks' I mean thoroughly stuck-up, arrogant personality traits.

I was so thrilled the boys had managed to make space in their pretty intense schedules. Joe worked in international finance, while Davie was our sports star, playing rugby professionally for Leinster. I'd give anything for Colm to see them now. When he died, the boys were twenty, and still in university, so he never got to see them achieve their success. If he was still here, he'd be finding excuses to go hang out with Joe in his swanky flat in Docklands and then he'd be flying over to Ireland every weekend during the rugby season to watch Davie play. He'd be so proud, so utterly ecstatic, to share their lives. Colm O'Flynn wasn't always a perfect husband – I think he'd be the first to admit that – but there was no denying that he was the best friend, the best company in almost any situation, and without a doubt, the best dad. His three awesome kids were living proof of that.

I blinked back the tears that had formed in my lower lids and chided myself for getting emotional. That was the last thing we needed this weekend. It was already a maelstrom of underlying tension.

Dan and Jess hadn't spoken since Thursday night, when she'd declared her undying love. Jess was pissed off that Lulu was now living with me and determined to get Dan back. And my mother was thoroughly disdainful of everyone on the face of the earth, except Beth.

'Is it just me, or does this feel like one of those murder mystery weekends, where someone ends up dead on the kitchen floor at the end?' Jess hissed, as we climbed into the van.

'I'm locking up all sharp objects as soon as we get there,' I replied.

Jess sat in the back seat, with Davie and Joe, while Beth sat in the seat in front of them, next to her Uncle Dan. She was already up on her knees and facing backwards so she could chat to her brothers. Despite the age difference, all three of them had Colm O'Flynn's genes, so they got on brilliantly and the hilarity started almost straight away, when Beth insisted that they join her in an impromptu singalong. God, she was her father's girl all day long. That's exactly what Colm would have done. He once got us thrown out of a posh restaurant in the Bahamas because him and Lulu started a singsong to 'Summer Loving' from *Grease*. 'Don't know what they're moaning about,' he'd countered as the door was firmly closed behind us. 'You usually have to pay extra for entertainment.'

'Oh no, she's deep in thought,' Lulu, sitting beside me, said with mock dread, before adding, 'Did I hear you saying something about a murder mystery? If you're trying to think of ways to knock off your mother, I'm in.'

'Lulu, dear, you do know I can hear every word you're saying,' my mother piped up as her flawless, Botoxed face appeared through the gap in the seat in front of us.

Lulu found that hilarious. 'Aunt Debbie, you know I was kidding. I knew you were there,' Lulu chirped, making my mother sneer before turning back to face the front. Lulu then mimed, 'I didn't know,' to me, setting us off on the same kind of irrepressible giggles that got us through our whole childhood. I sometimes wondered what would have happened if her parents, Charlie and Gwen, hadn't had Lulu. I'd have spent my formative years pretty much alone, being ignored by four adults who were only interested in each other, in gallivanting around the hotspots of Europe and in maintaining a glamourous lifestyle that made all their friends jealous. As far as I was aware, none of their chums knew the truth – that these paragons of respectability had open marriages that allowed cross pollination of their naked bits.

Thankfully, my mother distracted me from that thought with another trip to Bitchy Town.

'Really, Shauna, you should pick your friends better. This one is abominably crass.'

I closed my eyes. *Dear God, beam me up.*

Lulu, queen of the barbs, just shrugged and said, 'I definitely think you've got a point, Aunt Debbie.'

I punched her on the thigh, making her yelp.

Thankfully, Taylor Swift and her backing singers were still otherwise engaged up at the back of the bus, and missed this whole conversation. Who knew that two twenty-five year old blokes would know all the words to 'Look What You Made Me Do'.

Another thought: Colm would love this. A trip. His family. His friends. Even my mother being a cow to everyone. His absence hit me like a wrecking ball to the gut and I turned to stare out of the window, teeth clenched, water in the bottom eyelids again. Sometimes, not often, it was just all too much. Even now, years down the line, I missed him so much it ached, and I got so tired of plastering a smile on my face and acting like I was fine. It reminded me of every single day that Colm was in that hospice after the doctors told us there was nothing else they could do for him. He'd refused to accept it, so I acted like I didn't believe it either.

Every day, I'd go to visit him and I'd sit in the car outside, breaking my heart until my chest ached and my throat squeezed shut. I'd allow myself five minutes, sometimes ten, to hold on to the steering wheel, my knuckles white with rage and pain. And when I was done, I'd fix my make-up, brush my hair, plaster a smile on and go in to see the man I'd adored since the first time I met him.

I'd try to make him laugh as soon as I got there, announcing my presence with jazz hands, then climbing into his bed and snuggling into him while I made up all sorts of amusing stories about my day. None of it was true. The reality was that I was doing three or four events every single day to cover the mortgage, and I was so tired that it actually hurt to speak. He didn't need to know that, so I never told him. I always acted like everything was absolutely fine, and it would be no time at all before he was home and life got back to normal. That's how Colm dealt with it – his trademark denial and optimism. He was the one going through it, so if he wasn't broken, rocking back and forward, devastated, then I had no right to indulge my feelings.

The irony was, growing up with Debbie and Jeff, in a house where my feelings really didn't matter, had been the perfect training for dealing with Colm's illness. I was an expert at burying emotions and just keeping on going, never stopping, just doing what I had to do. I still was.

'You okay?' Lulu whispered, her hand now curling into mine. That's what people didn't understand about Lulu. Yep, she was a bolshy nightmare, but for forty-five years she'd showed up every day for me, in her own caustic, infuriating way. She was as much a product of her environment as I was. And underneath all the bluster and bitchiness, we loved each other like sisters.

'I'm okay,' I whispered. 'But if we're playing Cluedo this weekend, it was the daughter, in the kitchen, with whatever she could find to take her mother out.'

'Mum, mum, join in,' Beth begged from the back. 'You know all the words to this one.'

I did. And thanks to Taylor Swift, I shook it off all the way to the West End of the city, and into the kitchen of our Airbnb. We'd already allocated the rooms. Davie, Joe and Dan in a triple room. Beth and me in a double room further down the corridor. Jess and Lulu sharing a twin. And my mother in the master, with en suite, because she was still claiming she was an unpaid babysitter, so she at least deserved some perks of the job. At least she'd dropped her previous demand for a cash payment.

We all found our own amusement that afternoon until it was time to leave for the party. Jess and I hung out with Davie, Joe and Beth in the kitchen, playing cards around the old, chunky wood table in the middle of the room. Lulu nipped out to a salon for a full pre-party makeover, which was just as well because the tension between her and Dan was excruciating. They hadn't said a word to each other all day, and barely glanced in each other's direction. Dan had sought refuge in the sitting room, where he had his laptop open, catching up with some work. And I had no idea what my mother was up to because she stayed in her room, door locked. She probably sneaked a Tinder hook-up in the window and was right now doing the kind of things that would shock anyone taken in by her terribly refined demeanour.

We only chucked in our cards an hour before it was time to leave for my Aunt Flora's shindig. It was in a hotel only a few hundred metres up the road, so the men had decided to walk and I'd called a cab for everyone wearing heels.

It was just as well.

Jess and I had just made it back to the kitchen in our party frocks when Lulu reappeared after her day of pampering. 'Tada!' she bellowed,

My jaw dropped. Holy shit.

Jess and I scrubbed up pretty well – both of us in little black dresses, with evidence that, for once, we'd managed to track down our make-up bags.

But Lulu? There was no other way to describe it than spectacular. Her long red corkscrew curls had been teased out so that they were pure Diana Ross. Her make-up was subtle, but stunning, and highlighted her feline green eyes and her expensively sculpted pout. And her size-eight curves were in a scarlet dress that was sexy, thanks to the body-hugging fabric, while the high neck and calf-length hem gave it an edge of class. Some women just knew how to turn it on and Lulu was one of them.

'What do you think?' she preened, obviously fully aware that there was only one realistic answer.

Unfortunately, Jess didn't go with that one.

'You do know this is Flora's night, don't you? Only you're dressed like you're about to shimmy off to the BAFTAs and it's all about you.'

Oh God, here we go. These two were tetchy at the best of times, but now that rivalry over Dan had been added to the mix – not that Lulu had a clue about that little situation – the barbs from Jess's side were quicker and sharper.

'Ah, Jess, don't be like that,' Lulu teased, glancing up and down at Jess's fairly run-of-the-mill black shift dress. 'You never know, someone might pop their clogs tonight and then you'll be the one who's perfectly dressed for the occasion.'

I'd been so looking forward to tonight. An evening of celebration for the birthday of my elderly aunt, surrounded by everyone I loved and cared for.

But as the taxi honked its horn outside, I had a horrible feeling that it might not be the warm and fuzzy night I'd envisaged. Definitely more of a murder mystery weekend. Although I still wasn't sure if I'd kill my mother or Jess would whack Lulu first.

Lulu strutted out catching up with my mother, who'd emerged from her bedroom in a beautifully cut Vivienne Westwood frock that made her look at least five years younger than me.

The blokes and Beth trooped out next, Dan, his gaze still religiously avoiding both Jess and Lulu, giving off vibes that he'd rather be anywhere else but here.

Closing the kitchen door behind us, Jess sighed. 'You know we've still got time to bail out, find a tequila bar and drink until we're nothing but mushy puddles on the floor?'

I'd never been more tempted, but as always, I tried to put a positive spin on it. 'Come on, it'll be fine. We'll have a great time.'

As we climbed into the cab with Cruella de Vil and Cher in her 'Turn Back Time' years, I wasn't sure if I was trying to convince Jess or myself.

20

SHAUNA

'And finally, I'd like to thank my family, my wonderful husband, Arthur, my nephew, Tom, and his lovely wife, Chrissie, and some other very special guests, my niece, Shauna, and her daughter, Beth, and all their extended brood who have travelled up from London to celebrate with me tonight. Tom is the grandson of my late brother, George, and Shauna is the granddaughter of my late sister, the firecracker of a woman that was our Annie...'

Aunt Flora, still tall and slim, her white hair pulled back in an elegant chignon, an ethereal vision in a long pale blue flowing kaftan, let her gaze fall on our table. I had only met my cousin, Tom, four years ago. He was a couple of years younger than me, but he'd become one of my closest friends, our relationship punctuated by my trips north and his trips down to London, two only children in a small family, thrilled at having found each other. He came into my life just when I needed him, although I so wish he'd met Colm. They'd have loved each other.

'Shauna,' Aunt Flora continued, 'you remind me of Annie so much: your strength, your kindness, your ability to love... She must have been so, so proud of you and I'm so grateful to have you, and your wonderful daughter, Beth, in my life.'

She went on to talk about Tom and then her husband, but I didn't absorb what she was saying because I was too busy trying to hold it together.

What was wrong with me lately?

Why did I seem to be constantly fighting the urge to fall apart?

Come on, Annie, give me some strength here.

And why did I spend so much time talking to dead people?

That thought made me smile, and Dan, sitting next to me, gave me a hug. 'I reckon you're going to be just like her when you're that age,' he said in my ear. 'A class act.'

My smile got wider. 'I doubt it. I'll be trawling nightclubs trying to find Lulu and keep her out of trouble.'

Shit. That was another one of those jokes that would have been perfectly normal a few weeks ago, but could now be taken as a dig or an attempt to interfere in their relationship.

Luckily, we were interrupted when the band started up again. Joe and Davie grabbed Jess and Lulu and swung them on to the dance floor. Beth decided that her grandmother shouldn't be missing out on the chance to shake her stuff, so she dragged my mum up to dance too.

The setting was spectacular. A ballroom in an architecturally stunning, grand hotel in Glasgow's West End, with floor-to-ceiling windows, intricate wood panels and cornices that were a work of art.

It was strange how comfortable I felt in this city. It was almost as if the DNA I'd inherited from Annie recognised that it was home. Which was a good thing, because I didn't feel particularly comfortable with my chums this weekend. This was the first time I'd had a chance to speak to Dan since Jess dropped the bombshell and then Lulu arrived on my doorstep. His avoidance of Lu today had originally given Jess some hope, but that turned to disappointment when she realised he was avoiding her too.

'Anyway, how are you doing, Mr Channing? Are you feeling the pressure of all these women chasing your body?' I asked, trying to make light of it.

He smiled for the first time since he left home and climbed in the van that was taking us to the airport this morning. 'You know that's exactly the kind of thing Colm would say, don't you?'

'Maybe his ability to make jokes in totally inappropriate situations has rubbed off on me.'

'That's not a bad thing,' he said, going along with it. 'I could do with a bit of Colm O'Flynn in my life right now because I've no idea what the fuck I'm doing.'

'And you want advice from Colm?' That surprised me. My late husband wasn't known for his profound wisdom and clarity of thought.

'Nooooo! He was shite at giving advice. I just want him to get drunk with me until all this passes and I figure out what to do.'

My giggle made me splash my gin and tonic onto my dress. I just brushed it off. Damp frocks were the least of my worries.

The band broke into Neil Diamond's 'Crackling Rose' and the dancers stayed on the floor, although I could see both Jess and Lulu shoot glances in our direction. This was ridiculous. Two women, my two closest friends, and both thought they had a future with the same man. This was the stuff of soap operas, not the kind of thing that anyone expects in their own life.

I leaned in closer to Dan so he could hear me over the sound of the music. 'Have you thought about it all? Do you know what you want to do?'

He shook his head. 'I don't have a clue. You know, I didn't ever think I'd walk away from Lulu, but she made the decision for me.

And much as I miss her so much it hurts sometimes, I'm not sure if I could go back to the eggshells I spent the last twenty years walking on. Like I said before, I was always suspicious. Always. Every day. Because I knew that she couldn't change. Her need for excitement and attention is who she is. I just don't think I can give it any more.'

'I understand that,' I told him, honestly. 'Although, if you tell Lu I said that, I'll deny it under oath.'

'Understood,' he said with a conspiratorial wink.

I decided that while the conversation was flowing and warm, I'd go right in for the other big stuff.

'Am I allowed to ask what you think about the other night? With Jess?'

Both of his cheeks blew up a little as he exhaled. 'That one definitely blindsided me.'

'Yeah, sorry about that. I know I should have given you a heads-up, but she'd sworn me to secrecy and right up until the last minute I didn't think she'd say anything. This life-coaching gig has definitely made her so much more assertive, which is great, but it's coming with a few surprises.'

'Do you think she means it?' he asked. 'Because you know... *it's Jess*. She's like a sister to me. I've never thought of her as any more than that.'

This felt like dangerous territory, as if I was walking between the front lines of two opposing forces and any minute now, I could get shot by friendly, or extremely unfriendly, fire. I kept going anyway. I was done with keeping my opinions to myself. Dan's happiness was more important than the fact that Lulu could kill me in my sleep.

'I get that, but I do think she's definitely serious. She says her feelings for you have grown over the last year, but she kept it to herself because she wanted to be sure. To be honest, I tried to talk her out of it... Maybe selfish on my part. I just didn't want anything to happen that could cause more rifts in our group. I loved things just the way they were. Beth and I wouldn't have got through the last five years if it wasn't for each and every one of you and I don't want to lose anyone else.'

'Shauna, you'll never lose me,' he said, so earnestly that I wanted to hug him.

'I know, but things change. It's already different with Lu gone... don't know that I'll ever get used to her not living downstairs.'

'Isn't she in your spare room?' he pointed out the obvious, making me chuckle.

'She is indeed, but she won't last there. Lulu can only go so long without her walk-in wardrobe and her hot tub. Anyway, at the risk of sounding like I'm auditioning you for *Love Island*, do you think there could be something between you and Jess?'

His eyes flicked over to where she was dancing with Davie now, her head thrown back, laughing at something he'd said.

'I honestly don't have a clue. I love her dearly, I just don't know if it could be that kind of love.'

'Do you think you'd ever give it a chance to be more?'

He winced. 'It's just... you know... Colm.' He stopped.

I could see he was choked up and my heart broke for him. Losing his best mate, his business partner, Lu leaving him, divorcing him after more than two decades together... That thought was swiftly followed by a realisation, as what he'd just said clicked in my head.

'Wait a minute, are you refusing to even consider a relation-ship with Jess because you're worried it would be disrespectful to Colm?'

His grimace, accompanied by an uncomfortable half shrug, gave me the answer. Call it emotional overload, or loneliness or damn fury at the hand we'd all been dealt, but I felt something like anger consume me. Hadn't we all suffered enough? Colm O'Flynn was the most special man, a shining light who we all adored. Now we were all paying the price for the strength of our love for him. And the irony was, I knew he'd hate that.

I leaned in even closer, so that I could be sure he heard every word.

'Listen to me, Dan Channing. There was no one that loved life more than Colm. Happiness was his reason for being and he snatched every opportunity for joy. Sometimes that was bloody irritating because it meant he had no time for the sad or hard stuff, but that's who he was. He told me so many times how much his life was made better by you. You were his best friend, his work partner, and he always said that you were the Robin to his Batman.'

Now Dan was the one blinking back tears, but in traditional Colm and Dan fashion, he laughed, shook his head. 'Fuck that, I was Batman. He didn't have the body for that suit.'

A flashback. Dan and Lulu's kitchen about ten years ago. The same argument. Colm defending his position. 'I mean, Batman is the brains in the relationship, and I love you, mate, but that's definitely me.'

Dan wasn't giving in. 'That might be the case, but if anyone has the legs for Robin's tights, it has to be you.'

Colm had paused, then he got that familiar twinkle in his eye. 'Fair point. I do look great in a pair of tights.'

The memory tipped me over the sentimental edge and I had to force myself not to crumble. I couldn't. Not here. Not now. Not when Dan needed me.

'I'm not telling you what to do here,' I went on, 'and I'll never judge you. If you choose to take Lulu back, I completely get it. She's the kind of life force that Colm was, and everything just seems a bit more alive when she's around. God knows, I'd forgive her just about anything. But if the only thing that's holding you back from exploring whether you and Jess could be happy together is some misguided loyalty to Colm, I'm telling you he'd hate that. He really would. All Colm ever wanted was to have a great life and that's what he wanted for you too. If you and Jess getting together gives you both another shot at happiness, I'm telling you right now he'd love it.'

I knew he was still listening, but his gaze was on the dance floor again, where Jess had swapped partners and was now channelling Tina Turner, busting out her best moves to 'Proud Mary'. 'I think I'm going to go join the dancing,' Dan said. 'Fancy joining me?'

Everyone else was listening to Tina, but I was hearing Colm in my head. 'Go on, m'darlin', get up there and show them how it's done.'

I had two left feet, but I didn't care. I took Dan's hand and we strutted on to the dance floor like the prom king and queen in a teen movie dance-off. And we shook our stuff. Song after song, swapping partners with others in the group, we danced until our feet hurt and our cheeks ached from grinning. Somehow, in every beat and twirl, it felt like Colm was there with us and it was glorious. In five years, this was the first time I'd danced, the first time I'd let go of my inhibitions and the tight control I held over my emotions every single day. I was loving every second of it.

I was doing a twist with my Aunt Flora, who, at eighty-five, still had the moves she grew up on. When the song ended, she leaned over and hugged me. 'Oh my darling, that was wonderful, but this old lady had better sit down before my hip replacement falls off.'

'I'll have a whip-round and we'll buy you a new one for your ninetieth birthday, Aunt Flora.'

'Just get me a second-hand one, dear, I won't need it for long,' she joked, sounding just like her sister.

I walked her back to her table, kissed her and made my way through the revellers, reaching our table just as the lights came up. It was a long way to come for a party, but I was so glad we'd made the trip. Even my mother couldn't burst my little bubble of bliss with her caustic...

Hang on, where was she?

'Dan, where's my mum?'

'Okay, don't kill me, but she met someone and she's just gone off for a drink with them. She said not to check up on her because she's a... How did she put it?'

Lulu, sitting next to him, filled in the blanks. 'A grown woman who couldn't give a flying fig what we thought.'

Chills ran through me. 'You let her go off with a stranger? What were you thinking?'

Lulu put her hand up to stop me. 'It wasn't a stranger, it was your Uncle Norry.'

'Whaaaaat?'

Oh, bugger. My uncle, Norry. My cousin Tom's dad, and my late Uncle George's son, a vile, self-centred creature of a man who had just returned from a twenty-five-year stay in Australia after divorcing his second wife. Or was it his third?

There was no way my mother should be anywhere near that man! He was rude, materialistic, shallow and dishonest. He once flew back from Australia when my Uncle George was ill, just to try to get his hands on the lovely old gent's money. He had absolutely zero redeeming features, so...

'You know, I actually think they'd be a pretty good match,' I said, making a swift climb-down from my outrage. My mother was a grown woman who was free to make her own mistakes.

We were the last to leave, in a flurry of goodbyes, hugs, and promises to see each other soon. Beth was objecting to calling it a night, and we only pacified her by promising a bit of karaoke when we got back to the house. Thank goodness it was a detached Victorian home with walls so thick we could let a brass band play inside and the neighbours would never know.

Back at the house, I warned everyone to set their alarms for 9 a.m., in plenty of time for the noon flight. It had been a flying visit, but worth every minute. While Davie and Joe belted out Proclaimers songs in the lounge, using the karaoke app on Beth's phone, I escaped to the kitchen to text my mother.

Just checking you're okay? Remember flight is at noon tomorrow. We can collect you on the way if that suits better. Let me know where you are and that you're good.

I'd poured a glass of water by the time the reply came in.

Very good. Something has come up. Won't be flying home tomorrow. Go ahead without me.

If anyone else's sixty-something mother texted that, when she was out with a man she'd only met that evening, alarm bells would ring. I took consolation in that – as far as we knew – Uncle Norry wasn't some crazed serial killer. And another plus, I wouldn't have to endure a flight home with my mother.

Thinking about it now, their attraction to each other made perfect sense. Although they never met due to the rift between my gran and her family, Uncle Norry was my dad's first cousin. There were definitely similarities in their appearance – both had the Marbella tan, the gold chains and thick heads of hair, swept back like less attractive versions of Michael Douglas. Of course my mum would fancy him. I just couldn't believe that I'd never thought of introducing them before now.

Buzz.

I picked my phone up, figuring it must be another text from my mother, with some kind of unreasonable request or instruction that would piss me off, but that I'd do anyway.

Strange. The notification said it was a message from a number I didn't recognise. Maybe Uncle Norry's? I clicked it open.

Not Uncle Norry.

Hey. I'm hoping this is still your mobile number. This is mine. Left a message on your landline a couple of weeks ago to let you know I'm home. Would love to see you. Vince x

My heart began to thud out of my chest. Vince.

Colm O'Flynn had been the love of my life, but Vincent had come a close second. Too close.

My breathing became laboured, my heartbeat got even faster, a bomb of anxiety exploded in my stomach, until I was interrupted by Lulu strolling in.

She had obviously been to her room, because her make-up was off, her hair was in a ponytail, and she was wearing cute tartan pyjama shorts with an oversized sweatshirt.

'Where is everyone?' she asked, opening the fridge and taking out a bottle of water.

'My mother is still shacked up somewhere with Uncle Norry and they must be having a great time because she's decided she's not coming home with us tomorrow.'

'Eeeew. Does she know he's a slimeball?'

'Probably. But that's her type.'

'So true,' Lulu agreed. 'Now that you mention it, he does look a bit like your dad too. It's like a sleazy stunt double.'

'I beg you to stop talking or I'll never sleep tonight,' I warned her, only half kidding.

'Noted. Ok, back to my life. Where's Dan?' she continued with her original question, wandering over to the window.

'Not sure. I haven't seen him since we got back from the party.'

Action Lulu was on a mission. 'I'm going to talk to him, while I've finally got him under the same roof. I'm over him avoiding me. Hasn't so much as glanced in my direction all day, and let's face it, I was stunning tonight.'

I tuned out as she wittered on, and read the last part of the text again.

Would love to see y—

I didn't get to the end because at that moment Lulu uttered a thunderous exclamation of 'WHAT THE FUCK!?'

I didn't jump to react. With Lulu, this kind of outburst could mean a life-changing crisis or that we'd run out of mayonnaise. The differentiation on her drama scale was tiny.

'You're going to have to give me more than that.' I told her, staying calm.

'Where did you say Dan and Jess were?' she asked, icy cold now, her voice deadly.

Oh God. When Lulu was furious and ranting, we were good. That kind of volatility was standard practice. This wasn't. I'd only seen her switch to this kind of restrained fury a couple of times in our lives, and it had never ended well. It was like the moment when a python silently, but with absolutely menacing intent, unhinges its jaw so that it can swallow its prey whole.

Powered by dread, I put my phone down and turned to see her peering out of the window. Oh crap.

'Eh, living room?' I said, with as much hope as I could muster.

'Then how come Dan appears to be sucking the face off her out in the garden?'

Again, oh crap. No. Not here. Not tonight. And definitely not in front of Lulu. Why did my friends all have spectacularly shit timing when it came to relationships?

'Lu, I'm sorry...'

She spun around. 'Sorry for what? You knew about this?' Her eyes were blazing.

'No! Well... Yes. Kind of.' I was squirming. 'I only found out a couple of nights ago, that Jess had feelings for Dan.' A slight fudge of the truth was necessary to preserve life. Mine.

'She told you that?' Lulu's voice was still low and deadly.

'She told him that. I was there. At our meeting.'

'Ah, your secret fucking squirrel meetings. So all along it's just been some kind of sham so she could get her claws into Dan?'

'No! Lu, come sit down. Let's talk about this.'

'I don't want to fucking talk about it! I just want to know what Dan said when she announced this?'

'That... that... he needed to think about it.'

'Well, clearly he's thinking about it now. I can't believe this. Why would they do that to me? Why?'

Okay, I had two choices here. Pacify her or call her out and make her see the reality of the situation. The latter had never, in the entire history of Lulu, worked out well. In the heat of any moment, she was incapable of climbing down, of backtracking, or of seeing any viewpoint but her own. But I had to try...

She was pacing back and forwards, so I chose my moment to reach over, take her hand, hold on to it, make her stand still. She tried to shrug me off, but I wouldn't let her.

'Lu, I love you, but you need to hear this. You left Dan. You moved on and you crushed him...'

'But it was a mistake and—'

I cut her off. 'It doesn't matter, Lu. You don't get to decide what he does any more. You don't get to just leave him and then snap your fingers and have him come running back to you when you change your mind. That's not how this works.'

She managed to yank her hand away. 'How does it work then? He just forgets what we had and fucks off with someone else?'

'Yes! That's exactly what he can do now, because you already did that to him. He owes you nothing, Lu. You left him and you marched up the aisle at Clivedon only a few weeks ago, while we, and Dan, watched you do it. So yes, he can now fuck off with someone else. He gets to choose his own happiness.'

Tomorrow she would understand everything I was saying, but right now, jealousy and rage were running the show. Before I could stop her, she wrenched the back door open.

'Shit!' I hissed, jumping up to follow her.

An automatic security light above the back door flicked on as she went under it, giving full view of the garden, and that's when I saw what she'd spotted a few minutes before. Dan. Jess. Sitting in an arbour at the end of the garden, arms entwined, faces spinning to see what had caused the light to come on.

If this was a movie, the next few seconds would have been in slow motion. The couple, pulling apart, horrified faces, as the bloke's ex, in pyjamas and furry slippers, charged towards them, pursued by her panic-stricken pal.

Dan and Jess didn't even get a word in before Lu unleashed a tirade.

'Really? What the fuck is this? I'm in the same fricking house and you two...' She didn't finish the thought before pivoting. 'Seriously, Jess? Is this how you treat your mates? Sneak in and hit on their men...'

'He's not your man, Lu,' Jess said calmly, refusing to rise to Lulu's accusations. 'Bobby is your man. You made that choice.'

'Let it go, Lu,' Dan warned. 'Go back inside. This has nothing to do with you.'

'Of course it has!' she blurted. 'We were together for more than twenty years.'

'And you left me!' Oh, Jesus, Dan was close to shouting now, and he rarely, if ever, raised his voice outside of yelling at the TV during a football match. This wasn't good. 'And I'm over it, okay?' he went on, lowering his volume to a level that hopefully wouldn't wake the street. 'You don't get to choose my life for me any more, Lu. We're over. I want something else.'

'This?' Lulu spluttered, pointing at Jess, who just smiled sadly and shook her head in response. 'You want Jess? You want my friend? The person who is supposed to have my back but thinks that friendship is hitting on my ex?'

'Yes! You know why? Because I'm done with the lies and the secrets and all the shit you put me through. I just want honesty. Decency. Someone who knows what it is to be faithful.'

Lulu spat out a bitter laugh and the slow motion thing kicked in again.

It felt like the temperature dropped ten degrees as I realised exactly what she was about to say. The wide-eyed fear that suddenly crossed Jess's face showed she knew too.

No. No. No. No.

'Honesty? Decency? If that's what you want, then you've got your tongue down the wrong throat, mate.'

Dan shook his head, speaking softly now. 'Don't do that, Lu. Don't make shit up.'

'Come on, let's go back inside,' I begged, trying to head off what was undoubtedly coming. 'Lu, let's go. You've said enough. You've made your point.'

For a second I thought she had heard me and was going to pull back. To retreat.

I was wrong. She was in full assault mode.

'I don't need to make shit up,' Lu spat, 'because your little *decent* one there has a few secrets of her own. Haven't you, Jess?'

'Lu, that's enough,' Dan's words oozed something that sounded like pity.

Lu must have registered it too. Jaw fully unhinged. Prey in sight. Time to bite.

'Have you told him, Jess? Have you told him about you and Colm?'

'You bitch,' Jess spat back.

Dan just looked confused now, while I closed my eyes, hoping beyond hope that I could block out the inevitable.

Dan turned to Jess now. 'What's she talking about?'

Lu answered for her. 'Ah, she hasn't told you then. Let me fill you in,' her smugness was painful. 'You see, your honest and decent new tonsil friend there spent the night with Colm...'

'They were married!' Dan countered.

Lulu paused, like a diver at the top of a cliff, knowing that if they shifted their weight forward, it could be lethal.

Stop Lu. Please God, make her stop.

But no. She jumped.

'No, not the last time,' she blurted. 'The last time they slept together was in the year before he died... and he was married to Shauna.'

The nausea is churning my stomach and it's nothing to do with the treatment for this bloody tumour. At least there might be a cure for the cancer growing in my head, but for what I'm about to tell Shauna? No cure. No way to soften the blow. Definitely terminal. And yet, I can't stand the thought of going to my grave with secrets. That's why, even though this is the worst idea in the fecking world, and any sane person would try to persuade me not to do it, I have to tell her what I've done, because I can't bear the dishonesty of leaving her with an inaccurate picture of who I am. Or, by the time she sees this, who I *was*. Past tense.

Christ, I was a dick. If my life ends soon, it'll be up there with my biggest regrets.

I pour a glass of my special lemonade, the one that I keep in the bedside cabinet. Lulu was in earlier so it's got a couple of shots of vodka in it. She comes every single day and, honestly, I don't know what I'd do without her. Over the years I've given her so much stick about the way she treats Dan, but as a pal, there's no-one better than Lu. Today we made a list of all the people I could haunt after I'm gone. Can someone let our politicians know that if things start flying off their walls, it's because Lulu thinks they're all tits?

I'm procrastinating. I know I am. But I've gone months agonising about whether I should tell Shauna face to face, and the truth is, I'm too much of a coward. More than that, I can't add any more pain to her life. I just can't do it. So this is my compromise. I'm telling her here. She'll find out after I'm gone. I can't expect her to understand, and I can only hope it won't make her regret her life with me, but at least she'll know the whole truth.

Okay. Time to do this. I can't keep putting it off.

I take another slug of my special lemonade. Dutch courage. I press 'record'.

'Hey, m'darlin', how're you doing?'

I have to pause and take a breath. The tightness in my chest is squeezing the air out of my lungs. I want to stop, forget this fecking stupid idea, but then I tell myself why I'm doing it and something inside me pushes me to keep speaking.

'Shauna, I don't even know how to start this, but I guess I'll kick off by saying that if Beth or anyone else is with you right now, you might want to save this one for later, when you're alone.

'When we got together, we promised each other that there would be no secrets. Christ, we were naive. I was already keeping a secret from you. I know I told you that Jess and I divorced because we just drifted apart and wanted different things. That was a lie. I need to tell you the truth, because, well, you'll find out anyway. Years later, I did something awful and I know that one day, probably after I'm gone, the truth will come out. I hope you've seen this before that happens. Maybe then you'll understand how I could have fucked up so badly.' I hesitate again, steel myself, then keep talking.

'I need to start by telling you that the reason Jess and I split up was because we lost a baby. Our Daisy. I don't know why I couldn't tell you about that. Or how my complete fecking inability to deal with it wrecked our marriage. Jess was so hurt, so grief-stricken, and I was feeling those things too, but of course I fucked up. I couldn't deal with the sadness, so I just blocked it out. When she needed me most, I wasn't there for Jess. Her pain... I couldn't handle it, Shauna. She needed me to grieve with her and to help her get through it and I couldn't – I didn't want to hold her when she cried, or talk through what happened a hundred times. I just wanted to shut it down so I didn't have to feel it. Denial and avoidance. My mantra for life. It's pathetic, I know and I'll never stop being sorry for how I handled it.

'But there's something else, Shauna. One other secret – and this one kills me. I should have told you before now, but I just... Well, the truth is, I just didn't have the courage. I couldn't hurt you. I couldn't stand the thought of you hating me. God knows, you have every right to, Shauna. I'm sorry. I'm so sorry.'

I could feel myself starting to unravel and I knew if I didn't get it out soon, I was going to lose it and I might never find the strength to do this again.

'Shauna, I slept with Jess.'

Fuck, I'd said it. Sweat beads were popping out on my forehead and my stomach was on a spin cycle.

Keep going, mate. This is the price of being an absolute prick. And how you feel now is nothing compared to how Shauna is going to feel when she watches this. Breathe. Just breathe.

'There are no words to say how sorry I am or how much I hate myself for hurting you. Everything I want to say right now sounds like clichéd bollocks and that's because it is.

'I didn't mean it to happen. I'd never want to hurt you. It meant nothing. It's not you, it's me.

'All the fecking clichés you could think of are absolutely true, but none of them even come close to explaining how I could do this to you. I have no defence. None. But I'm going to give you the facts, because the least you deserve is to know what happened.

'It was the night last year, not long after my surgery, that I was going to Manchester to do that presentation. I was on the way to the station to get the train, when I had to stop in to see Jess. Can't remember why. Anyway, the boys weren't there, and Jess was upset. Steve had just left her and she'd found out their marriage was over.

'We were two wrecks in the same place at the same time. I had a drink and we got to talking and... You know, we'd never talked about the baby in all those years. That night we did. It all came out. All the pain. All the regret. Years of shoving down feelings because we couldn't handle them.

'We kept on drinking and we talked about my tumour and the fact that the bastard was going to kill me and for the first time I wasn't avoiding it, wasn't telling myself it wasn't going to happen. And then... Feck, I don't know why, but we slept together. It was like, just for one night, we wanted to be those young people who met when we were nineteen and didn't have a care in the world. We weren't parents. We weren't sick. Or divorced. We hadn't dealt with all the shite life had thrown at us. For a few drunken hours, we were just us, locked away where real life couldn't touch us.

'Oh, ma darlin' Shauna, I'm so sorry. I know this will slay you and I'd do anything to take it back, to rewind. You've been the most incredible wife and I've repaid you with this crap. I'm gutless not to tell you when I can still look in your eyes and take the punishment of seeing how much I hurt you, but I can't bring myself to do that now.

'I did come home the next day to tell you, to beg you for forgiveness, but feck, the gods don't make it easy. That was the day your dad died. I couldn't tell you then, and I've never been able to do it since. I'm a coward, Shauna. I just can't look at your

●

face as I say the words. So I'm taking the easy way out and telling you here.

'I don't expect you to forgive me because I'll never forgive myself. The only thing I want to ask... And it's a huge ask that I've got absolutely no right to expect... but please forgive Jess. We were both out of our minds with sorrow and sadness. Please forgive her, if nothing else, for the kids' sake. After I'm gone, the boys are going to need you. You're a better stepmother to them than I could ever have hoped for and they love you. Don't let them lose us both. And don't let Beth lose her brothers. She loves them. And I need some blokes around to kick arses if any boys come to the door for her.'

My voice is cracking on almost every word now and I know I haven't got many left in me, so I wrap it up, chest thudding, head banging, heart broken.

'Shauna, I love you. If I was going to live a long life, I'd spend every single day trying to make up for what I've done, but... well, we both know that isn't going to happen. Just don't let it take away even a tiny bit from what we've had. I know I've fucked up, but I love you, m'darlin'. You and me, whether I'm with you or not, we're always. I hope this doesn't change that.'

I stretch over to press the damn button that'll switch this recording off, but I miss it because the tears are blinding me. Feck it, I'll trim the video later, cut it at the end, before the tears started.

Eventually, my thumb finds the right spot, just right before I buckle forward and my chest heaves with sobs. Every other time in my life, I'd dry my eyes, straighten up, open a beer and call Dan to go down the pub and watch some footie. Not today. Today I'm just going to let this pain shred me. Because that's what a cheating fecker like me deserves.

Lulu, Jess and I were silent, while Dan snorted, like Lulu's claim was the most preposterous thing he'd ever heard. 'Oh, that's low even for you,' he said, venom in his voice. 'How could you make shit like that up about Colm. He'd never...'

'He did.' Jess this time, no emotion, like someone in a trance repeating a fact. I expected her to say something to Lu too, to rebuke her for her crass indiscretion, but she didn't. She didn't even glance in her direction. Somehow that was worse.

Dan was staring at Jess now in painful disbelief. 'You slept with Colm while he was married to Shauna? How could you? How could...' He stopped, as if his brain was just catching up with the implications of what he'd just found out. He spun round to me, searching my face for emotions, for clues. 'Oh God, Shauna, I'm so sorry. I didn't know. I'd have told you, I swear.'

'I knew.'

'What? You knew he was doing this? And you didn't stop him?'

'It was only once. I only found out after it happened.'

'And you didn't tell me?'

'I didn't tell anyone. Not even Colm.'

That stopped him in his tracks. He froze. Then, his gaze went to each one of us, as if he was seeing us for the first time, didn't recognise us at all.

'What are we? Seriously, what are we? You know what? Jess, Lulu, you two deserve each other. And Shauna, I'm sorry. I'm done with this.'

With that, he got up, turned and walked back inside, leaving the three of us out there, staring at each other, wondering who was going to let it rip first.

In the end, it was Jess.

'Feel better now, Lu? Got what you wanted?' she asked, in her very best chipper voice, as if she was enquiring about what Lulu had for lunch.

Lulu stuck with defiance. 'Don't ask me to apologise, because I won't.'

Jess gave a bitter laugh. 'Oh, I know. The prize bitch, Lulu Jones, unapologetically ruining lives since... what year were you born?'

Lulu didn't take the bait. 'If you're going after Dan, he needs to know what he's getting himself into. I was just putting it out there. Don't blame me for your mistakes.'

'You know nothing about my mistakes!' Jess shot back.

'I know you're not the Miss Perfect you make out to be. I've done you a favour. Would have been worse if he'd found out after you'd started seeing each other.'

'Don't you fucking dare...'

I didn't hear the rest. I had no stomach for it. There was nothing about that time that I wanted to revisit in a Glasgow garden at 1 a.m. with two friends who were locked in battle. I had another relationship to worry about. If Dan knew one side of the story, it was important that he knew the rest. I had to tell him, even if he'd hate me for it.

They didn't even notice that I slipped away, closing the door behind me so that no one in the house could hear them.

I checked in the living room, where Davie and Joe had both cracked open beers and were watching a *Fast & Furious* movie. I was tempted to just grab some popcorn and join them, and let Vin Diesel run right over the crapfest that was going on in my life right now.

I scanned the room. 'Where's Beth?'

'She went to your bedroom to watch the new Taylor Swift video. Apparently it just dropped. We're not supposed to tell you, so you didn't hear it from us,' Davie said, grinning that same smile as his dad, the one that got him out of trouble no matter what he'd done.

My heart melted. These guys were such testaments to Colm and Jess. They were both decent, level-headed men, who loved their family and knew how to have a good time – and those were Colm O'Flynn's mantras for life.

I thought again how he would love this weekend – everyone he cared about in the same place. Although, obviously he'd have completely ignored any fighting or bitching and zoned it out because, well, avoidance was his other mantra for life.

I had a wave of missing him so fierce it took my breath away. I'd give anything to have him back. Anything at all.

'I love you two, you know that?'

Davie, always the more outspoken one, flashed his dad's smile again. 'Wow, Shauna's getting all sentimental. Is this what a few of those Porn Star Martinis does to you?'

I flicked the top of his head, making him yelp.

He jumped up and threw his arms around me. 'Aw, wicked

stepmum, you know I was kidding. We love you too,' he crooned, kissing my cheek.

'What he said,' Joe added, laughing. 'Is everything okay out there. Sounded like Aunt Lulu was kicking off.'

'I love how you rushed to intervene,' I teased.

Joe shook his head. 'Noooooooo, ma'm. Uh-uh. Above our paygrade. Head down, ignore enemy fire, bollocks to the drama – that's what Dad always told us.'

I'd never heard that before. 'Really? Why didn't I know that?'

Joe shrugged. 'Maybe it was just our thing. He told us that since we were kids. I think maybe he didn't want Mum to know that he encouraged us to say "bollocks".'

My world was fragmenting, my friends were fighting, Dan was disgusted with this latest turn of developments, and yet these two, Davie and Joe, could still make me laugh until the muscles in my face hurt. Swap them out of this scenario for their father, and that was pretty much the story of my life.

I vaguely wondered if Lulu and Jess had killed each other yet, but I had no intention of rejoining them. Instead, I peeked my head into my bedroom to check on Beth. There she was, tucked under the duvet, her phone on the bedside table. I moved it away. At home, there was a 'no phones in the bedroom rule' and I stuck to it religiously, encouraging her to read at night. She only got her phone when she was leaving the house, and even then it was because her Aunt Lulu had bought it for her for Christmas a couple of years before. She spoiled her. Typical Lulu.

I kissed her forehead and went to the room Dan was sharing with Joe and Davie. Hopefully, my stepsons would be downstairs for a while. The conversation I needed to have with Dan was not for their ears.

I knocked.

No reply.

'Dan, it's me.'

His voice was husky when he said, 'Come in.'

Inside, he was lying in bed, one arm behind his head, still wearing his suit trousers and white shirt. There was a double and two singles in the room, and he'd obviously got the long straw, or pulled rank, because he was on the double bed.

'Nice modelling pose. You could definitely get work for the House of Middle-Aged Men,' I said, trying to lighten the mood.

His smile had a tinge of sadness. 'Did you come here just to boost my ego?'

'Yes. Is it working?'

'No.'

I lay down next to him, on my side so that I could see his face as we talked.

Dan went first, staring at the ceiling as he spoke. 'I just can't believe he did that. Not Colm. It's so out of character. He was the most truthful, loyal guy I've ever known.'

'Try not to judge him too harshly. He was sick. He knew he was dying. He was a lost soul just trying to turn back time to when he still had a life in front of him.'

'I don't get why you're okay about it, why it didn't cause problems for you.'

We were veering into dangerous territory.

'Because, in a way, I understood. He was a man whose love of life and refusal to deal with tough stuff got him through every day. Suddenly, he was faced with his life ending and every day was tough. It was nothing to do with me and everything to do with him just wanting to escape a reality that he couldn't bear.' I knew it would be difficult for other people to understand that, but I really believed it was true. I could see that Dan got it too.

His gaze went from the ceiling to me. 'What about Jess? How can you even look at her after what she's done?'

'Because... Okay, I know this is going to sound crazy, but she was there for him when he needed that escape. It was only a few months before he died, and I'm not saying it didn't hurt, because it did. At that time, Jess and I were co-mothers in a blended family, but that's as far as it went. We weren't friends at that time and we didn't get close until after it happened.'

He opened his mouth to speak, but I guessed what he was going to say and cut him off with an explanation. 'I know, there's an irony there. But back then, when it happened, there was no betrayal on her part. That day, she was as vulnerable as he was. When I found out, I figured I had two choices: call Colm out and add a whole load of heartache and conflict in his final months, or just... let it go. Let it ride by. Take it for what it was. A moment between two people, that, just for a couple of hours, could make them feel whole again. If it was at any other point in our marriage, I would have looked at it differently, but at that time... something inside me told me to keep my eyes straight forward, take care of him for whatever life he had left. I owed him that. In a way, it was the easiest thing for me to do too, because I loved him, and I knew it was the right thing to do. For both of us.'

He turned on his side so we were facing each other. 'And it never came up? You never even hinted that you knew?'

'No,' I answered truthfully. 'He was supposed to be staying in Manchester for a meeting the next day. I only found out he hadn't made there because I called the hotel and he hadn't checked in. I panicked, thought he'd keeled over somewhere, so I checked our Find My iPhone app and realised he'd spent the night in Jess's house. I went there the next morning, banged on her door, but he was already gone. Jess was totally up front and honest about what had happened and weirdly, that helped. She understood even then that it was a one-night physical thing, not the start of an illicit affair and I got that too. I know most people in the same situation would have been at each other's throats, but there were too many added layers to this and I understood from experience how grief could make them do crazy things. Jess was truly sorry, and I believed her, so that morning I made a pact with her that we'd never mention it again. Colm had apparently been planning to confess, but when he got home, I'd just found out that my dad died, so he couldn't. I got Jess on board, told her to persuade him not to tell me. It would have served no purpose, other than to cause us pain. For once, and only that once, I went with the Colm O'Flynn theory of crisis management: denial and avoidance.'

Dan shook his head, taking it all in. 'He was so lucky to have you.'

'I was so lucky to have him. Although, I'd be lying if I said I always felt that way. I was severely pissed off every time he smashed the kitchen window playing football.'

The daft comment lifted the mood a little, giving me an opening to move on to my next point.

'So... how are you feeling about the whole Jess and Lulu situation?'

He groaned and rolled on his back. 'If you ever told me I'd be pissed off that two women were interested in me, I'd think you'd lost it.' He paused. 'I'm not going back to Lu, Shauna. I'm definitely done.'

'And Jess?'

He was shaking his head again.

'I don't know. When we spoke earlier, you helped me see how good we could be, and the fact that you thought Colm would have been okay with it...'

'He definitely would. He'd be happy for you.'

'Yet... She slept with him when he was married to you.'

'But I've explained all that, Dan. It wasn't that simple. And if I can forgive her... You know, we all make mistakes, Dan. I wasn't perfect either.'

'But you never cheated on Colm,' I countered.

For a second I thought about holding back, about leaving the padlock on Pandora's box, but I couldn't do it. There had been too many secrets. Too many lies. If we were ever going to repair the cracks in our friendships we were going to have to start with the truth and hope our love outweighed the disappointment.

'That's the thing, Dan,' I began, sadness seeping from every word. 'You see, I did.'

23

SHAUNA

I'd never been so happy to turn the key in my front door and be home. The one-hour flight back to London had lasted about a week. The taxi ride from Heathrow to Richmond added another lifetime. The worst thing was the silence. Jess wasn't speaking to Dan. Dan wasn't speaking to Lulu. Lulu wasn't speaking to anyone. Dan could barely look at me. And I was too damn tired to deal with the lot of them. So I didn't. Instead, I coaxed a very tired and hung-over Davie and Joe to join Beth and me on a browse around the shops at Glasgow Airport, then cuddled up with Beth on the flight and shared headphones – she had the left ear and I had the right – as we watched *Pitch Perfect 3* for the hundredth time, next to the spare seat my mother should have been in. Thankfully Beth didn't even suss that anything was wrong. I told her my mum had decided to stay on in Glasgow for a few days, and that the solemn moods were all down to hangovers, and that's why she shouldn't drink alcohol until she was at least forty-five.

Jess had got a separate taxi home to her house with Davie and Joe, but that still left Dan, Lulu, Beth and me in a Ford Mondeo for long enough to age me at least ten years. The only blessing was that my mother wasn't there. I'd texted her before we left Glasgow, only to be informed that she was busy and wouldn't be returning my calls or texts. She just asked me to pack her things up and leave her case at the reception of the Grosvenor Hilton. Standard mother. Uncle Norry was a sleaze, but he'd no idea what he'd let himself in for.

Once we got back home, Lulu didn't even speak – just went straight to the spare room and I let her go. I loved Lulu beyond words, and to anyone else, I'd defend her to the ends of the earth, but the reality was that in this situation, she wasn't in the right and she was standing in the way of other people having the chance of finding happiness. One of the most important aspects of our friendship was that we'd called each other out when we were wrong, even if we didn't want to hear it or say it. That's what true friends did, and I just had to hope that, like every other time, we would find our way through this.

Beth followed me into my room and we collapsed in a hug on the bed. I was dreading the day when she'd reach the age where she didn't want to do that any more. Right now, the very best times in my life were when we were cuddled up on the sofa or here, watching movies, reading books, doing our nails or some-times, like this, just lying, her head on my shoulders, my hand stroking her crazy curls, as we chatted about silly stuff or serious stuff – either was good with me.

'You okay, Mum?' my lovely, sensitive girl asked.

'Sure am. How about you, cookie? Did you have a good time?'

Her hair tickled the side of my neck as she nodded. 'Can I ask you something...?'

'We're not going to Nashville, and you're not allowed to marry that singer from BTS because we're still hoping that when you're thirty you'll fall in love with Cruz Beckham and me and your

Aunt Lu can sneak into his mother's wardrobe and borrow her handbags. Did that answer your question?'

'Nope, but good to know,' she replied, chuckling. 'Are Aunt Lulu and Aunt Jess okay? I know they were fighting and they didn't speak all day.'

I sighed. I thought we'd managed to keep the ructions from the kids (I still included Davie and Joe in 'the kids' even though they were twenty-five-year-old men and several inches taller than me), but clearly we hadn't.

'Och, they'll be fine, my darling, don't you worry about them for a second. They'll work it out.'

'You always tell me I should help my friends to make up when they fight.'

'I will do, sweetheart, I promise. What else do I tell you?'

She gazed up at me, grinning. 'Be Switzerland.'

'Exactly. Help them work it out, but don't take sides. Except if one side is me, because I make your dinners. Tell you what, why don't we have an early night? How about shower, quick supper, bed, and then read until you fall asleep?'

'Can I argue?' Beth asked, her cheeky grin telling me she was weighing up that possibility. Usually in the school holidays, I let her stay up until after 10 p.m., but not tonight. It was going to be 8 p.m. at the latest, but she could read for as long as she wanted.

I kissed her forehead. 'Nope,' I said. 'It's another thing that's off limits because I cook your dinners. Now, go shower and I'll be back in a while. I just need to go and be Switzerland with Aunt Lu.'

She reached up for my hand, and I took it, pulling her up with only a mildly dramatic groan. She gathered her dressing gown and pyjamas, while I fetched a towel from the airing cupboard and left it in the bathroom for her.

Okay. Lulu. Deep breath.

I hadn't even taken a step into the hall on the way to her bedroom, when I heard the front door open.

'Lulu?'

No response. And much as my friends just seemed to wander in and out of my flat, I couldn't hear any footsteps coming towards me.

Stomach flipping, I stepped into the hall, and realised I'd got there just in time. Lulu was standing at the door, clutching the handle of her suitcase in one hand, her other hand on the door latch.

'What? Not even a goodbye? Or I'll call you? I must have been a crap date.' Under normal circumstances, humour was always the way to go with Lu. I just wasn't sure these circumstances could ever be called 'normal'.

'Yeah, pretty crap,' she told me, with no hint of amusement whatsoever.

I could hear the shower switching on, so I knew Beth couldn't overhear, but even so I walked down the hall towards Lulu. 'Lu, what exactly are you pissed off with me about? What would you have wanted me to do differently?' It was a challenge and for a heartbeat I hoped she would sigh, hug me, tell me – in true relationship speak – that it was her, not me.

No. The chin went up, the jaw set, and all I could see in her eyes was fury.

'You knew Jess had feelings for Dan. You should have told me.'

'Lu, I'm not going over this again. I only found out a couple of days ago, and I didn't think she'd act on it, and I didn't think she'd actually tell him. I also didn't see how it would matter to you, given that whole divorce and remarriage thing.'

I knew I was being brusque, but honestly, I didn't have the energy for this.

'Well, it mattered. But it mattered even more that you didn't have my back.'

I've no idea what button that pressed, but it caused something to snap. 'Don't you dare,' I said, and I saw her flinch as she registered the tone that only came out for politicians and seething anger. 'I have had your back all our lives, Lu.'

'But not this time.' I thought she was going to stay and argue the case – I'd never yet seen her walk away from a fight – but for once she didn't. Before I could say another word, she opened the door, walked out and the last thing I saw was her Gucci trolley case disappearing down the stairs.

I pushed the door closed, and slumped against the wall. 'I fucking hate being Switzerland,' I murmured to no one in particular.

A few minutes later, I heard the shower switch off, so I knew Beth would be through for supper shortly. I padded through to the kitchen to assemble something edible. Microwave rice. Some Cajun chicken strips. Corn. Tomatoes. Cucumber. I threw it all together and left it on the breakfast bar, shouting to let her know it was there when she was ready.

I'd just switched on the coffee machine when my mobile phone rang. Jess.

I answered with, 'You must be psychic. I was just about to call you.'

It was good to hear a laugh. 'Aw, were you thinking about me. I'm so touched.'

'Okay, now that I know you're not distraught, I'm hanging up if you're going to throw that kind of sarcasm around.'

'Don't! Okay, I'll behave,' she promised, clearing her throat, before going on. 'Good trip though. I love a drama-free jolly.'

Despite myself, I could feel one of those giggles rising, the kind that could quite easily flip to hysteria at any moment and end in tears. 'Me too. I always think we are so lucky to have such a mature, balanced group.'

Her laughter turned to a groan. 'So on a clusterfuck scale of one to ten, where do you think we landed?'

'I think we slid right off the board. Lulu just left. I think she's gone back to Bobby. He still doesn't actually know that she left him, so at least she had somewhere to go. She's still furious at me because I didn't tell her how you feel about Dan. Dan's upset with me because... well, I told him what happened with Vince. It looks like it's just me and you left. No offence, Jess, but since you appointed yourself as my life coach, my whole life has pretty much gone down the toilet.'

'I'll put that on my advertising leaflets. Jess McLean – Life Coach Who'll Put Your Whole World In The Crapper.'

A pause. 'So are we going to talk about it or just do a Colm and ignore the problem and carry on making bad jokes instead?' I asked softly. 'How are you feeling? And how did you come to be snogging the face off Dan in the middle of the night?'

She sighed. 'God, it seems so long ago already. I went out for some air, and he came out after me. He said he'd been thinking and maybe we should give things a try. I kissed him before he could change his mind. Then he was kissing me back and, oh, it was so good... right up until Lulu decided to stage an intervention.'

'Honey, I'm so sorry. Have you spoken to Dan since we landed?'

'No. I'm just going to leave it. I've said how I feel, and to be honest, much as I'm pissed off with Lu, maybe it was for the best that it all came out because this way he knows everything about me and I won't have to worry about him finding out somewhere down the line. It was one mistake that I made six years ago, we've come to terms with it, and moved past it for the sake of our family.'

I wholeheartedly agreed with her. In fact, in a strange way, it had brought us closer together. Although, I didn't let her completely off the hook. 'I still stick needles in a Barbie that looks a bit like you though.'

'I was wondering what was causing that pain in my arse,' she quipped, but there was a sadness there that was palpable when she added. 'If he can't live with me being imperfect, then he's not the right guy for me anyway. In fact, there's a bit of me that's pissed off about how he reacted. I've never judged him. Not once. Not when he was taking Lulu back for the tenth time, despite the fact she was wrecking him. Not when we were picking him up off a pile of beer cans a few weeks ago...'

'We did judge him a little for that one,' I teased softly.

'Okay, we did. But not to his face,' she conceded. 'That aside though, everyone our age has fucked up at some time, they've done things they regret, they've made wrong moves and bad decisions. We're too old for fairy tales.'

'Don't make me stop watching *The Princess Diaries*.' I know I was being a little glib but I was just trying to cheer her up, to stop her venting about my other friend, and well, Switzerland liked the occasional cinematic happy ending.

'Apart from that one, obviously.'

'Jess, I'm proud of you. Not for sleeping with my husband, because, you know – cow – but I'm proud of you for putting yourself out there and taking a chance. And if it doesn't work out, you've still got me. Although, I'll need to sneak you in here under a blanket because Dan's my landlord. And Lulu probably has a hit out on you.'

I heard her sigh. 'I think you might be right when you say my life-coaching skills need work. I'm not exactly a glowing reference for personal success. Do you think you and I are going to end up in adjoining rooms in an old folks' home, playing bingo in the afternoons and still trying to kickstart our dating game?'

'Don't be crazy,' I blurted, then climbed down a notch. 'We'll share a room, it'll be cheaper. More money for bingo.'

My eyes fell on Beth's supper and I realised that she hadn't come through for it. 'Listen, I have to go and check on Beth. Are the boys still with you?'

'No, they've both headed home.'

'Okay, well if you need me, you know where I am.'

'Yep, right upstairs from the bloke who thinks I'm a tart. G'night, Shauna. I love you, you know. Colm was a lucky guy having you.'

'He was a lucky guy having you too. G'night, Jess. Love you.'

I tossed my phone down on the breakfast bar and went back through to Beth's room. I heard the gentle sounds of her sleeping as soon as I opened the door. There she was, freshly showered, pyjamas on, lying on top of the duvet on her bed, with one of her favourite C.S. Lewis' chronicles open beside her. How many times had she read those books and she still loved them? I did too – as long as they didn't make my girl want to take a mallet to the back of the wardrobe.

I gently rolled her so that I could pull the duvet over her, then leaned down, kissed her head and whispered the same thing I told her every night when she was asleep. 'Good night, angel, your mum loves you. And your dad loves you too.'

She murmured, a half-smile playing on her lips, and then her breathing slowed again. Every time she did that, I wondered if it was Colm, stroking her face, maybe whispering something in her ear. He'd loved her so much. If there was any way in this world or the next that he'd have a front-row seat to his children's lives, I knew he'd be there.

Back in my bedroom, I pulled the first pyjamas out of my drawer and shook my head when I saw them. I should just have put them back in, but I figured they'd give Beth a giggle in the morning. It was July. No-one should be wearing pyjamas that were bedecked in fully decorated Christmas trees, with a message across the chest inviting onlookers to 'Go on, tickle my tinsel.'

A gift from Lulu. Along with a piece of tinsel that she suggested I place in a strategic position. As with ninety per cent of her advice, I ignored it. Thinking about her now made my stomach churn again. For a moment I thought about calling her, but I couldn't face another strained conversation. I loved her. She knew that. I just hoped it was enough for her to see my point of view and realise that I wasn't betraying her, I was just trying to let things work themselves out. I hated conflict. I hated drama. I hated being ambushed by emotional situations I wasn't prepared for.

Back in the kitchen, I binned Beth's supper, poured a glass of wine, grabbed a bowl of strawberries from the fridge, and trudged over to the sofa in the living area, where I picked up the remote control and pulled my cream cashmere throw (another Christmas gift from Lulu – and Bobby's platinum AMEX card) over my legs. I pressed a few buttons on the remote. Yes. This was exactly what I wanted. Peace. Quiet. And two new episodes of *Fixer Upper*, a programme where Chip and Joanna Gaines, two of the loveliest people in Texas, renovated houses while making you jealous of their sweet marriage and perfect lives.

I took a sip of wine and I exhaled.

Tomorrow, in between the lunch I was catering in Earls Court, and a kids' party at a regular client's home in Acton, I would track down Lulu. I would call and check on Jess. I would drop in on Dan and I would contact the Missing Obnoxious Person's Helpline about my mother.

But for now, I would breathe and witness a house refurbishment that would make a woman on the show sob into her brand-new dish towel.

They were still at the demolition stage when the doorbell went. Dear. God. I know this makes me a terrible person but please... Give. Me. Peace.

I ran through the options. It wasn't Lulu, because she would use her key and she was too busy hating me right now. It wasn't Jess, because she was just off the phone. So that left... Bobby, looking for Lulu. That was a long shot, because he'd have to have asked Dan to let him in the main door. My mother, with the announcement that she'd stopped in Gretna Green to elope with Uncle Norry. Or – and all bets would go this way – Dan. Of course he had a key, but he never used it, preferring to respect my privacy by knocking.

For a split second I thought about not answering but relief took over. He'd come to talk. He'd thought things through and had found a way to forgive me... Or he was evicting me and replacing me with a nun who'd never sinned and who would pay full rent.

I trotted down the hall, pulled open the door, and...

Not Dan. Definitely not Dan.

He was way over six feet. He was dressed all in black. He looked horrific. He was holding his nose while blood spurted into his hands.

He was the only other man I'd ever truly loved.

He was Vincent.

'Oh crap, I take it you met Dan?'

That was the first thing I'd said to him since Colm's funeral five years ago, when I'd asked him to give me space, to stop contacting me until I felt ready to speak to him again. I wasn't sure I ever would, and that wasn't his fault. It was down to guilt. Pure, stomach-churning, guilt. All mine.

'Yesh, I did,' he spluttered, through blood that sprayed when he spoke. A slick of red liquid was spreading down his white T-shirt. 'To be honesht, I was jusht exshpecting a "hello".'

'Come in, come in.' I beckoned him, immediately going into crisis-management mode, which was just, but only just, over-ruling my 'Vincent Is Here' panic mode.

I steered him into the bathroom a couple of metres down the hall, then grabbed a couple of charcoal towels from the shelf and thrust them towards him. 'Here, I'll go get some gauze out of the first-aid kit.'

'No, no, ish okay. Jusht... let me get cleaned up and I'll be out in a shec,' he said, backing into the loo.

I made a mental note. Fucking. Kill. Dan. What were we?

Teenagers? Didn't we grow out of all this punching stuff when we became middle-aged and secretly preferred staying in and watching *Strictly* to going out on a Saturday night? Adrenaline was pumping, my heart was thudding and my knees were about to give out, but I somehow made it back to the kitchen. At the sink, I flicked on the tap and started washing the blood off my shaking hands.

Vincent was here.

'Sorry, I've... erm... made a mess of your towels.'

'That's okay, I'll...' I turned around, stopped in my tracks, and then the absurdity of this hit me and I... laughed. 'Seriously? This is how we're playing this game? Did you really have an altercation with Dan or did you just smack your face off the wall outside so you could do this?'

The undeniably beautiful, way out of my league, former model, Vincent Palmer, was walking towards me, naked from the waist up, denim-clad from the waist down, his six-packed, tanned torso rippling as he moved. Even in his forties, he looked, as he always had, like the bloke off the kind of romance novels that had titles like 'His Throbbing Heart Was Mine' and 'The Prince Of Lust'. Lulu and I once spent a highly amusing couple of hours coming up with our own titles for his books. I couldn't remember them all but, 'My Loins Were Girded' was in there, and so was 'Ovaries Shaken, Not Stirred'. If I remembered correctly, the winner was, 'So Hot I Had To Turn Off My Electric Blanket'. We mocked up the front cover on his next birthday card and mortified him by putting it on the company Facebook page. Vince wasn't happy, but we got sixteen new clients that week, and all of them, unsurprisingly, were highly disappointed when I showed up to cater their function instead of the hot bloke.

'Which answer would you like best?' He began to grin, then winced about halfway as more pain kicked in.

'The one that gives you an option to sue for a nose job. Ouch, Vince, that looks so painful. I'm so sorry.'

'Give me some ice and a beer and I'll forgive you,' he offered. 'And sorry about flashing my nipples – my T-shirt was soaked. If I can shove it in the washing machine...'

I handed him the ice pack first, the beer second, then grabbed my wine off the coffee table and carried it to the breakfast bar. 'No worries. I've got a couple of oversize T-shirts you can borrow. Mine, not... erm...' I was going to say Colm's name, but I couldn't. Instead, I just flushed bright red, mortified, flustered, and dashed into my room.

I suddenly felt the need to make it absolutely clear that I wasn't giving him, of all people, one of my dead husband's T-shirts. That's why, five minutes later, he was still sitting at my breakfast bar, but now he was wearing a 'Hold My Beer (for 9 months cos I'm Pregnant)' T-shirt that I'd worn on many occasions between the blue lines on the stick and Beth being born. I'd pulled it from a box of Beth's baby things and family mementos that lived at the back of my wardrobe. It had always had so much sentimental value that I couldn't bear to throw it out.

Vince had already abandoned the ice pack, and instead was holding his beer bottle against his ever-growing hooter.

'Is there an "inappropriate outfits" rule in this house?'

'What do you mean?' I asked, confused until I saw that his gaze was on the message on my top. Ah, crap. Tickle My Tinsel.

'I like to wear these pyjamas all year round,' I shrugged, making that up on the spot. 'Get my money's worth.'

Once again, his laugh quickly deteriorated into a wince and an 'ouch' before he fell silent and I realised I was all out of things to say too.

This was one of my oldest friends – only Lulu had been around for longer. We'd met on the first day of college, two sixteen-year-old catering students who were handy with a piping bag, but that was about it. Weirdly, and unlike every other woman in our class, his tall, dark, chiselled jawed, young Jamie Dornan looks did nothing for me. Nor did the fact that he modelled to pay his way through college. Not a lust button was pressed. I was more into the quirky guys who made me laugh, so that left Vince and I free to have a genuine friendship, where I teased him mercilessly about the succession of unfeasibly beautiful women with forty-inch legs that went through our student apartment and then later, after we'd both set up successful companies and then merged them, his minimalist bachelor pad in Fulham.

It would have been easy to sneer at his lifestyle and avoidance of any form of commitment, but the problem was he was so respectful and so honest, that even the women he dated always walked away with only good things to say. He was a sweetheart. He'd also passed the biggest test of all: my gran loved him. High praise given that Annie had – as she would proudly announce in any company – the sharpest dickhead alarm in the free world.

He'd passed with flying colours, as I knew he would.

We'd worked together. We'd hung out together. He was a firm member of our squad. He'd grafted right by my side when I was trying to earn enough to support us after Colm and Dan started their own business. Vincent had showed up for me every time. Hell, even Colm liked him. Although, he did get frustrated with the regular work calls on my rare days off. 'That's Delia Smith on the phone again,' he'd mutter. 'He's got his banoffee pies in a twist.'

All that time, I'd had no idea Vincent was in love with me. None. I only found out years later, after...

'This isn't how I ever saw this moment playing out,' Vince said, cutting into my thoughts.

'You sitting there in a pregnancy T-shirt with a face like a hot dog and me in my Christmas pyjamas inviting inappropriate fondling? This is exactly how I pictured it,' I told him, feigning seriousness.

I rallied. *Come on. This is Old Friend Vince. Not One-Night Stand Vince.*

A bolt of something visceral shot through me at the very thought of that night. Noooo. Not now. I'd shut it down thanks to equal measures of shame, and fear about how good it had felt, and I didn't want to reopen the memory.

Another pause.

He broke it first, his one good eye piercing my soul. 'I've been trying to get in touch with you for a while.'

'I know. I've been avoiding you.'

'I figured. I'm pretty good at spotting the signs.'

I spun my wine around in my glass. 'I doubt that. It's not like you've had much practice,' I teased gently. It was hard to imagine anyone avoiding this man. Before we got distracted by nostalgia or cute stories from the past, I cut to the important stuff. 'So tell me.'

He raised an eyebrow in question.

'Why you're sitting in my kitchen?' I prompted.

He smiled again. At least, I think he did. It was hard to tell with the swelling. 'Can I go with "Because Dan punched me and you felt sorry for me and let me in"?'

'No.'

'Then it's because I missed...'

My heart dropped. No. Don't do this. 'Vince, don't...'

'... London,' he finished, chuckling at my obviously incorrect assumption.

Embarrassment made my cheeks flush. Had he been going to say me? Or was I making stuff up in my head. Urgh, my nerves were on the outside of my skin and I couldn't think straight, so of course I went for caustic sarcasm. 'I've no idea why we were ever friends. I only liked you because you were a great cook.'

'I only liked you because you were funny,' he sparred back, with a grin, repeating our mantra for most of our friendship.

I couldn't decide whether this felt way too comfortable or way too uncomfortable. Either way it was giving me the fear.

'You were pretty hard to track down though,' he went on. 'When you didn't answer calls or texts, I got worried. Went to your old house...'

'We moved,' I said, stating the obvious. 'After Colm died, the old house didn't seem like the right place to be any more, so I sold up.'

'The new owners told me that,' he said, nodding. 'So I thought I'd come here and ask Lulu and Dan. I figured they'd still be here because, wasn't this originally Dan's uncle's house?'

'Yes. Lulu and Dan converted it into two flats.'

'I realised that when I saw the buttons on the front door. Only one of them had a name...' That was true. Five years and I still hadn't put my name on my button. 'So I pressed that one and Dan answered and buzzed me in. I'd only taken a few steps into the building when he came out of his door and punched me in the face.'

Jesus. I knew his feelings were running high, but this was so out of character for Dan. I would have sworn he didn't have a violent bone in his body. 'Did he say anything?'

'Just "You're a fucking prick, mate. If you're looking for Shauna, she's upstairs." Then he turned and went back inside as if nothing had happened. Does he punch all your visitors in the face, or is that just me?' He was trying so hard to be flippant about it, and I knew that was for my benefit, but it wasn't working.

'Just you. It's a long story. He's... going through a rough week.'

'Oh God, don't tell me – Lulu's bought a yacht and put it on the credit cards.'

'She only did that once! And she cancelled it when he found out.'

'So what's she bought now then? Private island? Ferrari?'

'She left him,' I said, deadpan.

He flinched, searching my face, as if looking for some kind of sign that this was a joke.

'No.'

'Yes. She married someone else last month. That's why he's a bit volatile. And we've just come back from a trip to Glasgow that was...' Now I was the one searching for words. I settled on, '... Emotional'.

'Sounds like Lulu hasn't changed much,' he observed, unruffled. He'd always loved Lulu, but he knew who she was, so none of this would be a shock to him. 'Why were you in Glasgow? Holiday?'

His question evoked a flash of realisation. 'Oh wow, you don't know!' I blurted, spirits lifting as I changed the subject.

He leaned forward, mirroring my grin. 'What don't I know?' That was the thing with Vince – when I was happy, he was always happy for me.

'Turns out Annie had a family she left in Glasgow when she was in her twenties. There was a bust-up over a man she was seeing and... It doesn't matter.' I waved the details away. 'What's important is that I found them, and her sister, Flora, is still alive, so now I have an aunt and cousins.'

'You're kidding. Tell me she's just like Annie. There isn't a day that I don't miss her. She remains my favourite woman of all time.'

If Annie was up there watching, right now she'd be punching the air and bellowing, 'Yaassssss! I knew it!'

'Mine too.' I had to blink back another rush of moisture to my bottom lids. It was like stepping back in time. Annie. Vince. Me. She'd adored Colm too. It was nothing but laughter and love, and the pain of the void that left was so strong it physically hurt. For years now I'd been just existing, going through the motions, and I knew it was because of the bloody great hole they had left in my heart.

'Weirdly, she's nothing like Annie at all. She's tall, and elegant and gentle, and she definitely wouldn't pretend you were her husband when you were in public.' All of those things were the complete opposite of the short, mighty, raucous, sharp, straight-shooting party animal that was my gran.

Vincent laughed as my words popped out another memory. 'Do you remember the first time she did that?'

I'd heard him tell the story so many times, it was imprinted in my brain. Annie had taken Vincent along to Selfridges to shop for my Christmas present. Of course, she thought it would be hilarious to march him into the lingerie department. She loved to add a little sexy something into my Christmas pile every year because she got a twisted thrill from seeing me turn the colour of Santa's Y-fronts when I opened it. Vincent was over in the unisex section, when he saw Annie holding up a sexy baby doll. 'Tell me honestly, am I too old for this?' she'd asked a shop assistant, who was immediately paralysed and struck mute by the struggle between truth and making a sale.

'Och, it's okay, love, I'll ask my husband.' At which point she'd bellowed, 'Vincent!' and this six foot four inch male model strolled over from the Calvin Kleins.

'Yes, my love?' he'd addressed her, as he always did.

'What do you think?' she'd wagged the baby doll in his direction.

'Perfect,' he'd answered, completely oblivious to why the shop assistant's jaw was now on the counter.

'She did that every time we went shopping after that,' he said, grimacing from the pain of laughing. 'It never got old.'

The release of talking about Annie with someone who'd shared those moments was exhilarating. Beth never knew her great-gran, Jess never met her, Colm was gone. Only Lulu and Dan knew her well and they'd had so much other stuff going on for the last couple of years that chatting about my late granny understandably never made it into our discussions.

'I miss her so much, Vince. I keep waiting for it to get easier, but it doesn't. Beth reminds me of her sometimes.'

'Where is Beth?' he asked, as if realising for the first time that there should be another person here.

'Sleeping. She was up late last night and then we had the trip back from Glasgow today. She crashed out just before you arrived at my door like something from *The Walking Dead*. It's probably a good thing. She'd have been scarred for life.'

Vince was mortified. 'I'm so sorry, I didn't even think.'

'I'm kidding. She's eleven. At that age, nothing freaks them out. Sometimes I think she's the most adult and grounded of us all.'

'I'd like to meet her some day,' he said, and my stomach immediately flipped. Why did the prospect of them meeting feel like a betrayal of my husband? Vince had left the UK before Beth was born, at my request, and I'd only seen him again at Colm's funeral. Beth had been there, but I'd deliberately not introduced them, so they'd never actually met.

Instead of answering, I got up, pulled three more beers out of the fridge, abandoning my wine. 'One for drinking, one for your face,' I told him, putting two of them in front of him.

He immediately took one of them and held it against his nose. I'd fricking kill Dan for this when I got hold of him.

It was so strange, I hadn't seen Vincent for five years, but now he was here, sitting across from me, and it was so familiar it felt like yesterday. Even looking like he'd just been smacked in the face by a shovel, he was so beautiful, I realised that it wasn't just my brain that remembered him. I had an almost irrepressible urge to touch him. To hold him...

The memory was back. That night. Vincent. Me. Naked. Limbs entwined. Our breaths shallow and quick. His hand on my face. His lips on mine. Nothing else existed except that moment and I wanted...

Aaargh. I shook it off. No. Can't go there. Another subject change required.

'I want to hear about your life. Tell me. Give me the last five years in bullet points,' I asked, my face flushed as I decided to get him talking for a while so I could concentrate on getting the image of the night we spent together out of my mind.

'Where do you want me to start?'

'From the last time I saw you.' That had been at Colm's wake. Most if it was a blur, but I remembered Lulu telling me that he'd literally flown over for the day.

'I went back to New York...' he began, and I almost sagged with relief that half of my brain could switch off while the other half pretended to listen and nodded at the right moments. 'To find Carole had left. She didn't want me to come over. Last straw, she said. You know how jealous she was with you.'

I did. Carole, a full time model with an exquisite face and legs that went on forever, had been Vincent's girlfriend when we ran our company together and she'd always had issues with our relationship. Despite that, Vince had tried to make it work with her. After we'd dissolved our business partnership, he'd moved to

New York, they'd married, and I'd really hoped they would get a happy ever after.

Apparently not.

I nodded on cue. All the while, against every ounce of my will, I was feeling my body temperature rise and my heartbeat speed up, as the memory of our time together pressed against the lid of the box I'd locked it in. Eventually I surrendered to it.

Twelve years ago, only a few months after Annie died, I was a walking shell who was barely functioning. And Colm and I, we were lost. He couldn't deal with my all-consuming grief, couldn't handle being so close to the flames of loss, so he'd backed off. Abandoned me. For months, he'd gone with his standard avoidance tactics, deciding he didn't have the skills or the courage to reach me. Vince was the opposite. He worked with me every day, and he never stopped trying to break through, telling me he was there for me, asking what he could do. I felt so alone. So utterly desperate. And one day I broke.

I went to Vince's home on our day off and I collapsed in the doorway. He took me in, held me, washed me, put me to bed in his spare room. He was about to leave when I realised that I needed more, I needed something physical, something that would take me away from the pain for just a little while. Every single moment of that night over twelve years ago began unfolding in my mind like a movie.

'Vincent...' I reached over, put my hand on his heart, felt it beating under my touch, fast, hard.

'Don't do this, Shauna. Not like this.'

I could hear what he was saying, but I wasn't listening. 'Please...'

'No.' It was soft, thick with sorrow. He ran his fingers through his hair, groaned, then touched my face. 'I love you,' he said simply, but he didn't have to, because right then I realised that I knew. I'd always known. 'I've been in love with you for so long I can't remember a time

when I wasn't. But I don't want it to be like this,' he said. 'Not when you're vulnerable and hurt. It would feel... wrong. Like I was taking advantage of your pain. And I know... Don't worry, I know. You love Colm. You always have. And I hate that he doesn't see you, doesn't know what he has.'

'Vincent, please...' I stopped, the words refusing to form.

He stood up. 'I'm going to go to bed now, before either of us says or does something that can't be undone. And tomorrow, we'll pretend this never happened, smile and carry on like everything is fine. The way you do every day.'

I should have listened. He was a good man saying honourable things, but I was too far gone to hear him. Later that night, I went to him again. That time, he didn't say no.

That was it, our one night. Afterwards, we agreed never to speak about it. I went back to Colm and Vince went back to Carole, his girlfriend at the time. We continued working together every day, for months, until something changed.

Carole wanted him to move to New York, but he didn't want to leave me, either emotionally or financially, until I appeared at his door a second time.

'Vince,' I said, serious again, 'Please go.'

'Why are you so insistent?'

'Because I'm pregnant.'

His head reeled back like he'd been slapped.

'You're... Is it mine?'

I'd known he would ask. Of course he would. And it broke my heart that there was a tiny hint of hope in his question.

'No,' I whispered. 'I'm sorry, but it's not. I'm only about two months gone.' It was October. We'd been together in May, five months ago. There was no question. 'It's Colm's baby.'

He closed his eyes for a long moment before he went on. 'I hope he *realises how lucky he is to get this life, Shauna. You, a baby... that's an amazing future right there.'*

Walking away broke my heart. I loved Vince. As a friend, as a partner, as a person.

But despite our deep rooted issues, I was still in love with my husband. And our child meant that there was no other life for me than with him.

Vincent left, and I only saw him again at Colm's funeral.

'Can I call you some time?' he'd asked me that day.

All I could think about wasn't the thirty years of friendship we'd shared. Just one night had ended it. I couldn't bear the guilt. 'No,' I'd whispered. 'Don't call me, Vince. If you love me, please walk away.'

He'd done as I asked. And now, six years later, he was back.

'Shauna? Are you okay?'

His question snapped me back to reality. I hadn't allowed myself to think about Vince for so long and now I couldn't stop, wanted to stay in that place, to rewind it and feel all those things again.

'Erm, sure. Yes. Sorry. Just tired. Like I said, it's been a long weekend. But I want to hear everything, I do,' I assured him.

He didn't look convinced, but he went on, and this time I tuned in. 'Carole and I separated. No drama. It was mutual and straightforward because we'd never had kids and had no joint assets. Afterwards, I bummed around a bit, travelled to some places I'd never been, then came home about six months ago. I've moved back into my old place in Fulham. I was only renting it out on Airbnb by then, so I just unlisted it and stopped taking bookings. Since then, I've been thinking about calling you and a few weeks ago, something made me do it.' He stopped, hesitated, obviously trying to decide whether it was okay to go on.

'Tell me. What "something"?' I probed.

His internal tussle ended with him carrying on. 'I realised it was twenty years since you met Colm. I remembered the date because you told me every single year...'

'And every single year, I'd moan because Colm forgot.'

'You would,' he agreed, with a smile. 'And we'd eat cake and celebrate anyway.'

I'd forgotten about that. Back then, we used to joke that Vince was Colm's stunt double. Anything my husband didn't want to do, didn't care about, wasn't interested in doing with me, Vince would step up and take his place. In some ways, what happened between us was perhaps inevitable. Vince had been with me when Annie died. He'd shared the pain. He'd loved her too. He was the only person who could truly share what had happened to me. Or maybe that was just me looking for a cop-out. It wasn't fate. It was me, shattered by grief, risking everything to feel whole again, just for a few hours.

'I just...' he stopped, trying to find the words. '... Felt like I needed to see you.'

'Why now and not any other year?' I was intrigued.

'I've no idea. I just got this feeling, like I had to speak to you. Had to check you were okay. And then... hang on – you still haven't told me why Dan punched me.'

'Because... because... Och, fuck it. Grab another beer. It's a really long story.'

For the next hour, I filled him in on everything that had happened, with Jess, with Dan, with Lulu, with all the changed dynamics and new feelings and the conflicts that had burst our self-made-family bubble. By the time I got to the last bit, the discussion I'd had with Dan, the confession I'd made to him that I'd slept with Vince on that one, painful night, Vince looked pretty much as stunned as that shop assistant in Selfridges.

'I did warn you,' I told him.

He exhaled, nodding his head. 'And I thought the Christmas pyjamas were going to be the biggest shock of the night.'

That – and the rack of Buds we'd consumed, mine on an empty stomach – set us both off again. When we eventually composed ourselves, the room fell quiet.

'I missed you more than London,' he admitted softly. 'Every day, Shauna.'

'I missed you too.' More relief, this time at being able to admit it to myself, as well as saying it out loud. The atmosphere between us had completely changed in the last... I checked the clock on the wall above the cooker – damn, it had been four hours. It was almost midnight. At the start, there had been tension, nerves, strain, not to mention a nose that may require surgery if it ever wanted to be straight again. Now, though, it was just the way it used to be, just Vince and Shauna, mates since we were teenagers at college, until the carnage of life broke us.

Vince leaned forward, resting his elbows on the breakfast bar. 'Shauna.' One of his hands crossed the table and took mine.

My brain began screaming orders of 'Pull back, pull back,' to my fingers, but the traitorous bastards didn't obey, too busy rolling over and loving being gently stroked by the enemy thumb.

My hand was lost, leaving only my head and my heart to find the power to resist and right now neither of them were stepping up to the challenge.

'I lied earlier,' he confessed quietly. 'I didn't just come back because I was done with New York. The only reason I came back was to see you.'

'Vince...' I warned him, but that was as far as I could manage before my throat went. Another traitor.

'Shauna, I love you, you know I always have. I respected your wishes when you told me not to contact you, but it's been five years since I saw you last. Five years of living without you and wondering why I was letting my life go by on the other side of an ocean from the woman I wanted to be with. Five years of wondering if we could have a shot.'

He didn't add, 'Now that Colm was gone', but it was there in the subtext.

I could feel the frustration seeping out from my gut. It still didn't reach my hand though – that remained firmly in his.

'Vincent, what is wrong with you? You're gorgeous, you're kind, you're one of the good guys. You could have anyone you wanted, but you're sitting in my kitchen, the victim of an assault, declaring your love for a messed-up middle-aged widowed single mum wearing Christmas fricking pyjamas in July. Why can't you find someone who is spectacular, and free, and a match for you and your sexy single life?'

His one open eye was blazing as he blurted, 'Because they're not you. You're it for me. And unless you've met someone else...'

'I haven't.' Now my gob was on the traitorous bench too.

'Then give us a chance. Come on, Shauna. It was never just me who felt what was between us. You did too. I know you did.'

He wasn't wrong. But back then there were so many other things in the picture. I was still with Colm, although at that time, I truly thought we were irretrievably broken. We often questioned if we'd have made it through that time in our marriage if I hadn't got pregnant, and the truth was, I didn't know. Beth solidified us in a way that balanced out our differences and made them work. I was strict mum, he was fun dad. I took care of the serious stuff, he minimised the impact of any crisis or conflict with his carefree, ah-feck-it attitude.

It just worked. We rediscovered all the reasons we loved each other and we stuck it out, tough as it was, absolutely certain that we'd done the right thing. Colm and I were meant to be together and no one could change that, not even the incredible man sitting across from me. I was Colm O'Flynn's partner for life. For always.

But that was then.

Vincent lifted my traitorous hand to his mouth and kissed it, setting of such a rush of heat that my tinsel came close to combusting.

I groaned and it took a moment to identify the feelings that were suddenly intoxicating me. I wanted him. Every single pore of my skin wanted to feel his body against mine. I'd closed down my sex drive a long time ago, unable to even contemplate being with another man, yet here it was again, alive and well and absolutely desperate to be with this man who was saying all the right words, doing all the right things, just being all kinds of right for a woman who'd been in the romantic wilderness for way too long.

Then a train of thought came along and shut it all down in one rapid beat of my heart...

For the last five years, every time I thought of Vince, I was consumed by the shame of betraying Colm, no matter what justifiable reasons I could shout out in my defence.

If I were to be with Vincent again it would compound the crime: every time I looked at him, every time he touched me, it would be tainted by the reminder that I'd broken my vows to the man I married, long before he broke the same vow to me.

I loved Vincent Palmer. But I could never, ever go there with him, because no matter how much pleasure it gave me, it would remind me of the biggest regret of my life.

Not being with Vincent now was the price I had to pay for betraying my husband.

And there was nothing I could do to change that.

'I'm so sorry, Vincent, but I can't. You need to go.'

I closed my eyes, prayed that he wouldn't argue, wouldn't

protest, because I was hanging on by a thread and knew I was on the edge of falling apart.

I opened my fingers, let his hand fall away, closed my eyes and held my breath.

Please go. Please. Because I don't trust myself not to love you if you stay.

The next thing I heard was the gentle thud of the door as it closed behind him.

25

COLM – 2016

This room is way too hot. Or maybe it's just the stuff that's being pumped into my veins. I'm tired. Way too tired to do this, but I'm getting scared that I'm running out of time. Not that I'd admit that, not even to myself. Nope, not how I roll. I am beating this fucking disease until I'm not. And by then, I'll be gone, so I won't know I was wrong. Denial, avoidance and optimism all the way, baby.

I pull my phone out and balance it against the poker chips on my overbed table. Lulu was in again today and we played cards and talked nonsense all afternoon. She won twenty quid off me, but she wouldn't take it. Said I've to use it to buy the first round in the pub when I get out of here. To be honest, I think my money's safe.

Every bone in my clapped-out body groans as I push myself up. I knew I was going to do this today, so I got Lulu to shave me and sort my hair out after she'd cleaned up at poker. Dan sometimes does it, but he won't be in until tonight, and I don't know if I'll still have the energy to do this by the time he leaves. Can't keep my eyes open these days. Just want to sleep.

I can feel my head slumping and I snap it back up, give myself a stern pep talk. *Okay, mate, you've got it. One more. Let's do this. Don't fuck it up, don't fall apart. Get in, say it, retreat, job done.*

Something Lulu said to me earlier is playing on my mind, though. And if this is the last one of these I'm going to do, I need to sort that out for her too. Okay. Two messages. I've got this.

I press 'record'.

'Hey, m'darlin', how's things? No idea why I ask that. You'd never admit it, but I know they're shit. Every time you're here, I can see the exhaustion getting worse, I can feel the toll that all this is taking on you. I've left it all to you again. Not that that's different to every other day since we married. I know I've done that, Shauna. In hindsight, it was yet another dick move. But you always had everything so sorted, so under control, that it was easy for me to just take a back seat and put everything on your shoulders. Beth. Work. Finances. House. Me. Thank Christ we never got a dog, or you'd have been left to take care of that too.'

I realise I'm doing my usual – drifting off on a tangent and making ten different points before getting to the main one. It makes me great company in the pub, but pretty crap at messages I need to get done before the lights go out. Okay, let's go. Let's do it.

'Sorry, love, I'm prevaricating again. Would you listen to me with the big words. They cut out the bit that lets me remember what I did five minutes ago but left in the bit that says "prevaricate". Life's a crapshoot, eh? Anyway, darlin', I need you to do something for me. Is Lu with you right now? If she is, can you ask her to listen to me for a minute. You might have to teach her how to do that because she's known me twenty-five years and she's never managed it yet.

'Anyway, this bit is for Lu. She just left here half an hour ago and something she said has got me thinking. She said she's never been on her own. Not ever. Do you remember that, Lu? You said you went from those cretins you call parents straight to a life where you had a couple of guys on the go at any one time, then on to marriage with Dan, which, let's face it, wasn't always monogamous. Lu, I love you. But I've got a horrible feeling you're going to take my man, Dan, down one of these days. You two are oil and water. Not right, not wrong, just different. Dan needs someone way more chilled, someone who'll always look at him and think he's enough. I'm not sure you'll ever manage that. So I guess I'm saying two things. Lu, he's more than enough for someone. If that's not you, please let him go. Let him find someone who wants the same things as he does. Feck, check me out, spouting all this emotional stuff. In my defence, they were in poking about in my brain and they've definitely rearranged the furniture while they were in there.

'Anyway, Lu, here's the second thing I need to say to you. You're enough too. In fact, yer fecking magnificent. You've been the best mate I could ever have hoped for in here and God knows I love you, pal. That's why I can tell you this. You're enough. And if you make things work with Dan, then I'll be the happiest dead pal in the cemetery. But if you can't, don't go off with some soulless twat because you want his lifestyle or his fame or his money, or whatever it is you think you need to be happy. You don't need any of that. You just need to be you and to live life on yer own terms. As soon as you start realising that you're enough to make yourself happy, then you'll be grand. I really believe that, Lu.

'Aw feck, listen to me. I'm gonna call a nurse and see if she can find someone to come and shoot me before I talk even more bollocks.

'Right, that's the gospel according to a dying man done for you, Lu, but I need to speak to ma darlin' again. I know you two share everything, but I kinda need us to have a private moment. Go spend that twenty quid you won off me today on one of those mad mental coffees you buy. Just take it out of the petty cash tin. I'll see you around, pal. I love ya.'

That one catches on the vocal chords, so I clear my throat, then force myself back on track.

'Okay. Shauna. You might want to stop this and get a coffee, love. Feck it, get a gin. Oh, and just so you know, when you were in here last night and thought I was drowsy, it wasn't the meds. Me and Lu had indulged in a couple of vodka cocktails in the afternoon and I was wellied. Don't be mad at her. She's kept a dying man happy these last few months.'

I pause for a second. Hopefully she'll just think the screen has frozen. Thing is, I could stop now. I don't need to do this. I can save myself the pain of saying it, and save Shauna the pain of hearing it, and just hope for the best. But... I can't. Because I might have the emotional intelligence of a plank of wood, but I know my girl inside out.

Come on, mate. You need to do this. Deep breath.

Just as I go to speak, I have a sudden realisation and it diverts me.

'Right, Shauna, I just thought of something. There's every chance you won't see this one because after my last video, you might have put yer phone on the road and ran over it with yer Constant Cravings van. Crushed to death by a thousand coronation chicken vol-au-vents.

'Sorry. I know I'm deflecting from serious shit by coming out with crap jokes. They didn't fix that part of my brain when they were in there.'

I take a breath. 'I hope you've found a way to forgive me for being with Jess. I couldn't go with that on my conscience. And I hope you'll understand in a few minutes the other reason I told you. Okay. Feck, I'm shite at this.

'First of all, I want to say sorry for something that happened years ago. Shauna, I know how much you loved yer gran. We all did. Christ, she was some woman. I fully expect her to be waiting up there for me with a tambourine, a bottle of Macallan, and a box of those caramel wafers she was always eating. She'll have the twelve apostles whipped into shape and she'll have organised a sports day and put Joan Of Arc and Mother Teresa in charge of crowd control. Sorry. I'm doing it again.'

Jesus Christ, Colm, get this done. My head is getting fuzzy and my eyes are desperate to shut.

'The thing is, Shauna, when she died, I bailed on you. I know I did. Just like I bailed on Jess, when we lost Daisy.

'I saw what was happening with you every day. You were so low, you needed me to scrape you off the ground and be a husband, yet I couldn't. But someone else could. I know Vincent was there for you, m'darlin'. And I can still picture the moment that I realised it. It was at yer gran's funeral.'

My brain was fried and I'd been on the vodka, but I could still see that moment clear as day.

The venue, the flash Surrey golf course that Shauna and Lu's parents frequented almost daily, had been Shauna's dad's choice. He'd chosen to have Annie's wake there, despite Shauna's objections that her gran hated this place. 'Full of jumped-up tossers with an overinflated opinion of themselves. A bit like you, son,' Annie would frequently tell her arse of a son. She'd add a wink on to the end to soften the blow, but everyone knew she meant it. In all the time I'd known Annie, she'd never backed down, never shirked the truth or turned her back on anyone who needed help. Shauna was a lot like her.

While the oldies were scoffing down their cucumber sandwiches (I'm pretty sure Annie sent a bolt of lightning down for that nonsense – she would much rather have seen them line dancing with a whisky in one hand and a caramel wafer in the other), I spotted Shauna nipping out of a side entrance.

'Back in a minute,' I told Dan, then headed out after her. Through the door, I looked left to the reception area and right to the corridor that led to another bar. Shauna was nowhere to be seen. I opted for left. I crossed the foyer to the entrance, two heavy, mahogany antique doors befitting a grand old building like this. I pushed one open, stepped out, the green grass of the practice area directly in front of me. I'd been here before, setting off on my annual round of golf with my wife's father. The irony was that for a shit parent, he was great company. Full of the chat and hilarious anecdotes. Full of the charm if there were ladies present. I couldn't work the guy out at all. Funny guy, crap father, Shauna always said, and she was absolutely right.

There was no sign of her and I was about to go back inside when I spotted the long bench off to the left, where the golfers stopped to make their final preparations before going on to the first tee. There were two people on it, their backs to me, facing off into the distance. I didn't need to see their faces to know who they were.

Shauna. Vincent.

Fair play to the guy, he'd been great. He'd been with Shauna when her gran died, helped give CPR, called the ambulance, took care of her and I was so grateful that he was there, that Shauna hadn't gone through that on her own. Since then, he'd called, dropped by, been there for her, and yes, I was well aware that some of those tasks should have been mine, but Vince seemed to do it so much better.

Like now. I could see Shauna's shoulders move, shudder, and I guessed she was sobbing. Vincent put his arm around her and her head fell on his shoulder. That was it. No talking, no drama, just a quiet moment of solace.

I thought about going over, but what would that achieve? Vincent was doing a great job of comforting her. Like I said, he did it so much better than me.

If nothing else, I knew my limitations, knew when I didn't have what someone needed. Right then she needed a partner, someone to hold her up, to soothe the pain. Coping with the death of a loved one rated pretty high on the scale of things that were beyond me. I didn't do death. I couldn't. The memory of losing Daisy made an attempt to surface, and I pushed it back down. I wouldn't go there, wouldn't be one of those people who constantly relived the past, killing themselves with a million small cuts. No. Not today. Not ever.

So I backed up, slipped through the door and headed back inside. And I never told Shauna I'd seen them or how I felt about it. Until now. I stare straight into the camera.

'You know the worst thing about it, Shauna? I was grateful to Vincent for taking my place. No fucking spine whatsoever. I was so scared of going anywhere close to the fire that burned me when Daisy died that I just couldn't deal with death, or pain, or anyone else's broken heart. I'm sorry, Shauna. That's all on me. But something has always bothered me and it's time I laid it out for you here, because God knows that I'm too much of a fucking coward to say it when I'm alive.' I take a breath, not sure if it's the drugs or the difficulty of this conversation that's squeezing the air out of my chest. Inhale. Exhale. Do this.

'Shauna, m'darlin', I'm pretty sure something happened with you and Vincent. The man was in love with you, always was, plain for anyone except you to see. I know you didn't feel that way about him – my ego is still healthy enough to know that what we had was special and if you wanted Vince you'd have been with him long before we met – but if there was ever a time when you needed him because I was a useless dick, then I... I... Babe, it's okay. I know. I know there was a moment that you were more than friends. At least I'm pretty sure, because for years after he went to New York, I'd ask about him and you'd shrug and say you didn't keep in touch. And then I'd see your eyes cloud and your shoulders slump and I knew how much it was hurting you. It took me a long time to work it out, but that's how I knew. You'd never have cut him off unless it was to save someone or something else. I don't need to know the details, but I'm pretty sure that something was us.

'So, m'darlin', I guess what I'm trying to say is that if there's a chance that you can have happiness with Vincent, or with someone else, after I'm gone, I need you to take it. Beth deserves a bloke around the house, otherwise she'll make the whole place so pink she'll go blind. I might have made that up, but the message still stands. You deserve another partner, an equal, someone who can be there even in the crap times, when you need someone to lean on. More than that, m'darlin', you deserve to laugh that gorgeous laugh of yours, to find true happiness and to have someone to love you until the end of time. I reckon I've got maybe a month or so left, so you'll be...'

I pause to make the calculation. Can't remember her birthday. Fuck this brain.

'You'll be early forties when I go. That's too young to spend the rest of your life alone. That man loves you and if you think you can be happy with him, I want you to try. And if not him, then find someone else, someone who'll adore you, who'll love Beth, and who'll take good care of both of you until we're together again. And whoever he is, please tell him I said thanks. Tell him I said he's the luckiest guy in the world to do the rest of your life with you. I just wish it was me.'

There. I said it. I hold it together for just long enough to switch off the camera, then I buckle forward as the relief floods through me, then clears the way for another wave of pain. I meant every word of what I just said. I want her to be happy. But fuck, I would give anything for this death do us part shit to be a long way away.

26

I waited. I hoped. I dreaded. Two completely opposing emotions and I wasn't sure which one I wanted to prevail.

So I waited some more.

I hoped beyond hope that if I walked into that hallway Vince was still there, maybe leaning against the doorway, unable to go.

At the same time, I absolutely dreaded going out there in case he was there, waiting, and I lost myself in everything that he was.

I waited. Nothing. The clock on the oven clicked with every minute. Only when I'd counted to ten did I get up from the stool and go through into the hall.

He wasn't there. Relief. Sorrow. Pain. The utility-room floor was calling me. If ever there was a time that I needed to sit, to think, to watch my knickers go round while I was trying to sort out my head and my life, this was it, but I couldn't bear to give in to it. Not tonight. If I started to think, I might never stop.

Keep moving, Shauna, don't let it catch up with you.

I went into the bathroom that Vince used. He'd cleaned up as best he could, but his T-shirt was still steeping in the basin, the water around it pink with blood. I drained it off, rinsed it, unable to hold back a smile when I realised that he'd marched out of here wearing a T-shirt announcing he's pregnant. I hoped he hadn't gone straight to a pub.

I got some Dettox from the cupboard under the basin, cleaned the whole place up so it looked like it did right before Vincent knocked on my door. Couldn't have Beth waking up to a blood bath in the morning. It could traumatise her for life.

When everything was pristine, I wandered into the utility room, emptied the washing machine into the tumble dryer, then refilled it with the crime scene evidence. *Keep busy. Just keep moving. Do not let any of this sink in.* As long as I kept going, I didn't have to process what had just happened.

I decided to toss my pyjamas in too. There were a couple of drops of beer on them and I wasn't going to bed with the lingering smell of Eau De Budweiser. Before I switched the washing machine on, I went back through to my room to change into fresh pyjamas. It was only when I got there that I saw the carnage. When I'd pulled the oversized T-shirt out of the box in the back of my wardrobe, I'd tipped the whole thing over. Now the box was upside down and the contents were scattered across my bedroom floor. Dammit.

As usual, my eyes went heavenwards. I couldn't stand the thought that Colm was watching events unfold tonight, so I went for Annie instead.

'Really, Gran? You got so excited about seeing your hunk hunka line-dancing love again that you wrecked the joint? Or was it because you don't think I did the right thing?' I knew the answer to that. Annie would have told me to snatch the chance of happiness with Vince and to go live my best life. She'd adored him, she'd adored life, and she wouldn't even have hesitated to make a different choice than the one I'd just made. Sometimes I wondered if I should be more like Annie. The guilt would keep me awake at night, but I'd have so much more fun.

I slid to my knees and began picking up the stuff that was scattered around, falling immediately into a heart-melting cloud of nostalgia. This was our 'special things' box, the one that contained everything that had sentimental value from when Beth was a kid, thus the pregnancy T-shirt I'd given to Vince.

There was a print of her hands and feet from the day she was born.

There was her first pair of tiny baby shoes – Dior, of course, courtesy of her Auntie Lu.

A little box containing her first tooth. Another with her first lock of hair. Her first babygrow. Then there was a diary of her milestones. The first time she crawled, walked, said mamma, dadda. I stroked each item as I put it back into the box, then twisted to pick up the rest. Her nursery graduation certificate. Photographs of her first day at school. Her first school tie and some stories she wrote about her family. And then... A piece chipped off my heart. A framed photograph, the last one that she'd ever had taken with her dad, the night we brought him home from the hospice. I'd always figured I'd put it up when I had the strength to look at it without falling apart, but that day was yet to come.

I picked it up, dusted it with the forearm of my pyjamas, placed it in the box, then froze. Underneath it, sitting on the thick cream pile of the carpet was a phone. Not just any phone. Colm's phone. I'd bought him the personalised photo case a couple of months before he died, a photo of him, Beth and I holding up our skateboards at the park, laughing at something I couldn't remember. We'd been in our gallows humour stage by then. His memory was so shot that stupid jokes and Lulu's afternoon poker visits were the only things that were keeping him going at that point, so we'd written 'WIFE' above my pic, and 'Daughter' above Beth's, and told him that was in case he forgot who we were. He never did. Not even in his last moments.

For once, I couldn't stop the tears, and they dropped onto the screen as I turned the phone over in my hand, trying to compute how it had got there. Everything was such a fog at that time. When we'd brought him home from the hospice, the house had filled up with people, with love and chat and desperation and false hope. It had stayed that way until after he'd taken his last breath, in the middle of the night, wrapped in my arms as I lay beside him, his face wet with my tears. Then, zombied with grief, we'd all stayed together, organising the funeral, taking care of Beth, holding each other up. It wasn't until a couple of weeks later that I realised I didn't have his phone. We'd called the hospice, but it wasn't there. We'd searched the house, couldn't find it. There were probably more places to look, but by that time I'd put the house on the market and I was in that place where dragging out boxes and the contents of cupboards wasn't an option.

I'd put it to the back of my mind, filed his lost phone under yet another disappointment in life.

And now, here it was, one of those wonderful surprises in life. Another link to him. Maybe photos. Chat. Anything that brought him back to us even for a while.

Heart racing, I tried to switch it on, but there was nothing. I raked through Colm's bedside drawers – I still thought of them as his – until I found an old charger. I linked it up, then put the refilled box back up onto the top shelf, took my pyjamas off, pulled on new ones, washed off my make-up and... ping. It sprang to life.

I gasped. There he was on the lock screen, a photo of us taken on the first night we met, barely in our twenties, right at the start of our adult lives. It had been the screen on every phone he'd ever had and sometimes I'd catch him just staring at it, as if he was trying to remind himself that that's who we were, that young couple, full of optimism and joy and love.

I left it connected to the charger, while I sat on the edge of my bed and stared at it. Password. What would it be? I tried my first option. Beth2001. His daughter and the year we met. It had been the password he'd used for everything, but I had no idea if he'd changed it. When it opened, I spluttered a giggle through the tears. He'd never been one for adding complications where there were none.

I spent the next hours sobbing until my throat hurt, laughing until my cheeks ached, thanking every higher being for giving this to me. The phone had been a SIM only, pay-as-you-go, and it still had a signal. I scrolled through our texts, all of them familiar because I had the same ones on my phone. I read his notes – everything from work stuff to reminders about birthdays and anniversaries. He clearly never checked them.

And then I scrolled through his photographs, snap after snap of Beth, of us, of our friends, our whole life pictured forwards or backwards depending which way you swiped. I started at the beginning.

When I was done, and up to his last days with us, I was broken but exhilarated at the same time. Beth would have this. When she was an adult, she could look at this phone and she'd see how much her father adored her and she'd remember how much she loved him back. It was right there in every photograph. I had no idea how this had found its way back to me, in fact, its arrival was completely baffling, but it was the best gift I could ever have hoped for.

It was after midnight and I was about to close it, when I spotted his video folder. For a second, I thought about leaving it until morning, about getting at least an hour or two of sleep before the sun came up. How many videos of him teaching Beth to ride her bike did one dad need? Still I couldn't put it down. I needed to see everything. This time though, I started at the most recent. I laid back in bed, on my side, the phone only inches from my face and I pressed 'Play'.

'Hey, m'darlin', how's things?'

I buckled as if I'd been shot in the gut when I saw his face, whimpered when I heard his voice.

There he was. Colm O'Flynn. And I knew without a doubt he was speaking to me. I could see from the background that he was in his hospice room and just for a second, I imagined that he was still there, still with us, that I could touch him, speak to him, and the thought brought indescribable joy. Of course, it wasn't true. But in some way, seeing him on screen felt like he was with me and it was like a warm blanket stretching round me on a cold day, smothering my sadness and the questions that were ricocheting around my mind. How could I not have known about this? Why hadn't he told me? It didn't matter. For now, he was here and for the next two hours, until the sun was up and the birds were singing outside, I watched my husband say his goodbyes, share his wishes, give messages to the people he loved. I got through a whole box of tissues as my heart broke time and time again, only for something in the next video to stick it back together again. He told me about his night with Jess and it broke my heart to hear his guilt and regret that he hadn't made that right with me before he passed. All that time I thought I'd been doing the best thing in leaving it unsaid while he was alive. Maybe not, but it was impossible to predict what would have happened if we'd done it differently.

I burned with shame and regret when he said he knew about Vince, then cried with relief when he promised that he forgave me. And when he said he hoped I'd love again... I couldn't even process the consequences of that, so I pushed it to one side.

When the last video ended, I realised that the anger that I'd felt about him leaving me without discussing anything was gone. He'd shared everything in his own way and in his own time. When it mattered most, when he knew he was leaving us, he'd finally broken the cycle of denial and faced the bleakness of the future, but he'd left no doubt about his wishes. He wanted us to be happy. All of us.

At 8 a.m. I texted Marcy's mum. She was already going to be looking after Beth today while I was at work – we alternated the days in the summer – and asked if she could keep her overnight tonight. She came back immediately saying she would be happy to – Marcy had missed her friend at the weekend.

I then sent messages to Lulu, Jess, and Dan. They were identical.

Please come over here at 8 p.m. tonight. I've got something from Colm to share with you all.

I pressed 'send'.

I knew that they'd come.

They might not show up for me or each other, but they would always show up for Colm.

27

It was like a school playground after a fight, when all the offending parties have been sent to different parts of the room to cool off, and they were all sitting there sulking and refusing to look at each other.

Bloody hell, what had happened to us? How had we, this group who had loved and supported each other through the toughest stuff life had thrown at us, managed to tear each other down? This wasn't who we were, yet this is what we'd become. All because each one of us had, really, just been seeking someone to love, and someone to love us back. The problem was, we'd over-complicated it all by adding layers of conditions and exclusions and rules. We'd all lived such intertwined lives that we knew the best of each other and the worst of each other, so there were no fresh starts, no hiding of flaws or failures. Just four open wounds looking for someone to heal us.

That 'someone' was gone.

But not completely.

I still had no idea how the phone had got into our treasure box. There had been so many people helping to pack, all in their own little fog of grief, that I could only think someone had put it there, without really thinking. It could even have been me. Looking back, there were so many days that were a blur to me, that I walked through with my brain and heart in bubble wrap, refusing to let anything in because I was already at capacity. Maybe on one of those days, I'd put the phone in there, knowing it would be safe. I'd no idea, but I'd come to terms with the fact that I didn't need to have all the answers. What mattered was that it was here. Colm was here.

Now I just needed his nearest and dearest to get here too.

Jess was first, dressed down in jeans, Converse and an oversized white T-shirt that hung off one shoulder. 'I didn't understand the text. What do you have to share from Colm?'

'I'll explain when everyone is here. Have you heard from Dan?' I asked her hopefully. Maybe we wouldn't need Colm's intervention after all with this one.

'Nope,' she shook her head. 'And, to be honest, the more time that passes, the more pissed off I'm getting. He's known me for twenty-five years and he's fully aware I'm not in the habit of shagging married men. It was one time, under the most exceptional circumstances. The only person we hurt was you and I'll always be sorry about that...' She hugged me, and while she was in at my ear, whispered, 'So sorry. Please don't slash my tyres.'

'I'm biding my time,' I quipped back. 'One morning you'll come out and your car will be on bricks.' I let her go and got back to the point. 'Anyway, you only hurt me for a moment. Given what I'd done, I understood. Grief screws you up.'

'I love you for understanding. I really thought Dan would too. Who is he to judge me?'

Switzerland. Colm could be the United Nations and try to forge peace, but I was staying in Switzerland.

I was saved from being forced to choose sides by the arrival of

Lulu, who waltzed in, wearing all black and a high ponytail that swished as she walked.

'Did somebody order Lara Croft?' Jess murmured.

Lulu ignored her.

'Hey,' I said, holding out a glass of wine, attempting to placate this situation. 'We extend this invitation in peace.'

For a second, just a split second, I thought she was going to play nice. Then I remembered that it was Lulu. She switched her gaze to Jess.

'How nice that you're here, Jess,' she began, and I closed my eyes, dreading whatever caustic comment I knew would come next. 'Run out of husbands to hit on? The couple next door just got married if you want to go flash the guy through the window.'

There it was. Round one.

I needed to bring Colm into the equation soon, or it was going to be a long night. Time to kick this off. But where the hell was Dan? Maybe I should have kept Beth here to make sure things stayed civil. My first instinct had been to show Beth the video when she got up this morning, but I'd changed my mind. This wasn't the time. Not when four of her adults were at war, and the fifth one, my AWOL mother, was last seen checking into the presidential suite at a flash hotel in Glasgow. I'd show her when the moment was right for her and I'd prepared her for what was coming.

In the meantime, I had to get all her adults back on an even keel. Again, where the hell was Dan?

I was about to go storming downstairs and drag him up here when he sauntered in, leading with a bottle of beer and a reluctant attitude.

He greeted us all with the driest 'Hey' ever.

Before anyone could reply, ignore him, begin to bicker or do anything else to derail the rest of the night, I put on a cheery smile, which probably completely confused him, because I knew he'd have been expecting me to tear strips off him for punching Vincent. His wariness was obvious, when I breezed on with, 'Great, you're here. Okay, can you all go sit over on the sofa. I need to show you something I found.'

'But your message said this is about Colm?' Dan asked. 'Was that just some kind of ruse to get us here?'

'Busted,' I shot back. Anxiety and emotional overload took control of my gob. 'You're right. I got you all here because I thought we could snuggle on the sofa and have a movie night.'

All three of them raised their eyebrows. Sarcasm and agitation weren't normally in my wheelhouse. I usually left the first to Jess and the second to Lulu. Maybe I should deploy them more often because my three chums were now filing over to the living area.

Jess sat on one side of the couch, Lulu sat on the other and immediately threw side eye in Jess's direction.

Jess spotted it too. 'Lulu, straighten you face. Frowning like that will challenge your Botox.'

Dear God, this was like dealing with stroppy kids.

After grabbing the remote control for the TV, I took the chair opposite Dan, with the sofa to my left, so that I could see all their faces. Only Jess was looking at me expectantly.

'Thank you for coming. Look, I know we're all pissed off with each other. It's been a rough five years for all of us and I think losing Colm changed us more than we realised. After the first couple of years of grief were over, something else started to happen. Maybe Colm's death gave us a fear of our own mortality, or maybe we slumped as we realised we could never replace him. Or maybe it made us realise that life is short so we have to snatch happiness where we can and live for the day. Or, what I actually think happened, is that we each experienced all three of those things in different ways, and the result is that we all made life changes and decisions, most of them fairly crap. But that's beside the point. Somehow we're here. Pretty broken, but still standing and he'd be proud of that.' I hesitated for a second. They were all still here. That was a plus. I smiled. 'He'd also knock our heads together and tell us that we had to cop on to ourselves and sort this out. No one loved life more than Colm O'Flynn and here we are wasting time on – as he would say – the bollocks.'

'You're right,' Jess said softly. I knew she'd be the easiest on to get on board.

Dan and Lu had both dropped their shoulders a little, but they weren't skipping through daisies yet.

I ploughed on. 'I feel like Colm was always the one who reminded us to enjoy life, to sort things out, move on, laugh, sing.' I cleared the boulder of emotion that had just rolled up into my throat. Time to get this going before I crumbled and lost the audience.

'When he died, you all know I couldn't find his phone.' Flickers of bewilderment crossed their faces. 'Last night, I found it in our keepsakes box. I've no idea how it got there. I haven't been able to look in there for years, so scared that I'd fall apart if I was reminded of our very best moments...'

'Oh, Shauna,' Jess said, oozing sympathy.

Dan was sitting forward now. 'Wait, does the phone still work? Can we see it? Shit, that's amazing. There must be so much stuff on there.'

It was the first time I'd seen a genuine smile on his face and energy in his posture for months.

'Yes, it still works, and yes, the stuff on there is pretty amazing. That's why I wanted you to come tonight. You see, turns out he had some stuff to tell us.'

'What, like messages?' Lulu asked, getting sucked into the intrigue.

'More than messages. Watch this...' I lifted the remote control and pressed 'Play'. I'd already linked it all up to my phone, and for once, the technology worked seamlessly.

There were three, astonished, emotional, joyous, gasps as my beautiful husband's face filled the screen.

'Hey, ma darlin', so I was thinking that we should probably have a chat about some stuff. I know what yer thinking... Wow, my husband is sexy and look at him lying there on our bed like some kind of drop-dead gorgeous hunk in an aftershave advert... but try to focus on what I'm saying.

'The thing is, ma darlin', we both know what's coming. You've been refusing to discuss it and, well, we both know that denial is one of my superpowers. No one wins a coconut for guessing that I don't want to give a single day of what's left to talking about what will happen down the road. But we have to, love. I'm planning to tell you what's on here at the last possible minute, so I know I won't be around when you watch it. You might wanna go get a coffee and get comfortable because this will take a while and I can't promise I won't ramble on or insert inappropriate jokes to break the tension. I can't have you keeling over with dehydration when I finally find the courage to get to bits that matter.

'Just in case, let me start with the good stuff. Shauna O'Flynn, I've adored you every day of my life. Even when I've been a daft prick or an insensitive arse. You're everything. You always were. And if I had the choice of living these fifteen years with you, or fifty years with someone else, I'd choose you in every lifetime. But this isn't forever, Shauna. We both know that, so I've got some stuff to tell you. About the past. About now. But mostly, about after I'm gone. You know I don't believe in all that "watching over you" stuff – and yep, I'll feel like a complete eejit if it turns out I get a ringside seat to the future – that's why I need you to know my hopes for the lives you and Beth will have without me. I need

to know that you'll take care of the people I love. And I need to ask your forgiveness for...'

'*Actually, I'll come to that one later, m'darlin'. I've got a whole load of other stuff to get through first. Let me start with a few messages that I need you to pass on for me. Okay, here goes...'*

The screen flickered to black for a second, then came alive again. I'd sussed now that these movies were made with no real plan ahead of time, so maybe he'd frozen at the end of that last one, or perhaps he was interrupted. We'd never know. All we could see was that he picked up his train of thought again on the next clip.

'*Right, m'darlin, let's get this started. By the way, I miss you. I miss you now when you're out at work, and I'm pretty sure that when you finally see these videos, well, I'll be missing you then too because you're the other half of my soul.*

'*Och, listen to me getting all sentimental again. Honest to God, I'm sure it's the drugs. Anyway, here's the first thing that's on my mind. Babe, after I'm gone, I need you to keep an eye on Dan for me, because much as I pray I'm wrong, we both know that Lu will break his heart again.'*

A low, guttural groan came from Dan, who now had tears streaming down his face, mirroring Lulu, whose hands were over her mouth. I'd wondered if she'd be offended by this, but I could see she wasn't. Colm wasn't saying anything here that he hadn't said to Lulu's face and their brutal honesty with each other was at the very core of their relationship.

When she took her hands away from her mouth, she was smiling through the tears. 'Ya big eejit, Colm O'Flynn. I hate it when you're right. Fuck, I've missed you...'

28

'Christ, I've sobbed my eyelashes off,' Lulu wailed after the first couple of videos. After watching those first clips in shock and awe, we'd paused to refill our glasses and soak up our tears. Already the atmosphere in the room was so different from half an hour ago. We were us again. The old us. Dan was getting drinks for Lulu and Jess. Jess was hugging me, her body shaking with emotion – she'd always been first with both tears and hugs. And Lulu, to everyone's surprise, came up behind me and threw her arms around both of us, enfolding me in a Jess and Lulu sandwich. It was the closest she'd go to an apology, but I'd take it. It felt good, but we still had a way to go to see how the cards were going to fall moving forward.

When we all made it back to the sofa, Jess and Lulu had scootched a little further into the middle, no longer acting like goalposts at either end of a football pitch. Progress.

'Okay, Jess, this next one is about you. It might hurt, but I think we all need to watch it, to understand what happened with you and Colm.' My gaze went to Dan and I could see he got the message, before returning to Jess. 'Is that okay?'

There was a twinge of apprehension across her brow, but she brushed it off. 'Yes. I trust you.'

The warmth in her voice went straight to my heart. Colm O'Flynn would be dancing a jig right now if he could see the relationship Jess and I had built. I pressed play.

As always, it began with, *'Hey, m'darlin', how're you doing? Shauna, I don't even know how to start this, but I guess I'll kick off by saying that if Beth or anyone else is with you right now, you might want to save this one for later, when you're alone.'*

The others all glanced over at me, questioning. 'It's okay. Like I said, we all need to see this.'

Colm carried on, explaining how he hadn't told me that he'd lost a child with Jess, sharing his pain, and his inability to deal with it. No matter how many times I heard it, my heart would still break for him. And for Jess too.

You could hear a pin drop in the room by the time he finally whispered, *'But there's something else, Shauna. One other secret and this one kills me. I should have told you before now, but I just... Well, the truth is, I just didn't have the courage. I couldn't hurt you. I couldn't stand the thought of you hating me. God knows, you have every right to, Shauna. I'm sorry. I'm so sorry. Shauna, I slept with Jess.'*

'Oh, mate,' Dan said, under his breath, voice breaking with sympathy.

Lulu got up and brought a kitchen roll over for Jess, then held her as her tears fell, but Dan was frozen, unable to tear his gaze from the screen as Colm explained everything. He only tore them away after Colm said, *'I don't expect you to forgive me, because I'll never forgive myself. The only thing I want to ask... And it's a huge ask that I've got absolutely no right to expect... but please forgive Jess. We were both out of our minds with sorrow and sadness.'*

'You'd already forgiven him,' Dan murmured.

I paused the video. I'd explained all this to him in Glasgow when he'd found out the truth, but he'd been too furious to really listen. Now, it was like he was hearing this for the first time. 'I had. I forgave him the next morning when I confronted Jess and she explained what happened. He never knew, though. Maybe I should have told him, but like I said, I was so scared of it damaging what time we had left. For once, I was the one going with denial and avoidance.'

Now, it was as if Dan got that this wasn't Jess, targeting my husband out of some whim or attempt to get him back. It was Colm too, just two people, numbing their pain, saying goodbye.

Dan put his beer on the table. 'That took guts. Colm always said you were the strong one.' He was mellowing towards me. I could see it. I just hoped he'd still feel the same after he watched the last video. In the meantime, though, he was reaching for Jess's hand. She didn't notice at first, because her head was on Lulu's shoulder, the two of them still curled up together. Lulu spotted it, and gave her a gentle nudge, pointing her in the right direction. 'I'm so sorry, Jess. I should have listened to you,' he said.

Jess shook her head. 'You'd just been hurt, and the fear kicked in that if I'd done something this terrible, then I could hurt you again. I get it. Nothing to forgive.'

I could have pointed out that she was furious with him earlier and actually there was definitely something to forgive, but I wasn't going to risk derailing this when we were making progress.

'Lulu, this next one is for you,' I told her.

'Don't,' she said, voice trembling. 'Shauna, I can't. I just can't.'

'Yes, you can,' I argued gently. 'Lulu, you need to hear this.'

I thought about explaining how she had to stop running, stop being a fricking nightmare when, deep down, all she was doing was trying to bury her demons with material stuff, trying to heal her scars by seeking out unattainable levels of attention and affirmation, then rejecting them as some kind of brutal test of people's love for her. It had been her pattern her whole life. But she needed to hear it from Colm.

I pressed play.

'Is Lu with you right now? If she is, can you ask her to listen to me for a minute. You might have to teach her how to do that because she's known me twenty-five years and she's never managed it yet.

Anyway, this bit is for Lu. She just left here half an hour ago and something she said has got me thinking. She said she's never been on her own. Not ever. Do you remember that, Lu?'

On he went, Lu's breath shallowed, as each point struck her gut. Jess was holding her hand so tightly, both their knuckles were white. In this together. Up until a couple of months ago, that was the way it had been. All of us. In this together.

Tears rolled down Lu's cheeks as she absorbed his words, his hopes, his love. And when he'd finished and I'd hugged her, and refilled her glass, she sat, uncharacteristically speechless, lost in her thoughts.

Then I braced myself for the toughest one of them all.

No more secrets. If we were going to move on, everything had to be out there, no matter how much it hurt when it was my turn to take the place in the centre of the storm.

My stomach churned and my face burned as Colm talked about me, about him, about Vincent, about the worst time in our marriage and the fact that he'd known all along that there had been something between us.

'More than that, m'darlin', you deserve to laugh that gorgeous laugh of yours, to find true happiness and to have someone to love you until the end of time.'

Despite that, Colm and I had made it through. He'd forgiven me. He'd forgiven all of us. I just hoped we could forgive each other.

A sad smile escaped me as I switched the TV off. 'That's it,' I said. 'I'll make copies of his messages for each of you and send them to you, so you can watch them again whenever you want.'

I didn't break the silence, giving everyone as much time as they needed to process this.

Lulu was the first to react, unfurling the arm that was around Jess's shoulders. That was the thing about my Lulu. God knows, she blew hot and hard, but she could extinguish her flames just as quickly. Now, I could see the fire was out. Still, I almost choked on my wine when she spoke to Dan. 'You know, you should really give this lady a chance. She's so much smarter than you.'

Jess spun round, met her gaze suspiciously. 'Are you high?'

If I had a single tear left in me, I'd have cried with relief that the bitching was back, because that meant the love was too.

Lulu's raucous laugh cut through the emotional overload in the room. 'Probably from your perfume – you really need to pay more than a tenner a bottle.'

She pushed herself up on to her Louboutins. 'Dan, I'm sorry. Truly. Colm's right. I need to sort some stuff out, but that has nothing to do with you. I just freaked out and was... I don't know... trying to get my security blanket back. Jess, you deserve an apology too. Like I say, if he's got any sense...' she gestured to Dan, despite the fact that she was speaking as if he wasn't even in the room, 'then he'll see that you could be the best thing that ever happened to him. And Shauna...' She took a couple of steps to the side and plonked down on my lap, making me yelp. Then she kissed my cheek a dozen times. 'I'm sorry.'

Now I didn't know whether finding the phone or Lulu apologising was the biggest shock of the week. Lulu didn't do sorry. Colm must be pulling some serious strings up there.

'So am I,' I told her, deciding not to question her new-found grace. Besides, I wasn't blameless in our rift.

'And I love you, love you, love you.' More kisses punctuated each love.

'Understandable. I'm quite fabulous. Didn't you hear Colm say that?'

The atmosphere was crackling with relief, with love, with something that felt almost like excitement. It was as if some power of osmosis had taken the sheer joy with which Colm lived every day of his life and deposited it equally between our souls.

'I did. He was right. About a lot of things.' With as much decorum as she could manage, she clambered off my lap. 'I love you all – but I need to go.'

My spirits dropped. Hadn't this brought us all back together again? 'Why? Don't you want to stay, have something to eat...'

'I do, but there's something else that's more important.'

Feck. Maybe Colm hadn't reached her.

'I need to go leave my husband for the second time this month. This time I'll actually tell him that I'm doing it. I've decided to listen to an old friend of mine who says I'm enough. Just me. Enough.'

With that, she blew us all a kiss and strutted out of the door.

'I know she's a nightmare, but I fucking love her,' Jess whistled, making Dan, who now appeared to be holding on to her hand, laugh.

'God, Shauna, can you believe those messages were there the whole time and we had no idea?'

I'd thought about that. 'Maybe that's the way it was supposed to be. You know, Colm didn't believe in any form of afterlife, but I'm telling myself that he made this happen so that I found the phone exactly when we needed it most.'

Dan's thumb was stroking Jess's palm. 'I'll go with that,' he agreed, but his gaze was on Jess, before he switched back to me. 'I owe you an apology. Or rather, I owe Vince an apology.'

'Why, what did you do?' Jess asked him.

'Punched him in the face.'

'Nooooo. When? Where?'

The redness in Dan's face gave away his embarrassment, so I decided to offer the explanations. 'Last night. Vince came round, and Rocky here met him at the door downstairs with a right hook.'

'You didn't!' Jess was wide-eyed.

'I did. I'm sorry, Shauna. I'll apologise to him too. I was just...'

'Sticking by your pal,' I finished, knowing that in his mind he was righting the perceived wrong against Colm.

'Yeah. If it's any consolation, I think I broke my thumb,' he said, holding up a bent digit.

'You deserve it,' I teased.

'What happened next? Did he come up here? Are you going to see him again?' Jess probed.

I shrugged. 'I don't know. I need to just take a breath. Absorb Colm's words. Watch the videos about a hundred times and sort everything out in my head. I don't want to make another mistake, so I'm just going to take my time with it all.'

'Wise move,' Jess approved.

'You know, if it's okay with Colm, then it's okay with me. I just didn't know the whole story before. Sorry for not listening,' Dan said.

'I'm sorry for not telling you before now,' I said honestly.

'So we're good?' he asked.

'We're great.' I told him, smiling.

He exhaled, his grin wide. 'Okay, I'm going to phone in food and let's get more beers and...'

'Actually, is it okay if we don't?' I interrupted him. I could feel the emotions sparking between them and I knew that what they needed right now was to talk to each other, to work this out without an audience. If I said that, though, they'd almost certainly object, so I took another tack. 'I... I feel like I want to be on my own. I'm so tired. I just want to light a candle, run a bath, just be still. Is that okay?'

'Are you sure?' Jess checked. 'Really sure? I could stay and we could just flop and watch a movie and...'

'No. Really. Thank you. But I need to sleep.'

'Okay, we get it,' Dan said, standing up first, then pulling Jess up by the hand he was still holding. 'I'll take you up on the movie though,' he told her, the look in his eyes saying that he meant so much more.

'Really?' Jess said, grinning.

'Really.'

I could have lit a Yankee candle off the electricity that was flying between them. I hugged them both, then waved them goodbye. Then I sighed. Slumped. Spent.

We were okay.

I'd been lying about the bath and the candles, but now it didn't seem like the worst idea. I picked up the glasses and bottles and took them over to the kitchen island. I needed to think. I'd sent Vincent away, because I couldn't handle the guilt, but now I realised that Colm knew, that he'd made peace with it, I needed to work out how I felt. Every bit of me had wanted him when he was here. I'd loved him for three decades, as a friend, as a one-night lover, even as a mistake that I'd made when I was crazy with pain. It had crossed my mind too that perhaps Colm had sent him to me, made all this happen at the perfect time. But maybe going backwards was another mistake. Maybe I needed to go on, make a fresh start.

I cleaned up the kitchen, and had filled the dishwasher when I realised I was singing 'These Arms of Mine'. Otis Redding. Our wedding song. For five years it had made me sad, but not tonight.

I had broken my vows out of desperation to feel something other than grief and agonising pain. Years later, Colm did the same thing. We both knew, we both forgave each other. Knowing that lifted a massive weight off my heart.

I poured a glass of wine, grabbed a box of Maltesers, and had almost made it to the bathroom when, at the end of the hall, the doorbell rang and I could see the outline of a person there. Probably Lulu. Maybe she'd packed up super quick, and was already back to claim the spare room.

Putting the Maltesers under my arm, I used my free hand to open the door.

Vince.

There.

Right there.

Leaning against the door frame, that gorgeous smile more prominent now that the swelling had gone down a bit.

'No assault on the way in tonight?' Colm would be proud – I was making bad jokes to cover up my racing heart and distract from the fact my knees appeared to have turned to liquid.

'Nope,' he said, then his eyes ran up and down me. 'No tinsel tickles?'

I shook my head. 'You can have too much of a good thing. Is that what you came to check? Tonight's slogan on my pyjamas?'

His laughter made something inside me melt.

'No. I'm here because Lulu texted me. Said I need to come here.'

'She did?'

Vince took a step forward. 'She did. And then Dan texted me.'

'No way!'

'Yep. He apologised for last night and said that maybe I needed to talk to you.'

Dan heard everything Colm said. I felt like his hug was reaching me from downstairs.

Vince took another step forward. 'And then someone called Jess – I assume that's Colm's ex?'

I nodded, overwhelmed that all the people I loved had intervened. We were a dysfunctional bunch sometimes, but I knew, with a bit of interference from Colm, that we'd find our way past every problem and we'd do it together.

'Thought so. Jess texted to check I was on my way.'

'My friends can be pretty persistent. I'm sorry.' We were only inches apart now, our gazes locked, our hands almost touching.

'Are you? Sorry? Because, Shauna, I'm so not. I just need to know that you want me here too. Do you?'

I closed my eyes. Colm knew. He told me to take another chance at happiness. Our friends had heard that and they'd made this happen. For him. For me. For Beth. And maybe for Vincent too.

Could I choose a new life? A new love? Could I choose Vincent?

I gave the second love of my life his answer when I reached up, put my hand on his beautiful, swollen face, gently pulled it towards mine. I kissed him until he picked me up and carried me back through to the kitchen.

Colm's mantra had always been that him and I were for always. It was more than that. Colm, me, our child, our self-made family, and now Vince too – no matter what life put in our way, I knew we were always. Colm would make sure of it.

EPILOGUE

Okay, okay, so I was wrong. At least I think I was. Up here, you never know exactly what's going on, so I can't be sure if this is a dream, a premonition, or if I'm really looking down and seeing a world that kept on turning without me.

Whatever it is, I like it.

Today would have been our twentieth wedding anniversary and I was beyond worried that ma darlin' would still be stuck in her grief. I can't tell you the relief that she isn't. That big eejit, Vince, who, by the way, is far too good-looking, even with the new nose my buddy designed for him, has got her down at the North Devon coast and they're playing in the sea with Beth. My Beth. My smart, funny, brilliant girl. She still chats to me every night before she goes to sleep and I listen, bursting with pride. Much as I wish it was me, I'm grateful that Vince takes such good care of her. Every weekend they do something different and Beth absolutely adores him. Just as well, because Shauna's mother has bailed on her grandmother duties now that she's found a man. Not exactly a shocker.

Lulu and Dan are there too, but not together. Dan and Jess are on their first weekend trip as a couple with our boys, and Lulu has flown in from Paris to join them all. The boys have totally accepted Dan going from being their uncle to their mum's new partner. He'll never be their dad, but he's always been one of their best mates and nothing will change that.

Lulu isn't fazed about Dan being there with Jess either. She's too wrapped up in some cracking new job over there and she's enjoying the city of love a little too much, but she wouldn't be Lu if she didn't. Bobby has been showering her with gifts since she left him, but she's not for going back – especially since she discovered he got his secretary to send them all. Couldn't even do it himself. Says everything about him and everything about why Lu couldn't stay with him. She's got herself a therapist and she's working on herself before she launches into another serious relationship.

I could watch them all forever. Not sure if that's allowed, but I'll try to pull some strings. It's just so great to hear them all laughing together. I'd give anything to be there – anything at all – but I can live with the fact that it's not to be, because I know they're good and they're not throwing away a single day.

When I slipped my phone into our keepsakes box, I wasn't thinking too far ahead. I just figured that it would be safe there and that Shauna would find it in the days after I was gone. I had no idea it would take years for her to open that box again. But then, as she says, maybe she found it when they needed it most. Now Shauna and Vince are working together again, living together, laughing a lot. I don't check in on their alone time. I'm a spirit, not a saint.

Hang on, Annie's calling me. She says we have a vitally important place to be.

My world, everyone I love is okay. So if you're looking for us, well, me and Annie will be at the line dancing.

Join us when you're ready, m'darlin's.

But not too soon.

ACKNOWLEDGMENTS

Once again, this book wouldn't exist without the encouragement, patience and editorial brilliance of the wonderful Caroline Ridding.

Thanks too, to Amanda, Nia, Claire, the rest of the team and all the other authors that make up the Boldwood family.

And to Jade and Rose, for knocking yet another of my books into shape.

To the book blogging community, heartfelt thanks for every lovely thing you've said about my books over the years.

And of course, huge, HUGE gratitude to every reader who has picked up one of my books. I hope you love this one.

Finally, to my pals, my family, and the man who's been beside me for a lifetime, thank you. You lot deserve a medal for surviving another deadline.

Love always,

Shari xx

MORE FROM SHARI LOW

We hope you enjoyed reading *The Story of Our Secrets*. If you did, please leave a review.

If you'd like to gift a copy, this book is also available as an ebook, digital audio download and audiobook CD.

Sign up to Shari Low's mailing list for news, competitions and updates on future books.

http://bit.ly/ShariLowNewsletter

Explore more from Shari Low.

ABOUT THE AUTHOR

Shari Low is the #1 bestselling author of over 20 novels, including *My One Month Marriage* and *One Day In Summer,* and a collection of parenthood memories called *Because Mummy Said So.* She lives near Glasgow.

Visit Shari's website: www.sharilow.com

Follow Shari on social media:

facebook.com/sharilowbooks

twitter.com/sharilow

instagram.com/sharilowbooks

bookbub.com/authors/shari-low

ABOUT BOLDWOOD BOOKS

Boldwood Books is a fiction publishing company seeking out the best stories from around the world.

Find out more at www.boldwoodbooks.com

Sign up to the Book and Tonic newsletter for news, offers and competitions from Boldwood Books!

http://www.bit.ly/bookandtonic

We'd love to hear from you, follow us on social media:

 facebook.com/BookandTonic

twitter.com/BoldwoodBooks

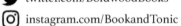 instagram.com/BookandTonic

Inheritance

Printed in Great Britain
by Amazon

27493840R00159